THE LOST AND THE HUNTED: THE COMPLETE NOVEL

AN EDEN ACADEMY PREQUEL

GRACE MCGINTY

For Amber,
Who never asks why; just provides an alibi.
G x

1

CELESTE

I let out a few choice expletives that would have made my well-to-do mother blush. Not that my mother cared much whether I lived or died; however right now, the latter looked like it would win out. I backed up another foot, hazarding a quick glance over my shoulder, cursing under my breath at the sight of the brick wall blocking my path. Sighing, I psyched myself up for a fight, curling my fists into tight balls, my jaw clenching and unclenching rhythmically. I ran scenarios in my head. There were three attackers, that meant I would have only one decisive move, and then I'd be back on the defensive. If they were normal, corner-a-girl-in-the-darkened-alley type of attackers, the odds would be much more in my favor. I had participated in self-defense classes like any good city girl. My instructor told me that I fought like a psychotic mongoose, but it was effective, at least.

Unfortunately, these weren't your ordinary drunken louts or sexual predators. They were highly skilled hunters that caught people like me for glory and huge monetary rewards. They dealt in preternatural trafficking. Of course, there were varying remuneration levels, and a lowly little shifter like me would probably only bring a couple of million, maybe more if the buyer had a fetish for snow leopards.

I gritted my teeth; if I'd already been in my snow leopard form, this would be a different story. I would shred these assholes into ribbons and then use their corpses as a scratching post. Unfortunately, it would take a full eight seconds to morph. Eight seconds where I would be completely helpless and for people like these guys, eight seconds was long enough to have me bagged, tagged, and off to be a kinky rich asshole's pet kitty cat.

I hadn't given up just yet though, and I let out a growl as I pushed off the wall, doing my best impression of a war cry. I managed to punch the one furthest to the left in the throat, making him crumble to the ground, gurgling noises escaping from his mouth. I might be in my human form, but I could still throw a mean fucking punch.

The other hunters barely spared a glance for their struggling comrade. I let out an ear-piercing scream and went to lunge for the middle one when there was a yell at the mouth of the alley. The hunters turned towards the uncertain threat, but that was all the opening I needed. I backtracked towards the dead-end at a sprint, morphing as I went, and used the wall as a springboard to launch myself at the remaining attackers. I had the benefit now of being hefty but small in snow leopard form, like a fluffy cannonball, and no matter how well trained the bounty hunters were, they couldn't fight gravity, and both went down. I put in a few deadly swipes with my razor-sharp claws, but didn't stick around to see if I'd done any damage. I ran as fast as my four legs would take me towards the opening of the alley and the relative safety of the crowded main road. I belatedly realized I couldn't exactly run around the streets of downtown Chicago in my shifted form. A snow leopard running through the crowd would raise the eyebrow of even the most jaded city dweller. I morphed as I ran, which was blessedly quick compared to the change to leopard, but it left me naked as the day I was born. I sent up a silent thank you to a design student I'd met in a refuge, who also happened to shift into a rabbit. She custom made clothes that remained somewhere on your person when you shifted. Being a prey animal made you aware of these things, I guess. Now I had a huge range of wrap dresses with studs that popped open when I changed into a snow leopard. I did up my dress as I ran, hooray for public decency, but I had to slow as I reached the entrance of the alley and almost ran into my accidental savior.

A guy stood there, and I guessed he was about twenty-five. His mouth was hanging wide open, his eyes like luminous satellites on his face. I couldn't blame the guy for looking shocked, but if he didn't get out right now, he would be unintentional collateral damage. I grabbed my savior's hand.

"Run!" I yelled. I couldn't really leave him here to face the bounty hunters alone, now that I kind of owed him one. I pulled him along the street, and he put up little resistance in his stunned state. I sincerely hoped that he'd just stumbled out of the bar next door and was drunk enough not to remember this later.

We were back out onto the main street, and we weaved in and out of the teeming crowd. I didn't give a shit how many people we smacked into, or the cross words that were shouted after us. I threw a quick look over my shoulder and swore when I spotted the hunters weaving their way through the crowd after us. I let out a double-fuck when I realized Hunter number three had recovered from his throat punch.

I turned to my blondhaired savior. I needed to ditch him and his tall ass, but the humane part of me knew I couldn't leave him behind until we lost the hunters. They weren't known for their compassion for human life and would be mad as a shaken hornet at the loss of their bounty. I knew I owed this guy, and besides, he was kind of cute with his floppy hair and dopey look.

"We need to lose them," I yelled back to the guy and veered off towards a shopping mall, tugging on his hand to hurry. Thankfully, there were crowds out already, partying their way through the wine bars or the harassed parents dragging their kids around the mall. Hordes of people moved in and out of the mall's entrance, and I quickly pushed my way through the entrance and then let the crowd envelop me.

We had to be as inconspicuous as possible, so I shook my hand out of the guy's and quickly plaited my hair into a long rope before twisting it up and tucking it into itself. My hero was quite tall, and he may as well have been a beacon with all that golden curly hair. Even though I was no longer holding his hand, he was still following along behind me. I sighed, looking around for something that would help disguise him. My eyes fell on a stall that sold hats and socks in the middle of the walkway. I picked up a dark blue cap with a wide, flat brim. It wasn't my style, but it would fit the purpose, making him look younger and obscuring some of his facial features.

I turned towards the guy. "Do you have any money? We have to obscure that big head of yours."

He just pulled out his wallet like a zombie and paid the vendor. I slapped the hat on his head, and walked away as casually as possible, but the guy next to me radiated tension.

I huffed out an exasperated breath. "Do you have a name?"

He silently continued to watch me. Maybe he was in shock. I looked over his pale cheeks and too-wide eyes. No, he was definitely in shock. "Do you speak English?"

Finally, he frowned. "Of course."

"Well, that's handy. You don't happen to see any of those menacing-looking guys lurking around back there, do you?" I still spoke slow; even if he did speak English, he didn't seem like he was firing on all cylinders.

"No, I don't," he said irritably, "and my name is Reese." His brow was knitted, and he had the funniest serious face I'd ever seen, like a toddler throwing a tantrum. It was probably the endorphins rolling around my system that made me start to giggle hysterically, and not his jutted out bottom lip.

"Luckily for you, peanut butter cups are my favorite. Come on; we should keep moving."

I continued to giggle, but Reese didn't join in. A group of loud college students walked past, heading toward the movie theater. Perfect. I grabbed Reese's hand again and walked quicker, pulling him along with me, attaching us to the back of the crowd of college kids.

"We need to find somewhere where there are a lot of bodies around. Stay close behind these guys like we belong." The collective heat of a mass of bodies enclosed tightly in a room would throw off their preternatural detection equipment. Shifters ran a bit hotter, and that's how they picked us out of crowds.

He nodded, but his eyes had lost that dazed look and were settling on wary. Why he was still with me was a bit of a mystery, and I wasn't sure if I wanted him to fuck off and make it easier for me to hide, or to stay with his hand clasped in mine. It was proof of how touch starved I was that I was clinging to him like this.

It was chaos inside the lobby of the cinema; parents chasing after children who were already too hopped up on candy and sugar drinks, and teens standing around doing their best to look like they fit in. I briefly glanced at the movie board, a talking animal flick, an action thriller with an explosion on the poster, and a movie that would probably win an Oscar but would be dull as hell. Eh didn't matter. I didn't want to wait in line to get tickets; I may as well just stand out the front for target practice now.

I looked over to where a pimply teenager in a genuinely hideous gold vest was ripping tickets. He looked bored, but I didn't think he was just going to let us in. However, next to the candy bar was a large set of double doors that said, "Do not enter. Staff Only."

It may as well have waved a red flag and said, "I Dare You!" underneath. Next to it was a self-service candy area, and I wandered over to it, going to the Hershey Kisses that were closest to the doors. I filled up a cup like I belonged there, waiting until Reese caught up and was standing behind me. I used him as cover as I took a quick look around, and then pushed Reese through the doors. With another quick look, I went in after him.

The hallway on the other side of the doors was empty, thank fuck. However, Reese was pressed against the wall and he didn't look happy. In fact, he looked about ready to snap. Maybe I shouldn't have been so damn weak and left him behind already.

"What. The. Hell?"

I rolled my eyes.

"Look, Peanut Butter Cup, please don't get all hysterical on me now. I promise that when we are done running from the very bad men, and I mean very bad, I will answer any question you want to ask. But right now, you have two options; you can keep it together for a little longer, or you can go off on your own and hope to God they don't catch you. But I wouldn't bet on you escaping their notice. You are as stealthy as a Thanksgiving Day Parade."

He wasn't the only one losing patience. High

tension situations made me a little bit testy as well. If I ended up a leopard skin rug because this guy was throwing a tantrum, I was going to be pissed.

I gently nudged him down the hall that led off the "Staff Only" area and he begrudgingly went. We moved at a steady pace until we came to the furthest door at the end of the hall.

I stuck my head through and looked for any gaudy gold vests, but it was all clear.

Sending up a thank you to the goddess of small fucking mercies, and I darted out into the hall, pulling Reese along with me. I tucked myself so close to his body that I could feel his warmth. He really could be quite pliable when he wanted to be.

I laced my fingers through his, justifying it to myself as maintaining our ruse, but I recognized that a part of me just liked the feel of his skin against mine.

My face warmed a little at the thought.

Before Reese could register the heat in my face, I pulled him through the double doors of the closest cinema. The noise and darkness swallowed us whole and I heaved a sigh of relief. I reluctantly released Reese's hand and beckoned him to follow. Walking slowly up the stairs to the middle of the cinema, I sat next to a group of people who appeared to be teenagers. Reese sat down next to me, hemming me between humans.

The action flick was playing in front of me and it

appeared that the bad guy was winning, considering the banged-up state of the hero. I glanced over at Reese, who was staring unseeingly at the big screen. A car exploded, and the flash gave me a clear view of his face. He might be a problem that I didn't want to deal with, but he was a very cute problem.

He was good looking in a nondescript way; a long straight nose ran into lips that were pressed thinly together, his eyes framed by long eyelashes and roundish glasses. The most remarkable thing about him was his golden hair. I briefly wondered if he was one of those guys who dyed their hair at the salon, but then I remembered how shaggy he was. There were limits to how shaggy you could go while still being fashionable, and Reese overshot that mark significantly. However, there was something else about him, something that wasn't physical, that my body responded to in a more primal way. Reese felt me staring and turned toward me.

"You never told me your name." His whispered words brushed against my skin, and I realized he was close enough to kiss. I frowned. I should give him a fake name, that was the smart thing to do. Unfortunately my impulsive, or stupid, side won out.

"Celeste." Reese nodded and turned back to the screen, his arm pressed against mine. My heartbeat quickened, but it was probably just the adrenaline from my near death experience. Yeah, that was it.

And to think, I never used to lie to myself.

I turned back to the screen, trying to appear as if I was watching the movie, but slowly my eyes drifted closed. Shifting always drained me, and coupled with the adrenaline comedown, I felt bone weary.

As much as my mind fought it, my body went languid and I fell asleep.

A POKE in the ribs jerked me awake and the noise around me was deafening. I sat up ramrod straight, trying to reorientate myself. Where the fuck was I?

"Celeste, wake up! They're here," an urgent voice whispered in my ear. My eyes shot open, any residual sleepiness long gone. Hunters. Reese. Fuck.

My gaze flew to the entrance and the three big shadows standing in the doorway to the cinema. They split up, one taking the front row and the other two taking either side of the central seating. I was sure we'd lost them and swore silently under my breath. It must have been a slow month for bounties if they were on my furry ass this hard. I looked for the exits, but they were down the front and we'd have to walk right by them. Damn it.

Tension thrummed along Reese's body, and that would be a giveaway in itself. Only one solution, but in the spirit of being truthful to yourself, I didn't try and think too hard about other options.

"Play along," I whispered as I swung my leg over his lap, pulling his face to mine and pressing my lips firmly to his. His body was stiff, but his hands wrapped around my back of their own accord. My thoughts were pulled away from the imminent threat when Reese's mouth softened beneath mine and he began to kiss me back. He ran his tongue along the seam of my lips with quick flicks, like he was tasting me, or maybe testing my defenses. My blood was already thumping in my ears, and as his teeth scraped over my lip, I had to stop myself from gasping as if he had burned me.

My hands gripped the back of his head harder, tangling in those golden curls that felt softer than imaginable. I opened my mouth and my tongue met his, quickly stroking it as he ran his hands over my hip, tracing a tingling line down my thigh. Heat flooded to my core and my chest constricted until I thought it would be impossible to breathe. I had to stop this, or we would be fucking in the back of the cinema like a couple of horny teenagers while people who literally wanted to sell me roamed the halls. Fuck, I was an idiot.

I pulled back from Reese's face enough to see the hunter descending the stairs, our faces so close together that if it hadn't been so dark, I would have been able to count the pale freckles that ran across the bridge of his nose. We sat there for a moment, Reese staring into my soul from barely an inch away, and I was suddenly uncomfortable with the scrutiny.

"We need to get out of here," I whispered. I needed the cold Chicago air to cool me down. We waited until the men left the cinema, and ran down the stairs two at a time to the emergency exit beside the screen. Reese pushed it open and the light above it started flashing.

"We better hurry before someone realizes the alarms have been tripped," Reese muttered, holding the door for me. Running down the corridor towards another red exit sign, I could feel the cold night breeze flowing into the room. It definitely emptied out into the street. Reese pushed that one open as well and this time an ear shattering alarm went off.

"Keep running. I want to get the hell out of downtown," I shouted back at Reese, leaping over trash and ducking around overflowing dumpsters. I wasn't going to get myself trapped in another back alley, that was for damn sure. As soon as we were back onto Main Street, I ran out in front of the first cab I saw, making it slam on its brakes.

Reese opened the door and pushed me in first, and then got in beside me. The cabbie was peeved about almost running me over, swearing in a language I didn't know and throwing me the stink-eye in the rear-view mirror.

"You know, you could have just raised your arm and whistled like a normal person. You don't have to get yourself killed hailing a cab, you know," he huffed. "Where to?"

I was surprised when Reese rattled off an address in Lincoln Park West before I could answer.

The cabbie nodded and drove off. I glanced through the back window one more time to see if the bounty hunters had caught up. Thankfully, I couldn't see them amongst the shrinking crowd. I settled back into the cracked vinyl seats of the old cab.

"What's at Lincoln Park? Are you going to put me in the Lincoln Park Zoo?" I didn't know if it was too soon to joke about such things. It also occurred to me that I probably shouldn't just hop into a cab with a stranger, even if we had just shared a near death experience and an unbelievable kiss. I just couldn't be bothered stressing about one more thing tonight. Besides, the chance of Buttercup over there beating me in a fight was non-existent, in my opinion. Not that he wasn't powerfully built, he had well-muscled forearms, broad shoulders and was well over six feet, but he couldn't take a snow leopard either. My eyes roamed over his chest and shoulders, hungrily taking in every inch of him.

"We're going to my place. I need a beer and you need to explain...everything." I was so distracted by the muscles of his chest I'd forgotten I'd even asked a question. I nodded, and it felt nice just to hand over control to someone else for a little while, at least while I was in the relative safety of the cab. Again, I wished I could explain away tonight's events on alcohol, or the effects of hallucinogens. I searched his face for any sign that he might be a heavy drug user. No shadowed, sunken eyes or haggard features. In fact, he looked in peak condition. Fuck it.

I sighed, the weight of my secret resting heavily on my shoulders. I might have been twenty-three, but on days like today, I felt a hundred. I really hoped that I wouldn't cast under the eagle eye of the Shifter Council because of this shit. Not that anyone would believe Reese, he was just one man. He'd probably end up on the front page of some trashy tabloid, a secondary story to 'Jessica Alba and Alien have a secret extra-terrestrial love affair'.

I looked at Reese intently. He looked solid, trust-worthy. But with secrets like this, you could never really trust anyone who wasn't a shifter. That was something I had learnt the hard way.

"Stop staring at me," Reese muttered. I was about to make a snarky comment when the cab pulled over, the driver slamming his brakes on with a little more force than necessary. Reese's hand shot out, banding across my waist so I didn't fling forward. Naw, he was back in my good books again.

"Seventeen bucks," the driver grunted, reaching his hand between the seats. I fumbled for my purse, real-izing I left the damn thing in the alley. However, Reese was already there, handing over a fifty and telling the cab driver to keep the change. I wistfully thought that one day I'd love to have enough money to say "keep the change" so cavalierly, but I only had fifty bucks to my name and a full time job was hard to hold down when there were always people chasing you. I got help of course, there was a group who called themselves 'Eden' that gave people like me a place to stay and some money if I needed it, but I didn't like staying there for too long. I was a loner by nature, and I liked it that way. There was no need to rely on anyone else for anything. I prided myself on the fact that I hadn't begged for help since my mother kicked me out at thirteen.

Reese slid out of the cab and held the door open for me. I stepped onto the sidewalk in front of a beautiful grey stone building with bronze arched windows. It had a small, dark green awning and green mat that rolled out onto the sidewalk. It was elegant art deco, and I let myself imagine for a moment that I was some kind of movie starlet in a beautiful gown, with a handsome date.

The cold chicago wind brought me back to reality real quick.

I would never have the opportunity to be anyone important. Hell, I wasn't even wearing damn shoes. A dirty wrap dress and bare feet were a far cry from an elegant ball gown. I'd lost my shoes, jacket, and my tights back in the alley, along with my purse. I never kept any ID in it though. I'd take my risks with the cops over the hunters learning where I lived.

It wasn't until the adrenaline wore off that the cold evening breeze even affected me. They were predicting early snow this year, and from the bite in the air, I believed it. Reese must have noticed me shivering because he shrugged out of his leather jacket and wrapped it around my shoulders. I pushed my arms through the sleeves and was immediately enveloped in his residual body heat. He looked down at my feet.

"You aren't wearing any shoes."

For some reason, his blandly delivered statement made me want to cry, but I blinked them back. Reese frowned at my feet again, then walked over and scooped me up into his arms like I was a child. Before I'd even recovered from the shock of being in his arms, Reese was striding across the icy cold pavement and didn't put me down until we were inside the warmth of the building's lobby. I just stood there, Reese's jacket almost covering all the way to my knee, its arms too long, and I just couldn't move. I stood there rubbing the soft leather between my fingers, staring around at the luxurious entryway like an orphan off the damn street .

Still, I looked over at Reese and smiled. "That's the nicest thing anyone has ever done for me." My voice could barely be heard above the wind. Reese looked at me dumbstruck.

"What, no one has ever offered you a jacket before?" He looked at me like I'd lost my mind, but it was true. With the exception of Eden, which was an impersonal organization, no matter how good their intentions, no one had ever offered me anything for free, even temporarily. I looked at his bare arms, which were starting to get goosebumps from the chill.

"I mean no one has ever gone without, for me." This time it was little more than a whisper, and I wasn't sure if he'd heard. I wasn't sure I wanted him to hear. He gave no indication that he had; he just ushered me further inside, muttering something about us both freezing to death.

We were greeted by an elderly man behind the desk, and he looked like the stereotypical doorman you'd see in movies.

"Evening Mr. Reese. It's a little breezy outside to be running around in just your shirtsleeves, don't you think?" Reese just smiled and shrugged, walking directly toward the bank of elevators.

They opened almost immediately and we were ensconced in luxury. He tapped a card he'd pulled from his wallet and the doors closed. The dark marble tiles and gold fittings made the elevator look far more luxurious than my crappy little studio apartment. There were mirrors on three sides of the elevator and I grimaced at my reflection. My hair was a tangled mess and my face was grimy. I looked ridiculous in Reese's jacket, like a naughty child who had to be dragged home after playing in the mud. I self-consciously smoothed my hair, watching the numbers rise until the door finally slid open, directly into his apartment.

He stepped in before me, beckoning me to follow as he reached around to flick on the lights. I gasped as I took in my surroundings. The place looked like it had been pulled straight out of the centerfold of an interior design magazine. The low modern furniture took up most of the space, with splatter wall art giving a bit of colour to a scheme that was predominantly mono-chromatic.

I sat down on the couch, perching right on the edge so I didn't soil it with my filth. "My God this is hard."

"Of course it is. It's for decoration, not for sitting on," he laughed. "That's a direct quote from my interior designer when I said pretty much the same thing. Do you want a drink or anything?"

I looked down at the pristine white couch and then my dirty clothes. "Would it be okay if I had a shower?" It only took one fancy room and I was back to a scared little girl all over again, out of place among the picture perfect life my mother had created. A cuckoo in the nest. I was terrified that I would stand up and there would be a dirt mark where I sat.

"Sure you can. There are towels under the sink in

the bathroom. Do you want to wash your clothes as well? I can give you some of mine to wear in the meantime?" I nodded, touched by his thoughtfulness.

Minutes later, I was under a steady stream of warm water, and I let it wash away the night.

2

REESE

I needed to get my head on straight. Everything about the girl seemed designed to fry my mind until I wasn't sure what day of the week it was. I went and got her some clothes out of my drawer, trying to find something that I wore in college so it wouldn't just fall off of her tiny waif body. The last thing I needed was to see her naked again. When I saw her running down that alley, the sight of her small, tight body was almost enough to make me forget that only a second before, she'd been a big cat. I shook my head. Maybe this was all just a really vivid dream, because there was no way in hell it could be reality. I knocked on the bathroom door. "I'll leave the clothes outside the door."

I stood there for a moment, unsure what to do. This wasn't like me; I knew my place and my purpose. I was one of the richest bachelors under thirty; I didn't get there by dithering.

But I couldn't shake the feeling of her tiny frame in my arms as I carried her across the pavement. She had to be half-starved. One look at her dirty feet had been enough to send me into Sir Galahad mode. I'd make her some food so at least she'd have a full stomach for tonight.

Decision made, I strode toward the kitchen. Unfortunately, the only thing I knew how to make that was guaranteed to be edible was grilled cheese. It would have to do.

As I prepared food in my ultra-modern-slash-easily-dirtied kitchen, I couldn't shake the image of her standing in front of me in the entranceway of the building, staring up at me with those big grey eyes like I was some kind of hero. The whole thing made my soul ache.

She emerged from the shower thirty minutes later, a rush of steam flooding from the bathroom behind her. She'd brushed her hair and scrubbed her face clean and I felt my knees turn to jelly. She had lost the dirty little orphan look, and her slightly damp hair, pink cheeks and kissable lips made me want to jump the bench and do unspeakable things to her. Instead, I offered her food.

"I made some grilled cheese sandwiches, if you'd like?"

Her hand flew to her stomach and she nodded gratefully. "That'd be great."

I grabbed the big plate of food off the stove top and set it in front of her. I looked down into her face and tried not to stare; her eyes were the most captivating thing I'd ever seen. They were a pale blue-grey, unlike any color I'd ever seen. She caught me staring and brushed absently at her cheek, as if self-conscious that she'd missed a spot. I mentally shook myself and went to the fridge, grabbing a soda and a beer.

I offered her both, but she took the soda.

"I hear sugar is good for shock." I sat down next to her and grabbed a grilled cheese for myself. "So, Celeste," I rolled her name over my tongue like I was tasting it. "Would you like to explain exactly what the hell is going on?" I was proud that my voice was even, my tone nothing but pleasant. I didn't want to scare her.

"We are eating melted cheese on toast, Reese," she quipped back sarcastically, playing dumb and innocent. Well, that wasn't going to fly with me. I wanted answers and I'd been more than patient.

"Okay, let's start with why you were running out of an alley naked." She let out a deep sigh, a look of relief on her face. Well, I wasn't about to let her off so easily, "and while you're explaining things, you can tell me why one minute it was a puma running at me and the next it was you." I just wanted validation that I wasn't losing my mind. She looked down at the grilled cheese in her hand, as if weighing up whether a crazy person could make such a good sandwich.

"A snow leopard," Celeste said as she stuffed more food into her mouth. She was eating like she hadn't seen much food this week. I blinked a few times, as if that would help me hear more accurately.

"Excuse me?" I felt like one of those clowns who get hit in the face with a cream pie all of a sudden.

"I said it was a snow leopard, not a puma."

The air whooshed out of my lungs. It was nice for someone to verify that I wasn't completely nuts, though perhaps we were both certifiable.

A look of resignation came over Celeste's face and she turned her body to face me. I remembered not to look directly into her eyes, because I couldn't do that and still process what was coming out of her mouth. Focusing on a spot in the middle of her forehead, I tuned into what she was saying.

"Okay Buttercup. I'm going to tell it to you straight, but remember you're the one who wanted to know." She took a deep breath and squared her shoulders, looking like she was ready to run at a moment's notice.

"I'm a shifter. I turn into a snow leopard when I feel like it, or if there's a full moon. The guys we were running from? They were bounty hunters who'd like to sell me to some rich old dude who'd, best case scenario, like to mount my head on the wall. Most likely scenario? Sex slave. You can't even imagine the worst case scenario, believe me." Celeste stuffed some more sandwich into her mouth and I watched as she chewed, her eyes daring me to call her crazy.

I had to avert my gaze to the wall just so I could process what she had said. If I hadn't seen it myself, I probably would've written her off as crazy. But I'd seen her transform, and even though I didn't necessarily trust my own eyes, it seemed a bit elaborate for some kind of prank. Also, those guys were no illusion either. When I'd hazarded a look back while we were running through the crowd, I'd never forget the cold look on their faces. It was detached, a soulless look of people who had killed too often. I looked at the tiny thing on my couch munching away on her sandwich.

"Are they looking for you in particular?" My voice seemed loud in the silence and Celeste startled a little.

"Uh... no, I don't think so. They usually just trawl through busy locations with heat guns looking for variances in body temperatures. Preternaturals tend to run a little hotter than the average human. Vamps don't have any heat signature, so that's also a dead give-away." Celeste giggled at her own lame joke, then sobered. "They also have special bloodhounds that can smell the difference between the paranormal and just plain old normal. But I've never seen one; they usually use them for the higher priced bounty, like super-naturals."

I couldn't help raising my eyebrows in disbelief. "Vampires? Are you serious?"

A pleased look came over her face at my incredulity. Obviously it was a response she was more familiar with, because she stood up and within seconds her body began to twist and change, swaying side to side before spurting upwards. If I had a moment to suspend my disbelief, I'd probably say that the magic reminded me of a butterfly emerging from a cocoon, but right then, I was too shocked by the fact there was a fully grown snow leopard on my living room floor. It sat down on its hind legs, like a well-trained dog, it's knowing eyes staring at me with intelligence. Scratch that, its eyes were laughing at me. It opened its mouth wide in a yawn, its sharp teeth glinting in the glow of the down lights. It licked its paw and rubbed it across its face, like your regular domestic house cat and then cocked its head to one side as if trying to judge my response. She smiled, a full toothy feline grin, and with a rush of air, the big cat shrunk back down into a small, naked Celeste.

She stood there, with the same predatory grin that was on the face of a snow leopard only moments before, completely comfortable with her nudity. My eyes wandered over every inch of her body of their own accord, trying to take it all in at once, hungrily devouring the curve of her breasts, the silhouette of her hips and gentle roundness of her stomach. As my gaze went lower, she quickly turned, giving me a great view of her ass as she slipped my sweats back on. Celeste looked over her shoulder and grinned at my rapt attention.

"Like what you see, Buttercup?"

I felt my cheeks flame and I immediately lowered my eyes. I liked to think I was raised well enough to feel abashed about my shameless perving.

I cleared my throat, looking at my hands. "That was amazing. I can't believe it, I mean... it's just that you were a cat in my living room and now you're you." *Yeah, real articulate there, big guy. Get your shit together.*

"Snow Leopard," she yawned, "and with two morphs so close together, it makes me really sleepy... sorry..." Her eyes drifted closed as she slumped down onto the couch next to me. She snuggled into my side before her breathing evened out. Within moments, she was sound asleep.

I couldn't help but run a finger over her smooth cheek, wanting to kiss its silkiness, but I drew my hand back. I wasn't going to creep on a sleeping girl. She didn't look any older than twenty. I reached over and placed my arm under her legs, appreciating all the damn planking Lincoln made me do as I maneuvered us both off the couch. I carried her down to my bedroom. Celeste snuggled against my body, her breath warm on my chest. If my jeans felt a bit tight before, they were like a torture chamber now.

I placed Celeste gently on the bed and pulled the covers up around her. God, I just wanted to climb in beside her and wrap myself around her. I consciously pushed myself away from the bed and out the door. A night on the hard couch was what I needed; it wasn't like I was going to be able to sleep anyway.

3

CELESTE

I woke up in a panic, my gaze slashing wildly around the unfamiliar room. Slowly the night's events seeped into my sleep addled brain and I remembered I was in Reese's apartment. I slipped silently out of bed and slowly grappled my way through the darkness to the living room. The light from the kitchen streamed in through the open door and I could see the outline of Reese's face clearly as he slept curled on the couch. I smiled as a wave of longing passed over me. What would it be like to be normal? To come home every night to a man like Reese, instead of constantly running from enemies I couldn't see until they were right on top of me?

Reese's bottom lip jutted out and I desperately wanted to taste it. As if I was drawn by an irresistible force, I felt myself leaning down and taking his bottom lip between mine. I sucked gently and he moaned in his sleep. I expanded my kiss, brushing his top lip with my bottom lip then gently nipping at it.

His eyes slowly blinked open and he looked up at my face like I was a damn dream come true. My heart thudded painfully against my ribs. He held his arms open, silently asking for more. I couldn't resist.

I twined my fingers through his and pulled him up into a sitting position and then onto his feet. Without saying a word, I led him to his bedroom and to his big, king size bed. I peeled his soft boxer shorts down over a delectable ass, leaving him standing gloriously naked in front of me. His big, lean body was perfect, his wide shoulders tapering down into a trim waist, his pale body luminescent in the darkness. I undressed myself, leaving Reese to take stock of my body as each inch of my flesh was exposed, until I was standing there as naked as he was.

I wordlessly closed the distance between us. I was so very alone, so I'd allow myself this moment to play make believe, to revel in one night of humanity, before I continued with the solitary existence that was my life.

Reese's hands roamed up and down my curves as his mouth gently explored my own. He turned my back towards the bed, laying me down before covering my body with his. He nuzzled my neck, tracing the rise of my collar bone with his tongue before it drifted over to take an achingly tight nipple into his mouth. I arched toward the sensation and my hands knotted themselves in his hair. He shifted to the other nipple and bit it teasingly, his hand ran up the inside of my leg until fingers skimmed over the wet heat of my core.

I gasped as he flicked my clit, my body bucking upwards to seek out the pressure that I so desperately needed. Feeling my urgency, Reese rubbed in light circles, making my legs tremble with need, the pressure building until I was moaning his name. I panted as the currents of pleasure coursed through my body. I wanted more, and I wanted it right fucking now. Reese raised himself over me, kissing me hard on the mouth, his tongue seeking entrance as his body did the same.

My nails dug into the hard muscles of his back, moaning as the thick head of his cock thrust inside me, filling all the empty places in my soul for just a moment. His soft groans matched my own as he pulled back and thrust in again, harder this time, wilder. I held on, rolling my body, trapping him between my thighs as he rolled his hips, sending ripples of pleasure through me like an electric shock. He leaned forward and took my lip between his teeth, biting it as he thrust harder, until my moans became shouts of pleasure. My orgasm washed over me until I was sure I wouldn't be able to breathe again if he wasn't inside me. Reese toppled with me, his groans mixing with my own, as my orgasm milked his cock.

He collapsed on top of me, sweat making our

bodies slick, and his arms shook lightly where he held some of his weight off of my chest. His hot breath burned against my neck as he pressed his face in the crook of my shoulder. An animalistic desire for him to bite me there washed over me, scaring the fucking shit out of me. That's where shifters bit their mates, and the fact my leopard wanted that to happen made my heart beat crazily in my chest with panic.

As if he could feel the sudden tension in my body, Reese raised himself up on his arms. I could feel his eyes burn into my face, but I refused to open my own in case he saw something in there that I couldn't take back.

"Celeste, I-" he started, but I rolled onto my side and put a finger to his soft lips.

"Shh. This isn't the time for words."

Yeah, it was cowardly, but I couldn't do this. I could make love to him, but words were dangerous. They were quicksand and I couldn't get stuck inside this dream.

I snuggled closer to his body, my lips pressed into the curve of his throat so I could feel his pulse race. I sat for a moment, before the stickiness of his release chased me to the shower. When I came back, he was sound asleep. I curled in beside him, resting my head on his chest, and fell into a deep, dreamless sleep for the first time in years.

In the early hours before dawn, I woke again,

spooned tightly into Reese's back. I pressed a quick kiss against his spine and silently moved from the bed. I dressed in his borrowed clothes and silently left the apartment with only the dullest thud of the door to mark my departure.

Chapter Four

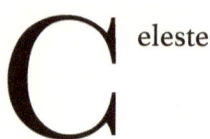 eleste

Five Months Later.

I stood under the large arch windows of the building in a baseball cap and thrift store sneakers. I played on my phone like I was just another twenty-something waiting for an Uber. The doors opened, and two well-dressed women stepped straight into a town car without so much as looking in my direction. I took advantage of the doorman's momentary distraction to duck in the doors. I sighed with relief when the desk was empty, and I didn't stop until I was at the elevator. I hid slightly around the corner, waiting for someone to swipe their key and activate the lifts.

When a man swaggered up to the golden doors, swiping his card, I strolled around the corner like I was meant to be here, still staring at my phone, a slight frown on my face to deter anyone trying to engage me in conversation.

Not that this guy looked like he was a big talker. He was frowning too, his cropped hair a sandy brown color. He watched me as I stepped in, and I hit the ninth floor. I'd jimmy the lock on the fire door to get to the top floor, because you needed the key to even press the button.

I stifled a relieved sigh and continued to fake-type out an email on my phone. When the doors opened on the ninth floor, the last of the floors with multiple apartments, I gave the guy in the elevator a tight smile and stepped out. I waited for the doors to close again before I walked easily to the fire escape door and went up.

I jimmied the first door easily. The security to the tenth floor wasn't quite as stringent as the penthouse.

Luckily, there was a maintenance hall that ran down the side of the building, allowing access to the elevator shaft along with the utility controls. I'd lifted the access card from one of the maintenance workers at a bar. He was still nursing a killer hangover that he was pretending was the flu. The guy couldn't hold his liquor or onto his worldly possessions. I scanned the maintenance card and stepped into the hallway. It wasn't pretty, a direct contrast to the rooms on the other side of the walls. Finally, I got to the small door that was the fire door for the penthouse suite. I took a deep breath and scanned the maintenance card, praying it worked.

This subterfuge was... probably unnecessary. But there was a chance that Reese was angry at me and I needed him to hear me out for five minutes. I figured if I was sitting on his couch when he got home, he'd be forced to listen to me, even if it was just while security arrived to escort me out.

I'd watched him get in and out of his town car every day for the last week, and I'd forgotten how pretty he was. Forgot the force of his smile. I thought maybe I'd put him on a pedestal after that night, like I'd set him up as this unobtainable mirage of what my life could be like.

But it wasn't a dream. He really was that freaking hot. I sighed and slipped the card into the slot, and when it turned green, I slowly opened it.

As I pushed it open, the room beyond looked exactly the same. Perfect interior decorating that was impersonal but beautiful. Uncomfortable couch with too many memories. When I stepped through the door, something was off, I just didn't know what, but my snow leopard swooshed her tail in my mind.

When a hand wrapped around my throat and slammed me into the wall beside the door, I guess I had my answer. The big guy from the elevator stood there, glaring down at me. "Who the fuck are you?" he growled.

I tried to swallow, but his hand was firm around my throat. He wasn't cutting off my oxygen, but his hold was firm. Could I break it? Probably. Was I going to out myself to prove that he wasn't as tough as he thought? Fuck no.

Did my Leopardess kinda like it? Yeah she did. But she was a kinky bitch.

He shook me a bit, and growled low in his throat. "I asked, who the fuck are you?"

Well, if we were playing it like that, I had some questions too. "Jessica Rabbit. Who the fuck are you?"

His lip curled. "I live here, bitch, so excuse me if I don't think strangers sneaking into my apartment is cute. Let's go, before I call the cops and tell them that I caught a dirty little thief."

This time my fear was real. I couldn't get thrown in prison. The bounty hunters had people on the police payroll just looking for supes like me.

"No wait, I need to talk to Reese," I said, as he grabbed my arm and dragged me toward the elevator doors. He pressed a button and they opened immediately.

"Like hell you do. You think you're the first girl who thought she could sneak into his apartment and wait for him naked? Like your pussy will bring him to his knees and he'll put a rock on your finger? You gold diggers are all the goddamn same. Granted, you are a little chunkier than most, but Reese was always a sucker for the doe eyes and a pretty face, and you got both of those."

I didn't know what I should be more indignant about. That he was dragging me around like yesterday's trash, or that he called me fat. What a douche.

Still, I let him stuff me in the elevator because I really, really couldn't go to the lock-up. I'd try to get to Reese a different way, one without the gorilla around. He mashed the ground button, and as the doors shut, he let me go like I was diseased. It really pissed me off.

"Look, you 'roided up asshat, I'm not up there to seduce Reese because I want his goddamn money. I just need to talk to him, that's all."

He rolled his eyes. "Then book an appointment through his secretary." As the car reached the ground floor, his hand latched around my arm again.

I huffed but didn't resist as he led me from the elevator to the front door. The man behind the desk was back, and he looked at me, his face scrunched up in confusion. He was probably trying to place my face, so I threw him a pleasant smile. Maybe I'd need him later.

The doorman opened the double doors, and the gorilla pulled me through. A town car pulled up in that moment, and the dude swore softly under his breath. "Great."

A confused looking Reese slid from the backseat, his eyes going first to the muscle-bound guy. I pushed my cap up with my free hand, and watched his face morph. Apparently, he hadn't learned a poker face in the last few months.

"Celeste?"

The gorilla dropped my arm like I was on fire. "This is Celeste?"

Well, it was probably good that my reputation proceeded me, but I wondered how much this guy knew. "Jesus, I thought you were dead. I looked..." Reese trailed off, and was in front of me in two long strides, wrapping his arms around my shoulders and pulling me into a hug.

I realized the moment when things changed. His whole body froze.

"We need to talk. Probably best to do it in your apartment," I whispered.

When Reese pulled away, he was so pale. "I think you're right."

The doorman opened the door again, his eyes trying to be uninterested but failing miserably. The gorilla guy was staring daggers into my skull as we walked back toward the elevator, Reese's hand on my spine. I saw the moment as the desk attendant connected the dots in his mind.

"Good to see you again, Miss." His eyes were slightly too wide, and I could sense his surprise. I saluted him, but didn't slow my steps.

The big guy's eyes were burning into my face, and I couldn't help the smug grin I threw him. "Told you I just needed to talk to him."

Reese looked between us. "You've met?" Neither of us answered him. "Lincoln?" he directed to the gorilla ass.

Lincoln. It suited him. Pompous. Strong. Jerkish.

The man in question glared at me. "Yeah, we bumped into each other while I was taking out the trash."

Well, shots goddamn fired. But being called trash was almost a compliment in my world. He was going to have to try harder to insult me. "You should be congratulated, Reese. I always wanted to train a dog to do menial chores too."

Lincoln's jaw tensed, and fortunately the doors slid open and we were back in Reese's apartment.

As soon as we all stepped into the foyer area, Reese was in front of me again.

"Celeste? Are you..."

I lifted my shirt and every set of eyes in the room dropped down. "Pregnant? Yeah, I am. Surprise?"

"Son of a goat bitching cock sucker," Lincoln swore.

I laughed, but it was a sad, miserable sound. "Amen to that. Guess I wasn't chunky after all?"

I looked at the rounded stomach of the chick in front of me, and knew this was going to be a problem. I loved Reese like a brother. Hell, I loved him more than my brother. Where my brother was a cruel motherfucker, Reese was soft. So damn soft with a heart so big he was asking for someone to crush it in their tiny fist.

And I had a feeling I knew who's tiny fist that would be.

Reese reached out and touched the pale globe of her stomach, and I could see his heart getting attached already. Fuck. "Is it mine?"

She nodded, her eyes haunted and sad. "Yes."

I scoffed. "We aren't going to just take your word for it." Reese looked like he wanted to protest on her behalf, so I raised a hand to stop him. "No way. Come on man. She fucked you and then fled in the middle of the night. Those are hardly the actions of a wilting virgin."

I expected her to screech or cry, but instead she flipped me off and then ignored me. "You told him?"

Reese looked a little sheepish. "I had to tell someone, just in case you were really a figment of a deteriorating brain disease, or tumor, or something. I told him I met a girl, we had unbelievable sex, and then she just disappeared like she'd never been."

She frowned. "That's all you told him?"

Reese nodded, his eyes flicking to me. That was his tell. He could never keep secrets. He was the world's worst poker player. How he survived in business was beyond me.

I looked between them and the heavy weight of the words left unsaid made the room tense. Maybe he wasn't such a bad secret keeper after all. He'd obviously been keeping a secret for months. For her.

I think I might hate her just out of principle.

She sighed and slumped down in the chair we used to put on our shoes. The interior designer called it an occasional chair. Stupid fucking name. "I can't give you a DNA test. I swear it though, Reese. I swear it's yours. I haven't even so much as gone on another date since you."

I rolled my eyes and pulled out my phone. I texted Vincent. I needed him back here ASAP.

911. I need you home NOW!

Within seconds, my phone buzzed.

OMW.

Vincent loved Reese just as much as I did. Hell, maybe more. Vincent would jump in front of a speeding car for Reese. Who was I kidding, we both would. In this case, we were going to leap in front of some little viper who was trying to wrap herself around the soft heart of my best friend. And I would not let it happen.

Even now, he was putting his hand on her shoulder and telling her he believed her. He wasn't lying either. He did believe her.

He was a sucker and I was here to make sure that people didn't take advantage of him. Because I knew more than most that the world was filled with shitty people who would stomp on you on their way to the top.

Problem was, there wasn't a conniving look on the girl's face. She looked tired. Defeated. But this was New York City, and it was filled with budding actresses.

Reese bundled her up into his arms, and I didn't miss the small kiss he dropped on her head. He'd been torn up when she just disappeared like a bad dream. Or a really, really good dream, as it happened. He searched for her for months, tracking her through his surveillance software until she just disappeared without a trace. I wanted to know where she'd been and why she was back now.

She'd been gone five months, and you didn't suddenly realize you were pregnant in your fifth month.

Something wasn't right, and I was going to work out what it was. Reese ushered her to the living room, and he looked over his shoulder at me. "We'll order in Chinese or something tonight."

I clenched my jaw and he sighed. He sat the girl on the couch, whispering something to her as he handed her the remote like she was fragile. She wasn't even a little fragile. When I'd had my hand around her throat earlier, she hadn't even flinched. If anything, there was heat in her eyes. Yeah, not exactly the damsel in distress she was painting herself to be.

Reese came back over and stared at me. "Don't start, Linc."

"Come on, Reese. Even you have to admit that there's something fishy about this."

Reese was shaking his head, denying my words even though they were true. "It's not out of the realms of possibility, man. Five months ago, I had unprotected sex with a woman. Now, I know my Catholic school education is a little light on the sex ed, but I'm pretty sure that's how babies are made."

I threw my hands in the air. Sometimes, I just

wanted to shake him. "So what? You're just going to take her word for it?"

Reese swallowed hard, and shook his head. "You don't understand. I believe her, but more than that, I don't think it matters."

The record scratch that sounded in my head was nearly deafening. "What do you mean it doesn't matter? Reese, this girl is going to milk you dry and you are just going to let her?"

He was still shaking his head and he lowered his voice until it was almost a whisper. Unnecessarily low. "I want her. Fuck, Linc, I haven't been able to get her out of my head and it's been months. I've slept with every girl Vince has thrown at me, trying to erase her from my brain and I just can't. She's back now and I intend to keep her forever. If she comes with a baby, all the better. I'll love it too, whether it's mine or not. Because they'll be mine, Linc."

Well fuck. Now we really had problems.

"Reese…"

He held up a hand. "Leave it. You can badger me about it later, okay? Let me just, I don't know, fuss or something for a little while before you tell me how she is just here to steal all my money. I get it. But I just want to believe for a moment that she could possibly be interested in me, the man, and not me, the billionaire. Okay?"

I gritted my teeth and forced myself to nod. Fine.

Let him play White Knight for the day, but I was watching her.

I sat across the room for the next thirty minutes as they talked softly to each other and ground my molars. When the elevator doors slid open, I breathed a sigh of relief. Thank fuck another voice of reason was here. Vincent strolled in with several bags of Chinese food. "Got this from the doorman on the way up, said I'd play sexy delivery boy," he said, winking at me lasciviously.

He dumped the Chinese food on the table and frowned. "What's crawled up your ass and missed the prostate completely?"

I lift my chin, indicating Reese and Celeste across the room. Vincent looked over his shoulder and his eyebrows hit his hairline. "Who's the chick?" he asked, and already his eyes were running over her body like she was a potential conquest. Vince was a manwhore. A stereotypical fuckboy. No, that was a lie. He loved women, maybe a little too much. What gave him hives was commitment. Given his childhood, I didn't blame him. His parents would put me off marriage too. "She's hot. Doesn't seem like Reese's usual type though. Not beige enough."

I snorted. "That's Celeste."

Now his mouth dropped open. "*The* Celeste? Like fuck 'em and forget 'em Celeste? Fuck me, she's nothing like I imagined."

Yeah, she wasn't like I imagined either. I had pictured this small, timid little thing that Reese had rescued off the streets and then boned between his thousand thread count sheets. The woman in front of me wasn't exactly timid, though she was tiny. But those eyes. They pierced your soul. They were eyes that would haunt the darkest of nights.

I cleared my throat. "Yeah, but we have bigger problems. She's knocked up and convinced Reese he's the father," I hissed and Vincent leapt back like accidental paternity was contagious.

"Fuck off," he gasped in disbelief. "Surely he doesn't believe her, right? He's going to get the test?"

I pinched the bridge of my nose because I could feel my frustration rising. "Nope. Says he doesn't care. Says he's going to keep her, baby and all. Doesn't matter if it's his or not."

Vincent's eyes went blank like the words did not compute. He blinked repeatedly until he finally shook his head. "He can't be serious, can he?"

I nodded, but eyed my best friend. There was a terror in his eyes that came from a well and truly fucked up childhood. Reese, Vincent, and I were as close as three people could be. All because of Reese. Reese was our linchpin, the warm safety net that kept us all okay. But Reese was so damn good, so ready to believe the best in everyone, that he needed someone to be cynical for him. That was me. Combination bullshit detector and bodyguard. Vincent was his wild side. Reese wasn't one of the youngest tech billionaires by luck. He was brilliant. But without Vince to drag him out, to make him live, he'd be stuck in his lab for days on end, completely engrossed in one project or another.

This girl? She was going to fuck up the balance. I could see it now.

Still, I rested my hand on Vincent's shoulder and he leaned into the touch. "It'll be okay, Vince. She obviously has commitment issues to match your own. She'll be gone before you know it."

She looked up, her grey eyes meeting mine like she could read my mind. I held her stare, my jaw set. Yeah. I saw her alright.

L ogically, I recognized that I was in shock. Celeste's return would have been crazy enough, but when you threw in a bulging baby bump, my brain was whirling as much as my hands were shaking. I could feel the heat of Lincoln's gaze, but Celeste seemed impervious to it. She'd come up against deadlier people than Lincoln, but when it came to me and Vince, Lincoln was a savage. He protected us with the ferocity of, well, a snow leopard.

"Your boy over there doesn't seem to like me much," Celeste laughed softly, completely unfazed.

I shrugged. "Lincoln is just protective of me. I've, uh, been burned before."

That was an understatement. I loved women. Unlike the guys, I'd grown up in a beautiful, loving home. My adoptive parents had been older and so damn enamoured by their quirky ass son that they'd doted on me. They believed in giving everyone a chance, offering a helping hand. They'd died in my first year of college. First my mother in a car accident, and then my father soon after of what I assumed was a broken heart, but science had said was a brain aneurysm.. I'd been so damn lost, but then I'd met Vincent passed out in a bush in front of my dorm.

I'd cleaned him up, made sure he didn't die by choking on his own vomit, and then he'd never really left. If it had even occurred to me, I would have been worried he was after my money, but Vincent was richer than God himself. Rich and completely, soul shatter-ingly sad. So there we were, two entirely different people brought together by our loneliness.

It wasn't until Linc came along, gave us something we both needed, that we'd found happiness. I owed him everything, not just because he was my bodyguard and best friend, or the fact he'd saved Vincent from dying at the bottom of a bottle. He protected me from everything, even myself.

I looked at Celeste.

But I didn't want or need saving from her.

Celeste wiggled on the couch. "You didn't get a more comfortable couch in the last few months. Jesus, how does your ass not go numb on this thing?" She squirmed, her face screwed up, and it was goddamn adorable.

I hadn't been able to shake her memory. Even when I'd woken up and convinced myself it was a dream, it was like my body still pined for her. I'd searched for her, of course, but I didn't know her last name. What was I meant to search for? Celeste Don't-Know-Her-Last-Name? Add that she sometimes shifts into a snow leopard.

Shifters.

I hadn't told the guys her secret, mostly because I promised not to, but also because it sounded freaking insane. But I'd quietly started researching. Message boards and the dark web. I'd stumbled across the sale of Shifters, everything from women, to children, to cage fighters. I'd nearly thrown up. Everything she'd said had been true, confirmation she wasn't a delusion. I'd seen those men with my own two eyes.

I looked down at her stomach. Now she was carrying my baby, er cub? I swore softly under my breath.

"It's just hitting you, huh?" she asked softly. I nodded and ran my fingers gently over the globe of her stomach. That was mine in there. I knew it as surely as I knew my own name. She tensed, and then let out a sigh that was so world weary, I wanted to pull her into my arms. "I'd prove it's yours if I could, you know that, right? But if the hospitals got hold of shifter blood, or if the bounty hunters tagged the files, decided to chase it up..."

I held a finger to her lips. I didn't want to think about what could happen to either of them. They were with me now, and I didn't intend on letting either of them out of my sight again. But instead of saying all that, I just nodded softly. "I know. I believe you, Celeste. You don't have to prove anything to me."

She shook her head and got an expression on her face that mirrored one that Lincoln often got when he was dealing with me. Bemused exasperation. "You shouldn't just take people's word for things, Buttercup."

I smile softly at the nickname. "I like giving people the benefit of the doubt. It's a happier way to live, rather than waiting for the next person to screw me over. Besides, that's what I have Lincoln for."

Lincoln was glaring, and when the elevator doors slid open, I wasn't surprised when Vincent stepped out. I was surprised it took him this long to get here though. He wandered over to Lincoln first, and they were talking in low voices. Something they said brought a smile to Celeste's lips. I frowned at her. "You can hear them?"

She lifted a shoulder and nodded. "Shifter hearing. It's a definite boon."

I winced a little. She probably heard what I said to Lincoln before. About keeping her. "What do you need, Celeste? Just tell me. I'll give you anything."

She shook her head at me again. "That's a big statement, Reese," she said, her mouth turning down in a sad expression. "There's so, so many things you can't give me. But I only need one thing and that's it."

I leaned forward and grabbed her hands, wrapping them in mine. "Anything." Honestly, I meant it. Money, houses, diamonds. Material shit I had in abundance. My heart? It was pretty much hers already. Or at least the idea of her.

"When the baby is born, I need you to take care of it."

I frowned. That couldn't be it. I'd already promised her that. "Where will you be?"

She let out a shuddering breath. "As far from here as possible." She stood up. "Excuse me, I have to go to the bathroom."

She all but sprinted out of the room, Lincoln and Vincent tracking her with their eyes. What the hell did she mean by that?

I ran my fingers through my hair, the sandy blond locks falling in my face. It was probably time for another haircut. I kept forgetting.

I rubbed a hand down my face. If I couldn't remember to get myself a haircut, how was I going to care for a kid?

Lincoln was putting out all the Chinese food on the dining table and Vincent wandered over to me. "Damn, Reese. You don't do shit in halves, do you?

Finally have a one night stand, then you knock the girl up."

I gave Vince a crooked smile. When it came to the idea of keeping Celeste and the baby, he would be easier to convince than Lincoln. Vincent had little to no regard for consequences. There were probably a hundred little Vincent's roaming the greater New York area, because he swore by four rules when it came to women.

Never give out your real name, never have more than a one night stand, never bring them back to the apartment and never, ever make any promises.

I'd broken all his commandments that night with Celeste. But still, he wasn't a worrier in the way Linc was. If I could convince Vince that this was a good idea, eventually Lincoln would have to fall in line.

"I'll introduce you when she comes back out. You'll love her. She's as tough as she is beautiful. She'll bring you to your knees and you'll smile while she does it."

He cocked an eyebrow. "You know I'm a big fan of being on my knees in front of a woman, but somehow I don't think we are speaking the same language here, bud."

I huffed out a laugh, because I didn't think we were either. But Vincent wasn't dumb, despite the stupid boozehound rocker persona he liked to project to the rest of the world. No, Vincent was as smart as me. Well, maybe he might have started off that way but he'd been pretty intent on massacring his brain cells with cheap vodka for a few years there.

I looked in the direction of the bathroom, but Celeste still hadn't emerged. I wanted to go and check on her, but I didn't want to overstep. Vincent slouched onto the coffee table, kicking his booted feet onto the couch. I pushed them off and sighed. "Just give her a chance, Vince. I really like her."

Vincent shook his head sadly. "That's the problem, brother. You really like them all. But Lincoln is out for blood. He isn't going to be swayed by your puppy dog eyes and her pretty face."

The door to the bathroom opened and I pretended like I hadn't been watching it like a hawk. I stood and waved her toward the dining table that delineated the kitchen from the living area. "Let's eat." I hadn't missed how thin she looked.

She eyed Vincent hesitantly from where he was lounging around on the couch, but she held her head high, meeting Lincoln's eyes like it was a battle of wills. I worried, but I briefly heard Vince chuckle. Yeah, he'd let me keep her around purely for the entertainment fact.

It didn't really matter what either of them thought.

I was keeping her.

The girl could put away food like a growing frat boy. She inhaled her food in a way that made me wonder if she even had a gag reflex. Then I felt like shit that I was even thinking that way about Reese's girl. And she was his girl. He looked at her like the sun rose out of her vagina every morning and set in her ass every night.

She was a way bigger issue than Linc could imagine, because while Reese professed his love for just about every hussy with big, fake eyelashes and a cute pout, the way he looked at this chick put them all to shame.

If Lincoln pushed this too hard, I think we'd lose him. That was the real reason I'd agreed to giving her a chance. Not because I gave two shits about her or the fact she was knocked up.

No, I agreed because if we didn't play this right, it could spell the end of everything I'd worked so hard to build and maintain. Real friendships. Love.

I'd grown up without either of those things, but there's that saying that you don't know what you're missing until it's gone. Well, it was the same the other way around. You don't know you're missing something until it pulls you out of a bush and makes sure you don't die.

"So, Celeste, is it? That's a pretty name. You kind of look celestial. Like a star," I cooed at her, and Linc snorted. The girl in question just raised an eyebrow.

Reese rolled his eyes, but he was used to my antics by now. I flirted like I breathed. It was interesting that he was so protective of her, so desperate for her to stay, but didn't mind me flirting with her. Maybe he didn't like her as much as I thought.

"Uh, thanks? It was my grandmother's name."

I ate an eggroll, sipping the beer that I was rolling between my fingertips. "Where have you been all this time? Reese here was quite in a tizz after you left."

Her face went carefully blank, but I didn't miss it. I people-watch for fun. "Here and there. Mostly women's shelters and couch surfing. A couple of house sitting jobs."

Yeah, that wasn't suspicious as fuck. I could all but hear the cogs turning in Lincoln's brain beside me. "Why no apartment?"

Reese gave me a warning look. "Vince…"

Lincoln pretended he wasn't completely invested in her answers. "It's a fair question, Reese."

Celeste laid a hand on Reese's arm, and it made something churn in my chest. Jealousy? Nah, that wasn't it. I was annoyed that she'd been with him all of two seconds, and now she was what, protecting him from us? What the fuck was with that? "They're right. It does sound suspicious. I pissed off some bad people, and they're chasing me. Well, not me in particular but that's neither here nor there."

I narrowed my eyes at her, rolling my eyes at her non-answer. "Pissed them off how?" I said, sounding suspicious even to my own ears. I don't know who looked more surprised, Reese or Lincoln, that I was taking this tact.

But Celeste looked me directly in the eye and grimaced. "By existing."

Well, that was about as clear as mud. There was more to this, a secret Reese knew but hadn't shared. Reese sucked at secrets, so it must have been a doozy. Lincoln could try and brute force it out of her, but I had different tactics. I sucked my teeth like I disapproved of people persecuting such a sweet, young woman. Well, I did on principle. The people who preyed on the weaker were the worst kind of scum. But they were prolific scum. Good people were harder and harder to find. They were everything wrong with the world, and it was the reason I trusted no one except the two men at the table with me.

I looked between Celeste and Reese. "So, is Star here going to stay? You don't mind me calling you Star, do you? It suits you. Less over the top than Celeste."

She pointed a dumpling at me. "You can call me whatever you like, names can't hurt me." But she wasn't looking anymore, instead her eyes had drifted to a taut Lincoln. Oh great, these two had a rocky acquaintance already. Yay.

I waved my fingers so she was looking at me again. "Star it is. Are you intending to stay?"

She nodded, her eyes drifting to Reese. "If it's okay with you guys. I need to get off the streets and out of the public eye before I get anymore pregnant."

Reese placed his hand over hers, his eyes earnest. "Of course you can stay. We aren't heartless enough to throw a woman back on the streets, especially not you."

My scoff reverberated around the room. "Especially not when you are carrying his baby. I'll bunk with Lincoln and she can have my room." Reese looked like he was going to protest, but I waved a hand. "She's going to need her own space, and Lincoln won't mind, will you?" I said to Lincoln, who was grinding his back teeth and looking like he wanted to murder me.

Instead of voicing the obvious 'fuck you' that was

written all over his face, he gritted his teeth. "That would be fine."

Reese looked torn. Like he wanted to invite her to live not only in his house, but in his bed. But he was raised too oldschool for that, he would never suggest she just jump back into his bed, unless she suggested it first.

I wasn't raised with his manners. "Unless you wanna bunk with me instead, Star?" Reese kicked me under the table and I grinned. "I'm kidding, obviously."

I stood and started clearing dishes and takeout containers. I felt the girl's eyes track me across the room. Well, maybe she wouldn't mind. After all, she didn't say no.

But then she looked back at Reese and her face softened. Dammit, he had that effect on people. You could be the most hard ass of bastards, but you turned to mush at the sight of his big earnest face, like a human golden retriever. Look at Lincoln. The guy went from 'I eat livers for dinner' to 'no one fucks with my Reesey-Weesey' in like three seconds flat. Unlike Reese and I, Lincoln was a product of his shitty upbringing. Well, that's not so different to me. The difference lay in the fact his was compounded by poverty, and mine was compounded by apathy of the rich and famous.

Poor little rich kid. It was a phrase I'd berated myself with often over the years.

I stacked the dishes and refrigerated the leftovers. "Give me a second to pack up a few of my things and then it's all yours," I told Star from where she was watching me like she wanted to eat me. Oh yeah, she was trying to hide it well, but I'd seen that look many times since I hit puberty and my mother's cougar friends started coming around for cocktails. They had made me uncomfortable as fuck, but my mother seemed to take my attractiveness as some kind of credit to her hard work, like she had any hand in the mixing of my genetics to create my aesthetics.

When Star looked at me, I was still uncomfortable, but it was only from the way my dick hardened in my jeans.

I wandered down the hall, pushing open my door and screwing up my nose. It was a bit filthy, but the cleaner only allowed it to get a certain level of messy before she held an intervention. That meant this week's clothes were on the floor rather than in the hamper. There were guitars and notebooks spread all over the place.

Other than mess and instruments, there wasn't much in the room that was personal. I hadn't brought that much with me when I'd abandoned the family of my blood for one of my choosing. I heard the shower start and then Reese was standing in my doorway.

He looked around and screwed up his nose too. Yeah. It was a bit like that. "I'll help you, uh, clean up a little." He picked up a handful of socks and aimed them at my hamper. I pulled some clothes out of my drawers, mainly just shirts and boxers.

He stopped me with a hand on my arm. "Thanks for this, Vincent. I really appreciate it."

Gah, I hated when he got all sincere. It made me feel like the shittiest person alive. Even if I hadn't done anything wrong.

"Whatever. It's not like I'm here much anyway."

That was the truth. Between touring and one night stands, I rarely spent the night here. And even then, I was rarely in my bed. As if reading my thoughts, Reese stripped the linen off my bed and replaced it with fresh silk sheets. Black. Always in black. Because if Reese was a saint, then I was a sinner. "When's your next tour?"

I shrugged. I'd just come off a world tour, and honestly, my heart wasn't in it. I didn't tell my best friend that though. He would worry I was burning out or something, and maybe he'd be right. But I didn't need him adding that to his lists of worries. Reese was a fixer. See a homeless man under the awning at your office building? Give him a job in the mail room. Find an angsty rich kid in a bush, bring him home. Find a girl in trouble? Fuck it, bring her home too.

Find out your best friend hates the very career he swore he wanted to do for the rest of his life, bankroll him until he finds his passion.

Reese must be protected at all costs. He was too fucking good for this world.

So instead of all that, I just said, "Record label wants me to cut another album first, so I'm home for a bit. But it doesn't matter. I'll bunk with Lincoln. We don't get to spend enough time together anyway."

Reese's eyes softened, and he reached out to cup my arm. "He misses you, I know he does. He just doesn't verbalize anything well. I missed you too. I'm glad you'll be home for awhile. We need you. It isn't the same here with just the two of us."

I cleared my throat before I did something very uncool like burst into unmanly tears. "Well, now there's four and a half of us." I stopped and drop-shotted my dirty boxers into the hamper. "How are you doing, man? It must have been a hell of a surprise."

Reese looked at the door, but the shower was still running. Yet he still dropped his voice to almost a whisper. Jesus, she'd have to have ears like a bat to hear him. "Don't tell Linc or Celeste, but I'm kind of excited."

Of course he fucking was. "Star isn't excited?"

Reese did that face he made when he was trying to find a lie that was close enough to the truth that he could get away with it. "Not really, no. I think she was a bit shocked. She wants to leave after the baby is born."

I frowned. "Why even turn up on your doorstep then, if she was just gonna take the kid and run off anyway? She had to know you'd want custody." Hell, you only needed to spend two minutes with Reese to know that he was all about doing 'the right thing'.

He stepped closer to me, his voice still pitched low. "She doesn't want to take the baby with her. She wants me to have full custody."

I reared back like he'd slapped me. "She doesn't want it?"

Reese shook his head sadly. "There's more to it. You don't understand."

Damn right I didn't understand. I was unwanted too, but at least my mother pretended she was a doting parent in public, even if she forgot I existed at home. But complete rejection? That was very uncool. "You're right there, Bud. I don't understand. Why don't you explain it to me?"

He shook his head, grabbing my full hamper to drag it to the laundry room. "I can't, Vince. It's not my truth to tell."

I fucking knew it. He was keeping secrets. "You've never kept secrets from us before."

He didn't say anything, just slunk out of the room.

Maybe Lincoln was right. Maybe she needed to go before she tore us apart.

8

CELESTE

I stepped out of the shower and sighed. It was good to finally be clean and warm. To have a shower without worrying about getting your shit stolen, or being attacked in the bathroom. Though the way that Reese's buddies were looking at me, maybe I should be on the lookout for an attack.

I found it hard to believe that a man as sweet as Reese would have friends that would attack women, but I'd been wrong before. So I'd keep an eye on them.

Yeah, in case of attack, not because they were both as hot as fuck. Lincoln was tall and broody, a long muscular body and a close trimmed beard that I wanted to rub my face against and purr. And those Alpha vibes he cast off? My snow leopard wanted to roll all over him. And Vincent... It had taken me a while to work out who he was, but when I did, I tried not to fangirl a little. It was Vincent Brazz, lead singer of Enlighten Me. I snorted. He *was* Enlighten Me. Every other member of the group had been replaced over the last couple of years, but Vincent was the one constant. He sang like an angel who'd fallen into a vat of whiskey, cocaine, and hookers. Probably not in that order.

His reputation didn't help. He was always on the front of the trash mags with a different socialite on his arm, who were probably just using him to get back at their parents. Because he was the quintessential bad boy, and it was hard to comprehend how he and Reese, who was the sweetest nerd you'd ever meet, were even friends.

You only had to glimpse the concern in Vincent's eyes, which was carefully hidden under his devil-may-care smirk, to see that he loved Reese.

I stepped from the shower, pulling on one of Reese's oversized shirts. I wasn't a tall woman, shorter and curvier than most, at least when I was well fed. For the last few months I'd been too worried to stay in one place for too long. To hold down much of a steady job. Because it wasn't just me now. Capture meant a two-for-one which would make the bounty hunters more persistent, and that wasn't a risk I was willing to take.

I was tired. So damn tired. My snow leopard wanted to make a den, wanted to settle down to prepare for her cub, and the moving was making her anxious and restless. Coming to Reese had been the right decision, even if his housemates thought I was after his money.

I wasn't. I wouldn't let myself stay for that long. A small part of me was glad that our child wouldn't have to struggle though. I'd left all my possessions in a train station locker that I'd have to go and collect tomorrow, but for now, I was happy enough in Reese's shirt that hung down to mid thigh. I looked down at my underwear and decided against it. I'd have to wear these clothes tomorrow, and the idea of putting my dirty underwear back on after I was finally clean made me screw up my nose.

I bundled them all up and tucked them under my arm. I stepped out of the bathroom door, and then there were hands gripping my shoulders tightly.

I huffed, and so did my snow leopard. Pregnancy was making her slow. Or maybe it was the fact she liked being pressed between a wall and the hard body that was Lincoln. Traitor.

He glared down at me. "I don't know what you're about, but don't think for a minute that I'm buying this whole thing. I don't know who's baby that is, but even if it is Reese's, I won't let him be a meal ticket for some conniving one night stand. Do you hear me?"

Oh, I heard him alright, but my leopardess was far too distracted by how close his body was, and the fact I wasn't wearing panties, and how strong his hands were, and how good he smelled. I physically had to hold myself back from curling against him.

With that, he turned and walked down the hallway, the way his jeans molded against his muscular ass making me bite my lip even as I flipped him the finger. Fucker.

I heard a slow clap behind me, and I looked over my shoulder at Vincent. "Not going to lie, Star. That was kind of hot." My face flushed and I glared at the sexy rockstar and his vapid expression. He waved me closer. "Come on, I'll give you the grand tour of my bedroom."

I huffed, calming my racing heartbeat.

At some point Vincent had lost his shirt and was walking around in low slung jeans and bare feet. He was bad for my heartbeat. Luckily he wasn't a shifter and couldn't scent what his wide tattooed shoulders, trim waist and that nipple ring really did to me.

I gave him a tight smile, and was a little relieved that his bedroom was close to the bathroom. Pregnancy bladder was no joke.

His room smelled like man. Not like stale socks or anything, but the faint hint of his cologne, and the scent of his skin just under that. It's decor looked how I imagined a hotel room would look if you lived in it long enough. Impersonal color scheme and furniture, but knick knacks and things strewn around. He had guitars on stands along the walls, and a picture of

Reese and Lincoln on the nightstand. A few posters from his concerts lined the walls. The comforter was a dark red, and the sheets were black silk.

"Reese has just gone to get you a couple of extra pillows. But this is it." He pointed to a door. "Ensuite. Excuse my mess in there." He turned. "Bed. The sheets are clean, for now anyway." He winked and my core clenched. I swallowed hard and attempted to keep my features blank.

I gave my snow leopard a stern talking to. I needed Reese to help me, and sleeping with his friends prob-ably wasn't the way to go about it.

Vincent cocked a brow, tugging his lip ring into his mouth. Fuck me. I wanted to do that, maybe more than I wanted my next breath. As if to remind me what was at stake, the baby moved in my stomach. It was like ice water to my overheated blood. I smiled politely, and he watched me with intelligent eyes. Yeah, there was more in there than a fickle party boy.

"Thank you," I said softly, and I meant it. I was kicking him out of his room and he volunteered his space without even blinking. Even if he was doing it for some nefarious reason, I was going to accept the good-will where it was offered.

"I emptied you out a drawer for your stuff. I guess if you are here more permanently, we'll uh, figure some-thing out."

I smiled at him then. I'd borrow his room for four

months, and then he could have it back. My brain shied away from the idea of leaving this all behind, of leaving the baby behind. But it was for the best. I was a known shifter. I needed to be as far away from my cub as possible if I was going to keep it safe.

My leopardess yowled in my head and my heart hurt. We both knew it was the best thing to do, but it hurt all the same. I shut the thought away. I'd deal with that when the time came. So I gave Vincent a strained smile. "I appreciate it."

He watched me with eyes that saw too much for a heartbeat longer, and then nodded. "Sure thing."

He grabbed a duffel bag of stuff and left. I climbed beneath the blankets of his bed, sliding between silk sheets that felt like heaven and sighed.

A gentle knock at the door and the scent of Reese told me he'd returned with the pillows.

"Come on in," I said softly.

Reese peeked around the doorjamb, his soft, golden curls falling in front of his eyes. "Hey, I grabbed you some pillows not covered in Vincent's drool."

I sat up on my elbows. "Thanks for letting me stay."

Reese sat beside me on the bed. "Of course, Celeste. I looked for you, you know, after you left. At first I was angry that you'd just snuck out, but when I thought about that fear in your eyes even though you were trying to hide it, I couldn't be mad at you. You had no reason to trust me, or anyone." He grabbed my hand and held it between his bigger ones. "But I promise you can trust me with this. You can trust me to keep you safe. Trust us."

I snorted. Yeah, I was pretty sure Lincoln would boot me out on my ass if he could wrangle it. And as for Vincent, I think he was apathetic to the situation entirely.

"Reese, I appreciate it, but you have to know that we can't possibly start up something more than this. I have to go in four months and that would just end badly for us both."

He smiled at me brightly. "I have to respectfully disagree, but for now, I won't push it. There's something here, Celeste. I felt it on that night, and I still feel it now."

I sighed, mostly because I felt it too, but I was going to be stubborn, dammit. Willpower. "Snow Leopards are not monogamous, Reese. We don't do well in one on one relationships. Even now, my snow leopard wants to climb all over your roommates."

Reese raised both eyebrows, looking between me and the door like he had x-ray vision. "I guess they are kind of hot. I get it." He frowned. "Okay."

"Okay what?"

"I can share you with my roommates if that's what you want and that's what it takes for me to keep you forever. Hell, it's the perfect solution. I want you, and I love them. They love each other. Actually, this would solve quite a few problems." Now he was talking more to himself than to me, and I just stared at him, my mouth hanging open.

"Are you for real right now?"

He just grinned, but I could see the cogs turning in his head. Fuck it. I was too tired for this shit. I yawned and Reese rocked back on his heels. "I'll let you rest."

He stepped toward the door and panic clawed at my chest. "Wait!" He stopped, a concerned frown on his face. I took a shaky breath. "Can you just, uh, sleep with me? Like on your side of the bed?" I cursed myself. I sounded stupid and pathetic. I'd just given him a big spiel about how we couldn't start anything and now I wanted him to stay the night. Mixed messages much?

His face softened. "Of course."

He peeled off his shirt and his jeans and climbed beneath the sheets with me. He kept a respectful distance between us, but the comfort of him being close soothed my animal.

"Want to watch 'The Witcher' before bed? I've been meaning to binge it, but I've never found the time?"

I smiled softly. When Reese wanted to Netflix and chill, I think he legitimately meant Netflix and chill. It wasn't a euphemism at all. I nodded, and he fiddled with the remote until the TV screen on the wall flicked on. He tapped something out on his phone, then the screen was alive with the sounds of Henry Cavill.

Reese switched off the bedside lamp and the room flooded with darkness. I reached out and entwined my fingers in his. I pulled them to my side of the bed and placed it on my stomach.

Something kept spiking inside my brain though. "What do you mean they love each other?"

He looked down at me. "Hmm?"

"You said that Vincent and Lincoln loved each other. What did you mean?" I was blinking rapidly now, trying to keep my eyes open.

Reese just grinned and pointed at the TV and I narrowed my eyes at him. I watched the show, but I was so tired that I was almost asleep in moments. I'd apologize to Henry in person if I ever got the chance.

Vincent threw his duffle bag on my floor, unzipping it and rifling through it just to knock shit on the floor and annoy me. He was doing it on purpose to distract me from what was happening down the hall, and it was working, the fucking asshole.

"Do you have to do that?" I growled, and he just looked up at me and grinned. That fucking grin was my achilles heel.

"I'm looking for my toothbrush. I'm sure I stuffed it in here, and don't particularly want to walk in on Reese and Celeste fucking like monkeys, you know?"

I huffed, picking up his duffle bag and taking it to my walk-in closet. I hung his band shirts and torn jeans in my closet, though they wouldn't stay on their hangers. Vincent didn't do order. I couldn't do chaos. How we coexisted was a mystery.

I looked up, and he was leaning against the door jamb, a smug smile on his face. I didn't know if I wanted to punch him or kiss him, but that was the way it was with Vincent. He needled me to make me feel, and I kept him anchored to his sanity. "Are you going to be huffy the whole time she's here, because I'm down for a few months of angry sex. But I think you need to come to terms with the fact she isn't a bandaid you can just rip off for him, Linc. He really likes her."

I slammed around my bedroom, putting everything back until it was in its place. Control and order. It's what we needed. She was the opposite of all that.

Vincent stepped toward me, his hands reaching out to grab my wrists. "Linc, he has to make mistakes like the rest of us miserable bastards. That's his kid-"

"Allegedly," I interrupted.

He rolled his eyes at me. "Allegedly his kid. He isn't going to abandon it. He isn't like your parents or mine. Even if it isn't his kid, he's going to look after it. We both know it. It's just the way Reese is, it's part of the reason we love him."

I hated it when Vince was fucking reasonable. When he was seeing clearly. "You didn't see the way she was eating you alive with her eyes," I growled and he laughed low in his throat. It always made me fucking hard, that sound. It was dark and dirty.

"Jealous, Linc?" he stepped closer until his chest was brushing mine. He was teasing, but I was a little. Not because she was eyefucking Vincent, because he was fucking hot. God, I knew trying to resist Vincent was an exercise in futility better than any person on the planet. But Reese would hang the moon for her and he's barely known her twenty-four hours, and she can't even keep her eyes to herself for an hour?

No. She was a one way street to heartbreak for Reese, and I would protect him at all costs.

"Not jealous. Angry that she can't even be loyal to him for a single minute."

He leaned forward and nipped my jaw. "Liar."

I leaned into his lithe body. He was walking art really. Tall, broad shoulders but a lean body covered in tattoos. He complimented my bulk like we were made to be together.

"I can see what Reese see's in her though. She has a heady kind of energy. I wouldn't mind fucking her," he groaned and I felt the hard line of his dick in his sweats.

My relationship with Vincent was another thing that was complicated, but easy at the same time. I knew I couldn't give him everything he needed. I didn't mean physically, because I could fuck the hell out of him any day of the week. I gave Vincent a sense of home that was wrapped in a parcel of danger. But it wasn't enough. Whatever he was still searching for was found between the sheets of a multitude of other lovers. I wasn't mad about it, it was how we worked.

I loved Vincent, but something in me was broken. If I loved something enough, I tried to break it so it couldn't leave. I'm sure Reese would say that was some kind of childhood PTSD bullshit. He was smart so he was probably right. Vincent was free enough that I didn't chafe against the urge.

"Then fuck her. It would show Reese how much she's just after his money like all the rest." The more I thought about it, the more I liked the idea. Maybe I would too. I wasn't blind to the way she'd eyed me in the elevator, or the way she looked at me from the corner of her eye. I didn't want to be conceited, but the few times Vince and I had taken the same woman to bed, they'd basically been on their knees begging for it.

Vincent was giving me his contemplative look, like he was trying to work out if I was serious or testing him. We didn't do that shit. Didn't test each other like that. To prove my point, I leaned forward and kissed him, sucking his pouty bottom lip between mine and biting it softly. It always made him groan; he liked to ride that edge of pain. He told me because he just wanted to feel; pleasure or pain, it didn't matter to Vince. I was happy giving him whatever he wanted too.

I traced my rough fingers over the black and white tattoos that spread across his chest and abs. He was fucking beautiful, and I wanted to lick every inch of him.

He pulled his lip from my teeth, even though it had to hurt. He grinned up at me, and I frowned. "Get on the bed, Vincent."

He slid out of his jeans, his grin getting wider. "Angry Lincoln fucks are my favorite kind. I might need to send the girl some flowers or some shit as a thank you."

I growled again and he sauntered toward the bed. He looked over his shoulder, his eyelids hooded. "Make it hurt."

I'd make it hurt for the both of us. I shed my own jeans as I walked toward him, kicking them off my feet but taking the moment to throw them in the direction of the hamper. It made Vincent's eyes light up with amusement, that I couldn't have disorder, even in a moment like this. Maybe more so in a moment like this. I strolled to the head of the bed and sat with my back against the headboard. The heat in Vincent's gaze was almost searing as he sucked his lip into his mouth again.

I beckoned him, curling my finger and he grinned. My lip twitched, but I didn't smile. I gripped my dick and stroked it, and he followed the action with his eyes. "Suck me," I growled, and I saw the shiver of pleasure roll over his skin. He crawled toward me, coming to kneel between my knees.

"How about you suck me?"

This time I did smile, but it was a savage expression. "Is that how we are going to play it today?"

Defiance overlaid the lust as he nodded.

I gave him a dark smirk. "So be it."

I gripped the back of his head and slammed my mouth to his, hearing the sound of his piercing scrape against his teeth. I gripped his bleached blonde hair with my hand and pulled his head back, exposing his neck. I bit it hard and he moaned. Even his moans of pleasure were fucking musical and it was my favorite kind of music. I continued to bite, then kiss, my way down his collarbone and over his chest, bending him further and further backwards, until he was stretched out for my pleasure. I tweaked his nipple, twisting the nipple ring until he whimpered and ground his hard dick against mine. I reached down and gripped it, stroking it roughly until he was thrusting into my hand.

"Linc, please," he moaned, and I stopped.

I pulled his head back toward mine, and ran my tongue along his jaw. "Not until you suck my cock."

He grinned. "Well, why didn't you fucking say so?"

What a brat. He moved down my body, running his tongue over my abs, until his lips were brushing the head of my cock. I loosened my grip on his hair, but kept the strands wrapped around my fingers.

Vincent slid his mouth around my cock, sliding

down until I was hitting the back of his throat. The guy had no gag reflex, and my eyes rolled back in my head. Jesus. I held his hair tighter and thrust up, fucking his face and he grunted around my dick. My balls pulled up tight and I dragged him off.

"I want to fuck you," I growled, and he grinned as he wiped his face across my thigh. "On your knees."

Vincent crawled up the bed, his smug smirk telling me I only had the illusion of control. I was fine with that. I didn't need him to submit. But I was going to fuck him until he begged me. I loved listening to him beg with that rough voice.

He put his hands on the head board and I took another moment to appreciate the long line of his back and the two big angel wings that were spread across his shoulders and down his biceps. His were shaded white, beautifully crafted like they were real, and when he stood under a UV light on stage? They turned blue and lit up like he was transported from heaven itself. They contrasted so perfectly with my tattoo, a rough, sketch style set of black wings across my chest. Chaotic and angry to his smooth and ethereal.

I reached into the drawer, getting out a condom and sliding it on. I wasn't a fool. Vincent was a party boy, and he gave zero fucks about his well being. We weren't exclusive and I didn't know if we ever would be. Until then, better safe than have my dick fall off because some hepatitis-riddled groupie fucked him in a toilet stall. I got the lube, slicking us both up when I reached around and stroked along his painfully hard cock. I grabbed his hip and slid myself inside him, and we both groaned.

"Fuck..." Vincent whispered, and I laid a small kiss between his shoulder blades. I pulled out the flogger from the drawer, every third cord tipped with metal. He wanted to hurt. This would be a pain filled answer to his wish.

As I pulled out and slid slowly back inside him, I flicked my wrist, and the leather came down on his back hard. He hissed out a moan. "Again."

I laid it across his back another six strokes, timing it with my thrusts, until red welts scored his flesh. "More," he whimpered, and I brought it down hard, just one more time, before throwing it to the side. I leaned down and traced the last, big welt with my tongue.

I pulled back, gripping his hips as I pounded out my anger into his body. The wet sound of our bodies snapping together became our music, even as Vincent swore rapidly under his breath. I wrapped my hand around his throat and squeezed, and his ass gripped my dick like a vice. Oh fuck.

I squeezed harder as I fucked him, and he let out a wheezing laugh. He might be bottom, but he was fucking me just as good as I was fucking him.

I reached around and grabbed his cock, thrusting

him into my palm, and then I bit his shoulder hard. I knew it would be too much for him and he came in hot spurts in my palm. I grabbed his hip and pulled him tight against me as I unloaded inside him. I pressed my cheek against his sweaty back as I pulled out. I slid the condom off and threw it in the trash.

Collapsing on the bed beside Vincent, I dragged him against my body and he pressed himself tightly against me.

"You know I kind of love you, right? I mean, I've always loved you, and Reese, but the way I feel for you isn't how I feel for Reese," he mumbled into the room. His fingers twitched and I knew he wanted a cigarette.

"I'd hope not."

He touched my chin and pulled my face in his direction. "This doesn't have to be chaos."

I knew he wasn't talking about me and him. He was talking about the girl.

"There's no other way it can be."

YEARS OF GROWING up in a crackhouse had made me a light sleeper. Vince was passed out, his head on my chest, red welts still criss-crossing over his back from the flogger. I ran my fingers over the raised skin, soothing them. A part of me relished giving them to him, but in the darkness, guilt ate me a little that I could hurt someone I loved like that. He enjoyed it, of that I was certain. My room smelled of sex and sweat because he enjoyed it so much. But still, a part of me thought maybe I enjoyed the violence because I was like them. Like my parents. Maybe I just enjoyed hurting people.

The soft steps in the hall weren't Reese's.

I slid Vincent off my chest, pulling the blanket up over his shoulders. He just splayed wide, not waking. I envied his ability to sleep through anything.

I padded toward the door on silent feet, opening it a crack and watching the girl walk down the halls. She was heading toward the kitchen, so I followed along behind her, staying in the shadows. She was probably looking to see what she could lift from the place, to hock when she inevitably left.

She walked to the sink, pulling a glass out of the dish rack and filling it up from the tap. Well, she wasn't stealing the silver yet, but I wasn't going to stop watching. I crept up behind her, watching her face.

"I know you're there. You may as well stop creeping in the corners like a fucking weirdo and just say whatever it is that's bothering you."

She didn't even turn and look at me. How the fuck?

I strode out into the open, so I didn't look like I was skulking. Screw it, this was my fucking house. I could skulk if I wanted.

"I don't have anything to say to you. I have a feeling

you know exactly what I'm thinking though. I'm onto you and your bullshit. Reese is a good guy-"

"I agree," she interrupted.

"He doesn't need to be taken for a ride because you somehow managed to talk him into bed and had unprotected sex to trap him. He might be blinded by your damsel act, but I've known too many girls like you."

She actually laughed in my face. "Oh, Lincoln. I'm pretty sure you've never met a girl like me. But we want the same thing. I know Reese is a good guy. The last thing I'd ever think of doing is hurting him."

I snorted. "Sure. So you're just here, why? Because you are on the run? Because you accidentally got knocked up? This is the twenty-first century. No one gets 'accidentally' knocked up unless they are conniving or just plain stupid. You don't strike me as the latter."

She grinned, and fuck she really was beautiful. No wonder Reese was blind.

"Aw, you think I'm smart?" She chuckled low, and it was a damn sexy sound. My dick twitched and I mentally scowled at it. "Gotta agree with you there, Lincoln. If it makes you feel better, I was surprised as hell. Trust me when I tell you I didn't plan this." She waved a hand at her rounded stomach.

I snorted. "I don't trust a fucking thing you tell me."

She nodded, and her smile was sad. "I'm glad he has someone like you. Protective."

My heart squeezed, but I didn't understand it. I frowned as I looked at the downcast lines of her face. She could just be a damn good actress, but that look of desolation? I knew that look intimately.

"I'm watching. You hurt him, and I'll hurt you."

Now it was her turn to snort. "We both know you aren't the kind of man who would hurt a woman."

I stared at her dead in the eye. "That's where you're wrong. I killed a woman once, and I'd do it again to protect him."

With that, I turned on my heel and left. Memories swam up in my brain, but I pushed them down. The nightmares would come tonight, but luckily I'd have Vince to wrap my body around and chase them away.

This board meeting was going on forever. I was tuning them out as they droned on, because my head wasn't in the room. It was at home, wrapped in my blankets beside the soft, warm body of Celeste.

It had been three days since she'd arrived on my doorstep, three days since she'd dropped her bombshell. I wasn't going to lie, it had been tense at home. Lincoln glared, Vincent flirted. I fussed. Celeste seemed to watch us all with the eyes of the hunted.

Today was my first day back and I was a little worried about leaving her home alone with Vincent and Lincoln. Not because I thought they'd hurt her; the idea was crazy. But I wanted her to stay and I was worried they'd chase her away if I wasn't around to stand between them. Well, Lincoln anyway. Vincent was more likely to chase her into bed.

I examined my complete lack of jealousy at the thought. That couldn't be normal, right?

I looked around the meeting table and my eyes stopped on Steve from PR. He was PR perfect. Blond and well groomed, he had a million dollar smile, and to make shit worse, he was a sweet person to go with it. I was pretty sure that every woman in my company, and at least half the men, had a crush on him.

I tried to imagine Celeste and Steve together. What if she told me she wanted to be with him too? I imagined what they would look like kissing, him having his hands on her body, and jealousy flooded me. No way. No fucking way.

Okay. So I wasn't broken. Then why didn't imagining Vincent doing the same thing create a similar response?

I was trying to look at this scientifically and coming up against a brick wall. The only difference I could see was that I loved Vincent and Lincoln. Not the way they loved each other, of course, I was straight, but we had been inseparable for years. A family unit, in our own bizarre way.

"What do you think, Sir?" Someone asked, and I turned toward the voice. Shit. I'd totally zoned out.

"Give me a report on it, and I'll think it over. Now is

not the time or the market to make rash decisions," I bullshitted and hoped it made sense. I checked my phone and frowned when there were no messages from anyone. None from Vincent or Lincoln, which wasn't actually weird. None from Celeste either, even though I'd programmed my phone number into her cell. I gave the boardroom a tight smile. "Excuse me, people, but unfortunately something has come up. Tad will reschedule something for later this week and we'll make a definitive decision on this matter."

Fake it until you make it. That shit got me through college, and it still works now.

Everyone shuffled their papers and left, most with their faces in their cell phone screens. I waited until everyone left and turned to Tad, my personal assistant. He was smirking at me. "Did I answer that appropriately?"

"You mean so they wouldn't know you were completely daydreaming? Yep, your response was fine for that," he teased back. Tad was in his late thirties and had a wife, three labradors, and two kids. I wasn't sure who he loved more, because they all got equal desk space for their framed photos.

Tad was an interesting guy. He was on the Autism spectrum, which made him super obsessive about some things, which in his case was Lego. The man loved lego as much as his wife. Hell, maybe more. But it also meant that his genius worked really well in a logical manner and he kept me organized easily. And he had an eye for detail that was unparalleled. He liked the comfort of being my personal assistant, of knowing what he had to do every day, of creating a routine for the both of us, so I never had to worry about him jockeying or playing office politics. I relied on Tad so much.

"I appreciate you, man. You know that right?"

Tad grinned and gathered up all the paperwork. "Yes. You tell me all the time."

I smiled and slapped him on the back. "Good. Just wanted you to know."

I walked back to my office, with Tad following along behind me, his face scrunched up as he looked at his tablet. "I can reschedule for Friday next week. Would that be okay?"

I nodded and flung myself down on the couch in my office. I rested my head on the back of the couch and sighed.

The other great thing about Tad? He didn't ask me questions like, are you okay? What's wrong? He just assumed that if I had a problem, I'd talk about it. I appreciated that about him too.

"Tad, if I took the rest of the week off, what would be the outcomes?"

Tad raised both eyebrows, but didn't ask questions. His fingers flew across the tablet screen, and he frowned a little. "We can make it work. Reschedule a few appointments for next month, move around a few things. There is the meeting with that Tech company down in Silicon Valley, but they have already rescheduled on you, so we should parry and return their gambit."

I wasn't sure if that was a chess or a fencing metaphor, but it worked. "Okay, reschedule everything for the rest of the week. I'm going home."

Tad nodded and left the room, his focus completely on his tablet. I sat down at my computer and booted it up.

I opened up my encrypted browser and went to the message board that I'd been loitering on while I'd been trying to find Celeste. I messaged the user called **Talbaloo**. He'd been a source of information when I'd been struggling to understand what the hell I'd seen. He, or she, was nice, but never, ever told me how to find Celeste. Said it went against the shifter code, which I could totally respect. He'd answered my questions, and warned me enough that I kept my mouth shut. I sent him a direct message.

BUTTERCUP: Hey Man. Are you around? I found her.

. . .

THERE WAS NO RESPONSE, but I didn't expect there to be. I was about to close my laptop when it dinged.

TALBALOO: Holy shit, dude. That's great. Is she okay?

BUTTERCUP: Scared. And pregnant. I'm going to be a father to a half-shifter and I am freaking all the way out.

TALBALOO: FUCK! Uh, congrats? She was a snow leopard did you say? At least you don't have to worry about multiple births.

BUTTERCUP: Not going to lie man, I am freaking all the way out. She keeps talking about leaving the baby with me and taking off so you-know-who don't get the baby? Cub? But I don't know what to do with a shifter baby? I can protect her, right? Hire good security or something?

TALBALOO: I don't know man. They aren't normal bad guys. Maybe she's right and you should let her go. I know some cat shifters if you need, like, pointers or something.

BUTTERCUP: Thanks man. I might take you up on that. I better go.

TALBALOO: No worries. I'm always here if you need me. Be safe.

. . .

I ALWAYS FOLLOWED THE RULES. Never be online long enough to be traced. Always encrypted browser and bouncing my signal off almost 300 servers. I didn't get where I was by not knowing my shit. Safety first.

I shut down my computer and stuffed it in my messenger bag. I was going home to see my girl. Despite what Talbaloo and everyone else said, I wasn't giving her up.

11

The sun on my cheeks was slowly warming my chilled bones. My chilled heart.

Sitting in Reese's penthouse apartment, soaking in the warmth high above the city, appeased the wild beast in my chest. I could pretend I was in a tree in the wilderness and not trapped in a cage of glass and concrete. I could pretend so many things; that my life wasn't roadkill on a freeway, just a mass of bones and gore and bad damn decisions.

I pulled my knees up under my chin and rested them there, an action that was getting decidedly harder given my bulging midsection. My brain shied away from the very real example of my bad decisions.

The front door opened and closed, and their scents hit me first. Humans always wanted to categorize people's scents as single, familiar smells, but there was so much more depth to it than that. Scents were ever-changing, given what you ate, your shampoo, whether you stood beside a smoker while waiting for the bus. But under all that superficial stuff was a person's real scent, and it was impossible to describe. These guys, together, smelled like sweetness and sin. Like violence and sex.

It made my heart race.

Vincent and Lincoln. Their scents were so inter-mingled that I wondered if it was because they were bunking in the same room or because they were a couple. No one had volunteered the information and I wasn't about to make our situation worse by asking and offending someone.

After Lincoln's little late night chat, we'd avoided each other the best we could, but he was always watching, just like he'd promised. And Vincent? He was sweet temptation all the fucking time. One thing they don't tell you in pregnant shifter school? The hormones make you horny as hell. And Vicent was sex on a stick. But he still looked at me with the same calculating eyes as his friend.

I could smell the lust on them. They might hate me, but they wanted me just as much as I wanted them. And my snow leopard wanted them really, really bad.

They circled me like sharks smelling blood in the water. Sexy fucking sharks. I raised my lip and snarled at them, despite the fact that my libido was going wild. They might be sharks, but I was no fucking unsuspecting tuna fish. I was an apex predator in my own right and I did not just lie down.

Lincoln stepped closer and I held my place. He was an Alpha, even if he was a human. His stare might make other humans quail, but I just lifted my chin and stared back.

"You're so fucking beautiful, no wonder Reese is blind to you. He sees your pretty face and your big innocent eyes and wants to be the white knight who rides in and saves you." He leaned forward, grabbing my chin, and pulling me easily to my feet. It was like my body would go anywhere with him, despite the fact my head thought he was an asshole. He pulled me close until his lips were a mere breath from mine. "But you are no princess and I'm no fucking knight." Then he slammed his lips into mine.

The kiss was rough, an assault rather than a caress, and the smoky chuckle of Vincent let me know his partner in crime had stepped up to my back. I was trapped between them, caught by hunters that I didn't think I even wanted to escape.

Pure lust clouded my brain, chasing away anything resembling good sense. I plunged my tongue into Lincoln's mouth, battling for supremacy with his, even as my body arched towards him for relief. My fingers scraped up the back of his skull, gripping the longer hair at the top in a hold that wasn't even a little gentle. Lincoln growled low, and heat rushed between my thighs.

When Vincent stepped closer, hemming me between them, I moaned. Their bodies were fire coated stone, and being pressed between them was bliss. Dirty, distracting bliss. Vincent's fingers trailed down my spine, making me shiver. His lips slid over the skin of my neck, then his teeth, and I moaned hard into Lincoln's mouth. It was too much like claiming, like being mated, for my leopard. My skin rippled with pleasure and I arched back into him, desperate to be mounted by this hot as hell asshole.

"Mmm, you like that, don't you, Star?" His teeth pressed firmly into my shoulder, and I reached behind me, groping for the hard dick I could feel pressed against my back, but he danced away. "Uh uh, not yet."

Lincoln, apparently disgruntled that I wasn't entirely focused on him anymore, bit my lower lip hard. I yelped, pulling away, my tongue flicking out to lick the bit of blood that seeped from my swollen flesh.

The tattooed monster didn't like me moving away though, reaching out to grab my chin and dragging me into another intoxicating kiss. He sucked my bruised lip into his mouth, making it better and worse all at once. He didn't let go of my chin, even as Vincent's hand slipped between us. His fingers slid beneath the waistband of my shorts, avoiding my stomach completely.

When his fingers brushed over my damp panties, I could feel his smug grin against the skin of my back. "You're dripping for us, aren't you? Dirty, dirty little Star." His finger slipped beneath the elastic, and as much as I wanted to punch him in the dick for his teasing words, I froze, desperate to feel his touch where I ached so bad.

When he pulled his hand from my jean shorts altogether and ran it down my thigh instead, I decided a dick punch was back on the table. I wrenched my face away from Lincoln, stepping from between them so I could fucking breathe.

"What are you doing?" I growled, my nostrils flaring as I desperately tried to suck in air that wasn't tainted with their scent. Ha! Good luck with that.

Vincent swaggered toward me, his lean body tattooed and the smirk on his face permanently etched there. "What you want us to do. I see how you look at Linc, Star. Like you want him to bend you over that uncomfortable fucking couch and make you scream his name." He crowded me again, but I didn't move away. I told myself I was holding my ground, but deep down I just wanted to feel his heat against mine again.

Vincent was a languid, white-haired god, and he knew it. Every movement was both effortless but purposeful, like he was wading through molasses, and the dichotomy of him made me want to sink my teeth into his flesh and run my tongue over every single one of his tattoos. "I see the way your pupils blow out when you watch me, how the little spot here," he leaned forward and took my pulse point between his teeth. He bit gently, before suctioning his lips around it and sucking. "How this little spot thrums as your heart beats wildly," he murmured in my ear, his raspy voice making goosebumps prickle my skin.

I needed to block out his words; Vincent could talk a nun out of her panties and into becoming an atheist.

I gritted my teeth and forced myself to stand stiffly, no matter how much it wanted to curve into the shape of his body. "So what? You're hot. You're still assholes."

Lincoln stepped forward, the grin on his face not even remotely pleasant. "You want me. Us. We are giving you what you want."

The scoff that came out of my mouth wasn't even remotely ladylike. "Altruistic of you."

Also fucking bullshit. This smelled of entrapment. A quick look at my watch told me that it was just past four in the afternoon. Reese would be home in about fifteen minutes, by which time they'd probably intended to have me spit-roasted on the couch between them. They needn't have bothered. After my chat with Reese the other night, where we stood was real clear.

The grin on my face was completely Cheshire. Because the dickholes were right. I did want them. My body wanted to rub all over them, to touch, taste, *feel,* everything they were offering right now. And if I got the joy of their little exposure plan blowing up in their faces?

So much better.

Lincoln's eyes narrowed at my returning smirk. But he didn't move as I reached out, gripping his shirt and dragging him closer. I thought he might resist, but he let me pull him in. Let me nip the tip of his chin, the stubble scraping my kiss sensitive lips. Let me nuzzle his neck as I kissed along his jaw.

When I tore open that fucking button-down shirt that strained across his chest, I enjoyed the slight widening of his eyes as the buttons bounced across the polished concrete floors. I scraped my nails down his chest, over the black sketched tattoo of wings, adding red stripes to the jagged strokes.

I bent, tracing my tongue down the raised scores on his chest, pushing my ass into Vincent. He grunted as my ass pressed against his hard cock. Yeah, they weren't doing this just out of the goodness of their heart. They wanted me too.

I was a shifter. I could scent lust a mile away. They might be telling themselves they were flushing a fox out of Reese's perfect little cock house, but they wanted my body just as badly as I wanted theirs. Like my ass was magnetized, Vincent ran his hands up the back of my thighs and gripped my cheeks. He groaned, pressing his hips against me, his dick straining.

I looked up at Lincoln, who was staring down at me with clouded, whiskey-colored eyes filled with lust and suspicion. "Get on your knees," he growled, and I grinned.

Yeah, you sexy jerk, I have you where I want you now.

Still, I dropped to my knees, looking up at him. My leopard wanted to submit, but instead I lifted my lip at him. Let him wonder if I'd suck his dick or chomp it in half. I always was one of those kids who smashed their lollipops with their back teeth.

To show that all men had no sense of self-preservation when there's a blow job involved, Lincoln didn't stop me from unbuttoning his chinos, slipping them over his perfect goddamn ass and down thighs that were pure muscle. Honestly, unwrapping him was going to make me spontaneously orgasm.

His underwear came next, and when the heavy fullness of his cock sprang free, I stifled a gasp. I didn't want to inflate his already swollen ego. I hadn't realized that Vincent had leaned forward until he was whispering in my ear. "Impressive, isn't he? You want to taste that?"

Neither of the men in the room seemed to care that Vincent's face was inches from Lincoln's cock. I raised an eyebrow like I wasn't desperate to bring the big man to his knees. Instead, I leaned forward so I could meet

Vincent's eyes as I dragged my tongue up Linc's cock, from base to head, making both men groan.

Vincent straightened, shucking off his jeans. That's all it took for him to be naked. He walked around shirtless with his jeans unbuttoned all the damn time, sans underwear. I'd been an inch from seeing his dick since I'd arrived. But I wasn't complaining. He was an artwork, intricate tattoos lining every inch of his body. I looked over my shoulder. Including his dick.

He held the head towards me, like he was offering me a lollipop, and I happily sucked Vincent's dick in my mouth. He moaned, but Lincoln wasn't having any of that.

He grabbed my head and pulled me back toward his own cock, like he was desperate to be buried somewhere inside of me. Putting him out of his misery, I slid him between my lips, pushing him further and further until he was deep in my throat. The full-bodied grunt was primal, and he pulled back slowly before sliding back into my mouth again. I kept the suction tight, letting him fuck my mouth until he was an unstable mess.

I was suddenly yanked from his cock, it slipping out of my mouth with a pop. Vincent dragged me to my feet, peeling my clothes off me with urgent hands. He continued to walk me backwards toward the couch, until he could collapse back onto the hard surface and pull me onto his lap, my back to his chest so I could see Lincoln stalk across the room after us.

When my heat slid across Vincent's hard dick, his fingers became frantic, lining himself up until he was notched against the entry, and my eyes rolled back as he pushed inside. Damn. This angle. That dick.

Hands on my hips, he dragged me down until I was fully impaled, before sliding me back up and doing it all over again. I rested my hands on his knees, arching my back in a way that was entirely feline. Lincoln's cock was back to nudging at my mouth, its tip weeping precum.

"You weren't finished," he growled and I raised an eyebrow at him.

I reached out, anchoring myself on his muscular hip as Vincent ground inside me like he was looking for the damn holy grail. "Don't blame me, blame your boy... oh holy fuck," I moaned, ruining my snarky comeback but Vincent's hand had slid around to flick my clit as his cock seemed to find that goddamn holy grail spot inside me.

Lincoln's eyes slipped from my face and over to watch his friend pound into my pussy, his hands clenched so hard on my hips they would've bruised if I wasn't a shifter. I looked over my shoulder and grinned at Vincent.

"Harder," I growled, and he smirked that goddamn

panty-dropping smile back, slamming me up and down his cock like a fucking jackhammer.

Lincoln had apparently had enough watching, because he grabbed my cheeks. "Open," he ordered, and I must have been riding a pheromone high because I did it without complaint. I sucked his cock into my mouth, letting him fuck my face in time with Vincent's thrusts.

My eyes watered, and all you could hear around the room was our moans and the sound of slapping bodies grinding against each other in the search for pleasure. Vincent flicked my clit just right, and I came hard on his cock, screaming to a god I didn't believe in.

As if summoned by my orgasm, Reese walked through the front door, his feet stilling as he took in the spectacle we must have made.

I pushed Lincoln away, my eyes darting to his just in time to see the pompous self-satisfied look in his eyes.

Instead of being outraged, which is what I assumed they thought would happen, Reese just threw down his briefcase and loosened his tie. "Good to see you're all getting along better," he said, teasing, but I didn't miss the heat in his gaze.

I slid off Vincent's still hard dick, smiling smugly up at Lincoln as his smirk shifted to a frown. "Just killing time until you got home, Buttercup." I sauntered over to him, naked and unselfconscious. I kissed his cheek. "Come on, I've been dying to know what happens at the end of "The Witcher", and I kept my promise not to watch it without you."

I threw one last look over my shoulder at the guys, with half-deflated dicks and confused expressions. "Sorry guys, you'll have to finish yourselves off. Henry Cavill waits for no woman."

With a low chuckle, I ushered Reese from the living room and into Vince's room. I pulled on a pair of soft pajama pants and one of Reese's oversized t-shirts.

"Are you tormenting my friends, Celeste?" Reese asked, fiddling with the remotes as he took off his shoes, but his eyes were sparkling with mirth and I was glad the conversation from the other night hadn't been just lip service.

I shrugged and climbed onto the bed, rubbing my hand on my stomach. "They deserved it."

He shook his head and climbed onto the bed after me, pulling me onto his chest. "I bet they did. Just... go easy on them. Their hearts are in the right place."

I wanted to tell Reese that their hearts weren't the appendage they were thinking with, but I resisted. Instead, I'd enjoy this moment with him and replay that beautiful moment when they realized their plan didn't work over and over again.

I looked at my dick. "What the fuck just happened?" I asked him like he knew all the answers to life.

"She was fucking with us," he answered back. Oh, no wait, that was Lincoln.

I snorted. "No shit, dickhead. She knew what we were doing all along. Crafty bitch." Apparently I didn't keep the awe out of my voice enough because Linc scowled at me.

"What the hell was with Reese's reaction? He didn't even seem... mad?"

Now it was my turn to frown. Did we want him to be mad with us? I wasn't going to lie, I didn't think this plan through, at least not much past the 'Put Dick into Pretty Girl' part. My heart gave a belated thump. Like when you wake up with a snake in your bed, and you realize you just cheated death. Happened once. Reese could have been mad, and not just at Star. He could have been mad at us too. "Linc, I think we fucked up."

What had we achieved here? Apart from a wicked case of blue balls, she'd gotten the upper hand. And now I knew how she tasted. How she felt wrapped around my cock. The noise she made when she came all over me. Lincoln's cock in her mouth. How the hell was I ever going to forget any of those things?

Lincoln was staring down the hall, like he could see through the walls and into my room. "Yeah, I think you are right."

I didn't miss the fact his hand was absently on his dick as he said it. Yeah, Lincoln might hate what she represents, but he didn't hate Star at all. He wanted her. That was almost worse for the girl in all honesty. Lincoln had a bad habit with relationships. He was too much. Too full on. Too attentive. Too panicky. I didn't blame him. His history was fucked. But inevitably, whenever Lincoln set his sights on a woman, there was exactly two months before the girl ran away. Because he's pretty, but he had more baggage than an airport carousel. So did we all, except Reese.

He was our rock. Our hearthstone. Without him? I shuddered. I didn't want to think about what hole we'd be in without him. "We got lucky. If he wasn't so, you know, Reese-like, he might never have forgiven us. This shit is dangerous, Linc. We are playing with fire and we will be nothing but ash if we keep trying to take her down."

I didn't know if Lincoln would listen. He liked order. He definitely didn't like surprises. And Star? She was chaotic, just like me. I closed my eyes, and I saw her face, twisted in pleasure, those blue eyes staring down into mine. She spoke to my wildness and I was helpless to resist its call. My dick got hard again and I groaned. "I'm going to have a cold shower," I grunted and stood from the couch. I strode toward the hall, ignoring the sounds of the television from my room. "Vincent?" he called after me, and I stopped, my dick still cupped in my hands like every single person in this house hadn't seen me naked and hard.

Lincoln raked his hands down his face. "I'll try. It's just hard, you know?"

I let go of my dick and pointed at it. Then it pointed back at me because it was that fucking rock hard again. "Yeah, I know what you mean."

A gruff laugh burst from Lincoln's mouth and I grinned. "Not what I meant."

I gave him an encouraging smile. Or it might have still been my trademark smirk. Sometimes, I had resting smirk face these days and didn't know it. "I know what you meant, Linc. I think it's better this way. She might be something good. We just have to trust that Reese knows what he's doing." I took a few more steps. "Are you coming? I don't want to waste a good hard on."

He shook his head, but gathered our clothes and strode down the hallway after me.

A HEAVY THUMP at the door heralded Reese into Lincoln's bedroom. Lincoln was awake and tense, partially clothed in boxers and sweats. I was still naked, but that didn't seem to phase Reese. Like it never occurred to him to be embarrassed by our nudity. It definitely never occurred to him that our relationship was somehow wrong. It wasn't that Reese was purposefully progressive, it just never seemed to cross his mind that our relationship was anything but natural. Which it fucking well was. I once headbutted a paparazzi for suggesting that my very well documented bisexuality was anything but normal.

That shit hurts, by the way.

Still, he shut the door behind him and his face was unnaturally solemn. "We should talk."

Ah, shit. I knew this was coming. I sat up in bed and pulled the sheet over my dick. This definitely wasn't going to be a dicks-out kind of convo.

He sat on the end of the bed, and gave us what I liked to call his 'intervention face'. It was somewhere between love and exasperation. "I love you guys so much. You're my family."

Yep, he was definitely about to kick us to the curb. "And it's only because I love you guys that I wanted you to know that I'm totally okay if you and Celeste start something. I know she's interested in you guys and obviously, if today was evidence of anything, you two want her as well."

My mouth dropped open. I... what?

Lincoln huffed. "You don't mean that. You just want her, and you are letting her walk all over you. That's not right, Reese."

For the first time in forever, Reese looked mad. It was like seeing Mickey Mouse covered in blood and holding a gun. The two things did not compute. "You don't get to tell me what's right, Lincoln. I'm not an idiot. If you think that I don't know you orchestrated me walking in at the exact moment you had your dick in the mouth of the girl I like, then you have a shitty opinion of my intelligence. You should take this for what it is and shut your damn mouth before you make shit worse."

Lincoln looked like Reese had just stood up and punched him in the face.

I reached out and gripped Reese's wrist. "We deserve that, man. For what it's worth, I'm sorry."

Reese sighed and finger-combed his hair, but it flopped right back down into his eyes. "It's fine. Celeste... well she's probably more than I can handle myself anyway. I'm not too proud to admit it. She likes you guys, and I'm thankful as hell for that. The thought of her being with any other men that aren't you two, fills me with a rage that I'm not sure I've ever felt." He turned back to Lincoln. "But I swear, if you fuck with her like that again, we are done. You aren't that guy, Linc. Deep down there is chivalry buried inside you. The kind that saves drug addicted rockstars and lonely, socially awkward nerds." He stood and slapped Lincoln's knee. "Try getting to know her. And have a little faith in me, hey?"

He paused at the door. "Dinner will be here in a minute. I'd like it if we all ate together."

With that, he shut the door behind him. I somehow felt chastised as hell, while hopeful for the future. I don't know how he managed that.

"He's going to be a good dad. I feel guilt-ridden as hell at his disappointment," I muttered.

Lincoln ignored me as he watched the door like he was waiting for Reese to pop back through and say, "Just kidding. I fucking hate you, now get out of my house."

I climbed out of the bed and walked around to stand in front of him. "We've been given a death row reprieve. Let's not fuck it up." I stepped back and twirled around so my dick flung out like a whirly-bird. "Now, do you think this dinner is clothing optional, or should I put on pants?"

13

Dinner last night had been... awkward. The sexual tension was intense, as was the hatred. Celeste somehow managed to look smug and pissed off at the same time. Vincent, in true Vincent fashion, had gone out, fallen to his knees, put his head in her lap, cooed out a, "Sorry, Star," and then kissed her.

Much to my amusement, she'd kissed him back, then reared away and punched him in the mouth. His lip had split and he'd grinned through the blood. "Fair call, Star. Truce?"

She shook her head and smirked back, but just like that, they were good. Like he hadn't had his dick in her hours earlier.

Me, however? She glared at me like I was scum.

So when I stumbled out into the kitchen this morning, another nightmare filled night chasing away anything resembling restfulness, and found her in the kitchen, I was tempted to turn around and go back to my room. Maybe climb back between the covers and try to sleep again. But I wasn't a bitch. I didn't run away at the first sign of confrontation. I'd spent the majority of my life looking for confrontation. So here we were.

I didn't say anything as I stepped into the kitchen, and Celeste didn't even slide her eyes toward me. Instead, she pretended like I didn't exist. Whatever. Maybe it was better that way.

Except she was standing right in front of the mugs.

I reached across to the cabinet above her head. Rookie move. Quicker than I could follow, she turned and nailed me in the gut with a hard punch. The wind burst from my lungs and I doubled over, gasping.

"The next time you try to use sex against me, or against Reese who is supposed to be your best friend, I will gut you like the coward you are," she hissed, and I looked up at her, my eyes blazing.

I growled, expecting to find the anger or even the smugness of last night. Instead, the sadness was back and that knocked what little air I'd dragged into my lungs back out again.

She grabbed my forearms and helped me straighten, and I jerked away from her. Fool me once. "Look. We got off on the wrong foot. I get it. You don't trust me. Apparently you don't trust Reese either. I get that as well. He's too fucking good for this world." She dragged in a deep, shuddering breath. "I need to trust you. Reese loves you, and you aren't going anywhere anytime soon unless you decide to use your dick as a weapon again and Reese decides to kick your fuckboy ass to the curb."

I snorted and held back the groan as I stood. I reached up to the cabinet to grab my mug, exposing my middle again. If that didn't say trust, what the fuck did? "I'm not a fuckboy," I grunted, filling my coffee cup. Without thinking about it too hard, I grabbed down a glass and filled it with milk.

I slid it toward her, not looking at her again. "Milk is good for pregnant women."

She raised both eyebrows but took the glass, daintily taking a sip like she was checking if it was poisoned. "Thanks. I need to trust you, Lincoln. I need to trust you with this," she rubbed her hand over her stomach, and I forced myself to follow the gesture. "You're protective and part of me appreciates that. Reese will need you. I need to know that my baby is safe with you."

I reared back like she'd slugged me in the stomach again. "I'd never, ever hurt a child."

She shook her head. "There's more than one way to hurt a person, Lincoln. It isn't only fists that hurt."

Guilt washed over me. It wasn't a sensation I was used to, because guilt was only for people who weren't desperate. I'd spent so many years surviving, I some-times wondered if I'd lost my ability to feel anything but apathy.

Today proved that I could because this sensation was more uncomfortable than the pain in my abs.

I swallowed hard. "I'm sorry. What I did was wrong." My mouth felt weird even forming the words, like I was testing a foreign language. Apologies meant I'd done something wrong. Doing something wrong meant second guessing myself. There'd been no room in my life for that up until now. Until the safety of Reese and Vincent.

"That looked like it hurt," she said softly, and I could feel the atmosphere lightening.

I raised my eyebrows. "Doesn't come naturally." I sipped my coffee, even though it was too hot. I enjoyed the burn. "I might have overreacted a bit. But Reese has been burned before. The last one almost broke him." Christina had been all big blue eyes and a cold black heart. She took one look at Reese and saw a meal ticket for life. He'd lavished her with gifts and a love that he gave way too easily. I should know, I lapped that shit up like a starved mutt when I'd met him. So when I'd busted her still sleeping with her ex, Reese had gone into his office and not emerged for six days, and I'd sworn to Vincent that I would never let another money-hungry bitch get in his head or his bed again.

Then Celeste strolled into his life.

Celeste jumped up to sit on the kitchen island with ease that should have been nearly impossible in a pregnant woman. "Look, Lincoln. I'm not trying to break him. I've been pretty damn clear with him how this is going to go. In three or so months, I'm going to hand over the best thing that ever happened to me, and then I'm gone. I don't want to hurt anyone else along the way."

She meant that she'd be the only one hurting, and that didn't make me feel better. "You're insane if you don't think leaving won't hurt him."

She gave me a dead-eyed look. "You say that like you didn't try and fuck me out of his life yesterday."

I have a very vivid flash of her on her knees in front of me, her pretty lips around my cock and her full lashes fluttering against her cheeks. My dick grew uncomfortably hard in my sweats, but I refused to adjust in front of her. "I said I was sorry. I didn't mean to take advantage."

She chuckled, and ran a finger down my chest. "Oh, Linc. The truly adorable thing is you still think *you* were taking advantage of *me*."

With that, she clinked her glass of milk against my mug in a fucked up cheers and left the kitchen, heading toward the balcony. I heard a wheezing noise and looked up to see both Reese and Vincent in the hallway. Reese was bent in half, sucking in lungfuls of air as he laughed. Vince just stared after the woman, a dazed look on his face. He slapped Reese on the back, and I wasn't sure if he was trying to help him breathe or not.

"Dude. I think I might actually love her," Vincent muttered, and Reese straightened, his shit eating grin aimed my way.

"Welcome to the club, asshole."

To PROVE that I'd changed my ways, at least to Reese because I didn't give a fuck what Celeste thought, I turned off the ball game looked at the other three occupants in the living room. Vincent was strumming his guitar idly, his lip piercing sucked into his mouth in a way I definitely wanted to replicate later. Celeste was lying in the sun again, stretched out on the blush faux hair rug that Reese had moved by the window for her. She spent a lot of time doing that, just lying in the sun, and part of me thought it was weird. But hey, pregnant women were damn strange anyway.

Reese was sitting beside her in an armchair, typing out emails on his insanely expensive laptop.

"We should buy baby shit."

Vincent gave a discordant twang. "You wanna buy baby shit?"

I frowned at him and he stuck his tongue out at me. "Baby supplies. Cribs and... I don't know. Stuff?"

Vincent frowned. "I'll pass, but have fun with that."

I snuck a look at Celeste, and her brows were drawn together but she wasn't protesting. Reese, however, was grinning like it was Christmas. "Awesome idea! We should do this as a family though. Vincent, you have to come. "

I don't know who looked more shocked. Celeste or Vincent. I felt my tense facial muscles and I consciously relaxed them. Okay, it was probably me.

Reese looked down at Celeste, something painfully hopeful in his expression. She gave him a soft look and lifted herself up onto her elbows. "Just let me get changed."

She didn't need help getting to her feet, agile and lithe. If I hadn't seen it for myself, I'd almost wonder if she was faking her pregnancy. She smiled as Reese grabbed her on the way past, pulling her into a hug and whispering something in her ear. But I could see the lines of sadness in her face when she walked past me.

Reese's frown told me she hadn't hidden it so well from him either. "You gotta tell me your end game."

Reese looked fierce. He dropped his voice low. "I want her to stay," he whispered.

"But what if she-"

"Shh," he said again, and I looked around. There was no fucking way she could hear us from the other room. But I whispered back to humor him.

"You can't make her stay. You need to be prepared for both possibilities."

Vincent sauntered over, resting his guitar against the arm of the couch. "I vote we keep her so sexed up that she can't even think of leaving."

Reese rolled his eyes. "Your dick is your solution to everything."

Vincent was so far from offended though. He just grinned and gave a little air-thrust. "I'm pretty sure my dick could bring world peace if the rest of me was willing."

"I'm sure," I deadpanned, and he winked at me. It always made an unholy cocktail of butterflies and lust cramp my gut when he did that. He was too fucking hot. I dragged my eyes away from him and back to Reese. "I'm just saying, we don't have a basement to lock her in, so just prepare yourself. She doesn't strike me as the kind of person who would enjoy feeling trapped." That was an understatement. Celeste felt wild in a way I wasn't sure I could describe. The room just felt different with her in it, and that undescribed sensation fucked with my sense of order. Maybe that was why I was so dead set against her. She felt like a storm and I'd spent years creating a safe harbor for us all.

Reese slapped me on the back. "I know, Linc. It will break something in me if she leaves but at least I'm going into it with my eyes wide open. But I want her to feel so safe and happy with us that she never even considers leaving. I need you to help me do that." He paused, and gave me that assessing look that seemed to unpick all my complicated walls and see right into my soul. "You like her." It wasn't a question. He was telling me what my brain refused to admit, but perhaps my body already knew. "You do. You just need to forget all that baggage from your past and let yourself get to know her. You're just a guy and she is just a girl. Give her a chance."

He'd asked this of me three separate times in the last week. Could I just forget my fucked up past and be her friend?

Sure. Why the fuck not? "Okay," I said and it was worth it just to see the smile on Reese's face. I looked at Vincent, who had on no shirt and unbuttoned ripped jeans. You could just see the dark curls of his pubes. I shook my head. "Let's go get changed before someone takes one look at you and calls child protective services before the kid is even out of the womb."

For someone who didn't want to come, Vincent was having way too much fun. The change occurred right around the time he realized the store had a full range of rock-inspired onesies. I swear, he put one of each in his cart.

"Pretty sure my child now has a better wardrobe than you do, Vince," I teased and he grinned over his shoulder.

"Our child, Bro."

My heart did a little splutter at that, but I tried not to let it show on my face and scare the shit out of my notoriously commitment phobic friend. Lincoln's words kept going around and around in my head about Celeste not staying. The idea hurt more than it should, considering I'd only known her a week, but if she did go, at least these two guys were with me for the long haul. The baby would be our baby. Even if Celeste stayed, we would be a family. I was going to make sure of it.

Both Vincent and Lincoln had crappy childhoods, so they didn't really have any life experience with the warmth, the security, that having a loving family could provide. But a baby? A baby would cement us all. A baby would need us all, and they both had huge hearts even if they kept them locked down behind impenetrable brickwalls.

As if to prove my point, Lincoln was over in the safety section, looking at some kind of weird crib pressure mat that told you if the baby rolled over or stopped breathing or something in its sleep. His cart was filled with safety stuff. I was pretty sure not even Fort Knox had as many safety precautions.

If anyone looked uncomfortable, it was Celeste. She wandered around, picking up and putting things down. I made a note of the product numbers with my phone camera, but didn't press her to buy anything. I walked up beside her and resisted the urge to pull her to my chest. The need to touch her, to comfort her, was almost overwhelming.

"Are you okay?"

She gave me a bright smile that didn't reach her eyes. "They are buying so much stuff."

I shrugged and lost the battle not to touch her. I pulled her into my side, slinging my arm over her tiny frame. "Let them. We are three guys with good jobs and no responsibilities. They have money to burn and it's making them happy."

It was making me happy too. I would have to look at converting my office into a nursery and I made a note in my phone to call a contractor. So far we'd picked a crib that had a matching wardrobe and changing table, and also a bassinet. A state-of-the-art stroller was another purchase and came with more accessories than my car.

I hadn't realized babies needed so much stuff until I printed out a list from the internet. When Celeste began to look weary, I decided it was time to wrap it up. I tilted my head at both Vincent and Lincoln, leaning down to kiss the top of Celeste's head. "Let's take this over to the register and then we can wait in the car for the guys."

The shop assistants fussed, probably because I was sinking money in the tens of thousands. Celeste looked pale at the amount, but I just held her tighter. Lincoln and Vincent looked like they were arguing about the number of stuffed toys in Vince's cart and I shook my head. I handed over my credit card and the girl was nearly gleeful when she swiped it, but Celeste remained unnaturally quiet.

I grabbed her hand and led her towards the entrance of the shops. "Did you know I was adopted?"

Her eyes shot to me and she shook her head. "No."

"Yep, as a toddler. A really wonderful older couple became my parents, and no matter what happened before they adopted me, I knew nothing but love for my entire childhood. They lavished me with gifts, which was great, but more than that they were so generous with their love." I sighed and gripped her hand harder. "What I'm trying to say is I have money, sure, and our child will have the best of everything. But more than that, it will know love like I did."

She smiled up at me then, her first genuine one of the day. "I know you will."

She froze and her face turned down in a frown. She glanced around, and I only got to see the flash of panic on her face a split-second before electricity shot up my spine.

I'd been tased.

I could only watch Celeste as my limbs went offline, and she spun, her elbow getting the guy trying to grab her in the solar plexus. I felt like all my muscles had been torched by fire. It was the longest five seconds of my life as I watched a second hunter come out of nowhere and make a grab for her, herding her toward a van that was now idling on the street.

"Get the fuck away from her!"

The sound of Vincent's voice made me want to cry with relief. Because if Vincent was there, then...

Lincoln came out of nowhere, his fist whipping out and catching the guy trying to grab Celeste in the side of the head. The guy stumbled, but it was long enough that Lincoln had Celeste behind his back and a gun pointed at the guy's face.

Finally, the ticking of the taser stopped and my muscles relaxed. I yanked on the wires and struggled to my feet. Vincent was there, grabbing both Celeste and me, his eyes whipping around the parking lot looking for more attackers.

There was a crowd of people now, watching from a safe distance.

"Don't fucking move," Lincoln growled, and the hunter just grinned. Bullets started flying from the van, and I ducked, covering Celeste's body with mine as we ran toward my SUV. Vincent was there before me, yanking the door open and pushing us both inside.

We heard the squeal of tires, and the van pulled away, mounting the sidewalk as it careened around a corner.

Lincoln was suddenly in front of us, checking Vincent over before wrenching open the car door and looking between Celeste and I. "Are you guys okay?"

I nodded, but I was still checking Celeste over. She was okay. Her eyes were wide and she was so damn pale. "Are you okay? Celeste? Are you okay?"

She swallowed hard. "I'm fine."

Pale faced people began to swarm into the spot in front of the store, and Lincoln eyed them all like they were possible shooters.

"Let's get out of here. The cops can catch up with us when they do their job."

Lincoln climbed into the front and tore out of the parking lot. He was silent and tense, his eyes watching the road in front of us and behind us, in case of a tail. Vincent was still in the back of the car with us. I had Celeste bundled into my chest and Vincent ran a soothing hand down her back. I realized she was shaking and I whispered soft promises.

When I felt hot tears soak my shirt, I didn't say anything, just held her harder. It wasn't until Vincent placed his palm over mine that I realized my hand had curled into a fist on her back. I relaxed it and it shook. I would make it safe for her, even if I had to break the world to do it.

BY THE TIME we reconvened on the couch after we got home, Celeste was drinking her third cup of herbal tea from a travel mug and Lincoln had called a private security team and the building's security to make sure it was airtight.

Vincent continued to pace around and around the room, unable to sit still. I held Celeste on my lap, and she had curled up against my chest, soaking in my warmth. "You have to tell them. They are going to find out sooner or later, and it's their safety at risk too."

She tensed, but whatever she was going to say in

response was interrupted by Lincoln hanging up his phone. "I have a private security firm coming in to tighten measures around the apartment. I told building security that no one is permitted up here if it isn't one of the four of us. No Chinese delivery men, no strippergrams, nothing."

I nodded, trying not to hold Celeste too tightly. Vincent stopped in front of us and dropped into a crouch until he was eye level. "I gotta apologize, Star. I thought the whole 'I'm on the run from bad people' schtick was a load of shit. I was wrong."

I tensed, waiting for her to lash out, but she just snuggled closer to my chest and sighed. "It was a week for misunderstandings. I get it." She sat up, and looked between Vincent and Lincoln. "I should admit that I was lying a little. Well, at least omitting all the facts."

I saw the moment when all the progress that Lincoln had made with Celeste evaporated. His body went tight and his eyes went hard.

"You should just do it. No matter how you explain it, they are going to freak. Better to just rip off the bandaid," I whispered and she shrugged.

"Okay, they are your friends. Just make sure he doesn't shoot me." She eyed Lincoln warily. She made a good point.

"Gun, please?" I asked, holding out my hand and he stared between us like we were crazy. "Trust me, Linc."

He narrowed his eyes at me, because I didn't often play the earnest card, but he unholstered his gun, taking out the clip and handing both to me. This was how Lincoln showed his love. Unless he was naked, he was always armed. And even then, he was within five steps of a weapon of some kind. We'd probably have to fix that when the baby came.

The fact he just handed his weapon over was like a child handing over their security blanket.

I took them and tucked them in the gap in the couch.

I looked at Celeste, her eyes sparkling with amusement. "You know this is my favorite part, right?"

I shook my head. "We'll see."

It finally got too much for Vincent, because he was frowning. "Are you guys going to let the rest of us in..."

He trailed off, because before he could finish his sentence, standing before him on four legs was Celeste. The snow leopard.

15

CELESTE

I laughed as Vincent let out a girlish squeal and fell backwards off the couch. Only, in my snow leopard form, it was a chuffing sound. Lincoln automatically went for his gun, but it wasn't there. I lifted my lip and snarled at him. Asshole.

He let his hand drop to his side when he realized it wasn't there, the act of going for his gun seemingly unconscious. He didn't take his gaze off me though, staring directly into my eyes like he was still the apex predator in the room.

My leopardess chuffed in amusement. She liked him, the alpha-douche.

Vincent scrambled back to his feet, but stayed on the other side of the couch. "What the actual fuck? I swear I gave up LSD."

My leopardess thought this was hilarious, or

maybe I did, and we slumped to the floor, rolling onto our back with our murder mittens in the air. Even in this form, my stomach was swollen with my cub.

Reese, who had the benefit of not being surprised, still looked at me with absolute amazement. "Hey there beautiful," he crooned, kneeling down beside me to stroke the soft underside of my fur. I purred a little, batting at him with my paw until he was closer. "Fuck you are just amazing."

I grinned, which probably looked a little nuts as a snow leopard, and I turned to the other guys. Vincent had come around from the couch, but was still standing several feet away. I rolled back to my feet and padded over to him carefully, not making any sudden moves. It was best not to make any sudden moves in front of a predator, but I didn't worry. My leopardess really liked them and when she looked at Reese, a thrumming purr began in her chest and a word rever-berated around our head that I refused to latch onto.

I butted my head against his thighs until he reached down, running his fingers across my head with tentative fingers. "Holy shit, Star. You are... Fuck I don't know if I can describe it. Magnificent." He looked over at Reese. "She's still in there right? She's not all snow leopard?"

Reese shrugged. "I don't know. This is only the third time I've ever seen it. But I figure Lincoln would be in ribbons if Celeste wasn't in control."

I chuffed again, and swung my head toward the man in question. He continued to stare unwaveringly down at me, and even my leopardess wanted to submit to his Alpha vibe. But he was still a human, so I raised my lip again, showing him my pretty pearly whites.

He dropped to his knees, and I rushed up toward him. Vincent squeaked out a warning, but I didn't stop until I was inches from his face. I stared into his eyes, showing him that it was me still in here.

Then I licked his face. Yeah, a snow leopard tongue felt like a cat tongue, but worse. That shit hurt like a bitch on human skin.

"Ugh," he protested, and I rolled back onto my side, huffing out more laughter. He dropped his fingers to my fur and I rubbed my face along his palm.

Then I turned back into a human and his hand rested on my cheek and not my head. "That's..." he seemed to run out of words.

Vincent walked over to the wet bar in the corner. "I'm going to need a drink and you're going to have to explain all this real slow, Star."

As Vincent got a round of scotch, Reese went and got me a glass of milk. Lincoln just continued to stand there and stare through me, like he was waiting for his mind to catch up with his eyes. At least, until Vincent stuffed a crystal tumbler into his hands.

Then Vincent whipped his shirt over his head and handed it to me. Oh yeah. I was naked. Whoops.

"I have no problem with your nudity, Star, but it's hard to concentrate when looking at your tits, and I feel like I need all my brain cells for this conversation." I laughed and it morphed into a yawn. Shifting when I was pregnant seemed to suck up more of my energy. Reese returned from the kitchen, handing me my milk and then dragging me back onto his lap like I hadn't just turned into a big cat.

I stretched and curled up, trying to ignore the fact that my naked ass was pressed to the front of his jeans. I also tried to ignore the hard line of his dick, but that was more difficult. "What do you guys want to know? I'm a snow leopard shifter. The guys today? Supernatural bounty hunters."

Lincoln spoke. "The baby?"

I shrugged. "I'm a half blood, and he or she would be even less. Maybe he'll be a shifter, maybe he will just be an average human with some extra perks. It's a bit of a genetic lottery."

"Do you have like a pack, or a family, or something?" Lincoln spoke for the first time, and in true Lincoln fashion, went straight for the jugular.

I shook my head. "No. I'm the bastard child of LA new money and the gardener. When my mother found out she was pregnant, she had my biological father deported back to whatever country he'd come from. When she realized I turned into this," I indicated myself, "she kicked me out. Told everyone I'd died in a skiing accident in Switzerland."

Vincent huffed. "Sounds right. How old were you?"

"Thirteen."

Lincoln turned away, but his body was vibrating with rage. Vincent was frowning at me. "Holy shit, you're Celeste Van Pell. Daughter of Prestcott and Winona Van Pell. Our families run in similar circles. I'm pretty sure I attended your wake."

I huffed, because it was an old emotional wound, but that bastard still hurt. "Figures. Selfish bitch would want sympathy even if she is a dirty rotten liar."

"She threw a thirteen year old girl out onto the streets?" Lincoln growled, and my snow leopard wanted to roll over and purr some more. But Lincoln was livid. Incandescent with rage. It was kind of something to behold.

I stood, and placed a gentle hand on his arm. I tried not to feel hurt when he wrenched away. "It's okay. I ended up fine. She prepaid for a little studio apartment for a year, and then I figured it out."

He whirled around and got in my face. "Was it, Celeste? How old were you when you learned about the bounty hunters, hmm?" I didn't answer, but he wasn't done. "How old were you when you realized that normal human men wanted to take advantage of a desperate young girl? It's not okay, Celeste."

He turned and stomped toward his bedroom, and I

watched him go with bewilderment. Vincent came over and hugged me to his chest. It didn't even occur to me to protest. I wanted his comfort.

"Don't worry, Star. It isn't you. Linc has his own demons. He'll be okay." He kissed the top of my head. "I, for one, am glad you aren't dead in the Swiss Alps." He pulled me back to the couch, stuffing me down beside Reese and then plopping down on my otherside.

"Tell me everything."

I WAS CURLED up in Reese's arms and it was blissfully nice. His warm breath puffed over my neck, and his arm was wrapped around my waist, his palm cupping my stomach. The baby fluttered against his hand, like it knew its daddy.

He was sound asleep, and he had the happy, restful sleep of a man who'd never had to live on the streets.

I could hear Lincoln roaming in the kitchen. I'd told myself he needed space, but as if it was completely separate from my brain, my body gently disentangled itself from Reese and climbed from beneath the covers. I was drawn to his pain.

I padded out into the living room on soft feet, and he was standing in front of the full length windows, looking out over the endless sea of lights.

I made a little noise so he knew I was there, and I watched the muscles in his shoulders tense, but he didn't turn to face me. I yearned to wrap my body around his and heal his pain, but I didn't even know what I was healing. So I just went with instinct. I walked up behind him and wrapped my arms around his waist, pressing my cheek against his back and holding him tight, anchoring him. He was still tense in my arms, but when he realized I wasn't going to move, he relaxed muscle by muscle.

He lifted his hand and placed it over mine where it rested against his abs and we just stood there in silence, only the sound of a clock and our heartbeats marring it.

We stood there for what felt like endless minutes before he spoke. "I grew up middle class. Not as rich as Vincent, or probably even you, but not too bad." His voice reverberated through my cheek where it rested on his back. "When I was five, my mother fell down the stairs and broke her collarbone. No big deal, she had to have a cast but that was it. The doctor prescribed her some serious pain relievers and she got hooked. She took more and more, until the Doctor stopped prescribing her refills and she got desperate. She started getting them off the street, and when they stopped working, she went into harder stuff." He sighed heavily, his muscles curling in on themselves. "One day, I came home from school and my father was gone. With him went our comfortable middle class life."

I didn't like where this story was going, but he obviously needed to get it off his chest. "Meanwhile, my mom was a ghost of her former self. She started hocking all our shit to pay for drugs, even though she said it was to buy food. Eventually, her dealer moved in and my older brother started pedaling shit on street corners for him." He shuddered. "It went downhill fast. Her boyfriend got her hooked on some hard stuff, things that would send her into rages. I was seven at the time. My brother eventually joined a gang and became this bitter, angry creature that was nothing like the kid I'd idolized. Eventually, the shadow of my mother got knocked up and had a baby." My fingers curled against his abs, but I said nothing. "They didn't have the mental faculties to take care of it, so she became my baby. I stopped going to school so I could care for her. In hindsight, I should have let protective services take her away, give her to a loving family who would have given her a perfect life."

"When she was about three, my mother got a bad batch of whatever the drug of the week was. When my baby sister toddled toward her, my mom freaked out, and backhanded her across the face. She bounced off the coffee table and hit her head on the floor. They tell me that she landed in a way that snapped her neck. A completely freak accident. My mom lost it. She picked me up, threw me across the room, and tried to stab me with a kitchen knife. I got hold of the knife and turned it. She slipped and it embedded in her chest."

I couldn't breathe. I didn't know if I wanted to hear the rest. It was so fucking tragic. Lincoln was shaking beneath my hands. "I called for help. She bled out on the kitchen floor before they could arrive. The cops took me away, questioned me, and I got sent to juvenile hall because they couldn't find anyone who would take me or pay my bail. Not my brother, that was for sure, or my mom's crackhead dealer boyfriend. My father was MIA. My mother's death was eventually ruled self defense, but by that time the damage was done. I missed my baby sister's funeral. I got sent to a group home. Bounced around foster care. No one wanted a killer for a foster kid long term. I aged out."

I just held him as he sucked in shuddering breath after shuddering breath. "I'm sorry I freaked out about you turning up, about you moving in, about every-thing. I just... I don't like things I can't control."

I pressed the softest kiss between his shoulder blades; a kiss that said you aren't alone anymore.

He spun in my arms, swooping down to kiss me. Suddenly, I was the one being held, his lips covering mine with a searing kiss. All that pain, the torment, he channelled into his kiss, and I ate his pain like it was a meal.

He dragged his lips away, panting. "I don't want to

control you, Celeste, but I'm not sure how to do this without it."

I kissed him back, gentler this time, and it promised him things that I had no right to promise. His hands ran under Reese's oversized shirt, stroking up my bare spine. They were softer than I'd have imagined, and spread wide, they covered most of my back.

He spun me so my back was pressed against the glass window, his body curving into mine, even though he had to stoop a little to kiss me.

He dropped to his knees, pushing my sleep shorts down to my ankles. He pulled one of my legs over his shoulder and I slid up the window until I was standing on my toes, my naked ass pressed to the glass.

He touched his lips softly to the tender flesh of my inner thigh, and I reached down to wrap my fingers in his hair, tugging a little. I didn't want it to be gentle. I wasn't breakable. He chuckled, puffing air across my wet pussy. Then he bit my thigh and I moaned, curling toward him. Grabbing my other thigh, he lifted my other leg up so I was suspended between the glass wall and his shoulders, his face burying between my thighs with ferocity. His tongue stroked and swirled, his nose nudging my clit as he lapped at me. He ate me like I was his last meal and it was heady.

He held me easily, and I felt my orgasm creeping up, my moans getting louder despite my efforts to stifle them. I was so fucking close, and that's when he stopped.

I snarled. My leopardess and I were in agreement right now. We were going to maim him if he didn't get back to it. But he just chuckled, dropping one of my legs to the ground as he slid up my body, his tongue trailing a wet line. "Fuck you taste like heaven. I'm about to blow in my shorts, and I want to feel you come around me."

I wanted to say something witty, but he had pushed up my shirt and had my nipple in his mouth and every smartass thought disappeared out of my brain. He picked me up, sliding me up the cold window. The chill against my back contrasting with the heat of his body was sending my brain into sensory overload. He lifted me easily and I wrapped my legs around his waist, grinding my body against his abs, seeking the relief.

"Lincoln," I moaned and he chuckled again.

"I like the way you purr my name," he whispered against my ear, and my whole body tingled.

I turned my face so I could capture his lips with mine, dragging his full bottom lip between mine and tugging. His dick twitched against my pussy, and I dug my heels into his ass. "Lincoln, please."

He pressed me against the glass with his body, pushing his sweats down with one hand. His dick sprung free and slid against the folds of my core. I wiggled, trying to get more. "Easy," he growled, and slid me slowly, purposefully down on his cock. I let my head bang back against the glass as he bottomed out inside me.

He grabbed my chin and held my face to his. "Why did you have to be so fucking beautiful?"

Then he pulled back and slammed into me again and any answer I may have had was washed away by pleasure. He drove himself up into my body over and over and I came on his cock so hard he shuddered and stopped, breathing hard through his nose. He pressed his nose into the crook of my shoulder as he panted. When the waves of pleasure stopped riding my body, he sucked in air and began to move again.

"You make me want to blow like a two minute man. You are so wet and tight," he groaned, driving up inside me, his pelvis rubbing against my sensitive clit. I couldn't do anything but grip his shoulders tightly, my nails scraping against his skin, making him hiss but thrust harder. His lips sucked at my throat and his fingers gripped my thighs roughly. There'd probably be fingermarks against them tomorrow but damn I loved it.

When he replaced his lips with his teeth, biting the column of my throat, my second orgasm smacked me into the stratosphere, all pretence of silence gone as I screamed his name. He slammed into me once more, roaring his own release as he came deep inside me.

I ran my hand up over his neck, burying my fingers in his hair. I sucked in air, my brain trying to catch up with my mind.

His body started to shake, and I felt his hot tears against my neck. I made soft noises, reassurances, nonsense that I was sure he couldn't hear. He just cried silently against me, both of us half naked and all the way fucked up.

I looked past his head and noticed Vince standing in the doorway, silhouetted by the soft lamp of the living room. He sauntered over until he was just behind us. He pressed a kiss to Lincoln's shoulder.

"Come on. Let's go to bed," he crooned softly, and Lincoln dragged in a shuddering breath. He slid his softening dick from between my thighs, but his arms remained around me. He held me as he walked down the hall, stopping at the bathroom so I could clean up, and then picking me up again like some kind of teddy bear. When we got to Vincent's room, somehow Reese was still asleep. I looked at Vincent, my arms tightening around Lincoln.

"There's room for all of us."

Vincent gave me a lopsided grin and nodded. We crept into the room, and I climbed in, sliding right up against Reese. He mumbled a little, and I pressed a kiss to his lips.

He blinked at me sleepily, then at Lincoln and Reese standing by the bed. I pressed my hand to his cheek. "Linc and Vince are going to sleep with us tonight," I said softly.

Reese, bless his goddamn heart, just nodded and shifted closer to the edge. He wrapped his arms around my body and snuggled me into the curve of his own. Lincoln climbed in beside me and Vincent got in on the other side.

I pressed my fingertips to Lincoln's cheekbones. "Sleep. I'll guard your dreams tonight," I whispered, leaning forward to kiss him gently.

Reese ran his thumb softly over my hip then gave it a squeeze. He approved. In that moment, I could see how you could love men like these.

But it wasn't in my future and I could almost hear my heart cracking in two.

"Night, Star," Vincent murmured. "Sweet dreams."

I wish I could have told him this was the sweetest dream of all.

16

I had to look up the signs, but I was pretty sure I was in a relationship. She'd met all my friends. Hell, she'd slept with them all, and me, and then we all had breakfast afterwards. We spent every weekend together. I want to take her places and show her things. Check, check, check. I want to talk to her all the time, kiss her all the time, and fuck her sweet, tight body all the damn time. Yep, yep, yep.

According to Cosmo, I was in a relationship. In the month since her abduction attempt, there'd been no other problems. Some of that was down to the fact that Lincoln had locked down security in our building tighter than a nun's vagina. But Celeste thought that perhaps it was a crime of opportunity. It happened. Apparently, shifters ran a little hotter and were easily detectable by heat gun.

My girlfriend was a fucking snow leopard. That was a bad acid trip I was never going to get used to because what the actual fuck?

We were on the couch now, her head on my lap as we watched some movie that made her cry even though it wasn't even remotely sad. But I stroked her hair and let her create a little puddle of hormone tears on my jeans because, I don't know, I liked her a fucking lot.

My phone blew up again, and I frowned. I'd been ignoring my manager, and the label, and they were getting upset.

She rolled onto her back, swiping her face with her sleeve. "Aren't you going to answer that?"

I shook my head. "Nope. They just want me to go to the label's Halloween party."

She frowned. "You don't want to go?"

I shrugged, because I didn't want to tell her that I'd rather stay home and let her cry into my jeans over the dog finding its way home in some kid's movie. "What if I came too?"

I slid my hand down her body and played with the elastic waistband of her sweats. "I'd like it if you came too. It's the gentlemanly thing to do." I winked and she laughed, slapping at my hand.

"Seriously. I need to get out of the house. The label will have lots of security to keep Lincoln happy. We could all go. You can pass me off as Lincoln's pregnant girlfriend to the media."

I booped her nose, because it was a pretty cute nose. "Star, you are Licoln's pregnant girlfriend. And Reese's pregnant girlfriend." I paused and stared down at her, the look in her eyes crazily vulnerable. "My pregnant girlfriend."

She gave me a soft, sad look. "Vince, you know I have to go."

I folded in half and kissed her lips softly. "Do you? Hasn't Lincoln protected you so far? We could keep you safe."

She shook her head, and I knew the stubborn look in her eye. We'd all tried to convince her that she could be with us, that we could be a family, but I think she was scared. Scared we'd cast her aside. Scared she'd be a shitty mother like hers was. But we had another two months to convince her.

She gave me a tight smile. "We're going to the party, Vincent! Pull out your sexy bunny suit, because I'm to be the envy of every girl there."

I rolled my eyes, but pleasure blossomed in my chest. It was a thrill that had nothing to do with drugs or driving my Maybach too fast around winding, mountainous roads, and everything to do with her. She sat up, and I knew she was done with our conversation. So when my manager rang again, I answered and promised I'd be there. I just needed three extra tickets.

. . .

WHEN THE LIMO pulled up to the warehouse, there was a fucking red carpet. Jesus, I was getting too old for this bullshit. Still, I looked at the people inside the limo with me, and thought maybe this party wouldn't be so bad if they were here too. Lincoln looked tense, but I leaned across and kissed him.

"It'll be fine. The security here is tight. No one is getting our girl."

Lincoln was dressed in a black tuxedo, his hair slicked back and a gold rolex on his wrist. I knew he had a crazy amount of firepower tucked beneath his expensively tailored jacket. Apparently, he was going as James Bond. But damn he looked delicious as hell. Reese was dressed as The Lone Ranger, complete with a mask that he got from the sex shop near his office building. If he didn't have the hat, I'd think he was about to pull out the riding crop and make me beg for mercy. Unlike Lincoln, his guns were entirely fake.

But Star? She had gotten an alien face hugger and stitched it on the front of a white cocktail dress, and it looked like it was exploding out of her pregnant belly. It was hilarious and terrifying all at once.

Someone opened the limo door, and I climbed out first. I was dressed as Willy Wonka, complete with a purple velvet suit and top hat. As I pointed my weird pimp cane at the crowd, there was a smattering of amused laughter from the paparazzi.

I walked a little way up the carpet, drawing the

paps so Star and the guys could get out of the limo, though I kept an eye on them as I worked it for the camera.

When I was happy that Lincoln had her situated between himself and Reese, I walked toward the doors. I waited for them as they got past the security, ignoring the calls to Reese about the mystery girl. The door girl fluttered her lashes at me, and six months ago I would have fucked her in the coatroom. But not today. I just strolled past her, herding Celeste and the guys inside the warehouse. It was decorated with about as much tastefulness as a highschool gym, but the food was good and the booze was free.

We quickly checked Celeste's coat and moved further into the room.

I saw my manager across the room, but I pretended I didn't. I had a booth reserved in the back of the room, because if I couldn't throw my clout around at my own label, what was the point? I ushered Star in first, and then Reese slid in after her. I sat on the opposite side, and Lincoln perched on the edge of his seat, his eyes roaming over the crowd.

"Relax, Linc. We're good." A waitress appeared with a tray of champagne flutes, and I took one with my trademark smirk. The waitress flushed, but it felt wrong with Star here. So, instead of flirting like I would have done, I just squeezed Celeste's knee under the table.

Her eyes were taking in all the faces too, but not in the same way that Lincoln's were. When her gaze stopped on a pop princess snorting coke on her table, her eyes nearly popped out of her head.

Never meet your idols. There was wisdom in that statement. "What do you think?" I said, waving my hand at the writhing crowd, the already drunk starlets and the wall to wall bodyguards hovering around. I should have stayed home. I could have given Star a foot rub that would have eventually turned into me rubbing something else fun.

"Can we dance?" she yelled over the music and I smiled. Hell yeah we could. Lincoln shifted out of the way, giving me a stern look. I just grinned and blew him a kiss. Later, I'd probably just blow him. Super protective Lincoln did wild things for my libido. Reese leaned over and kissed Star's cheek, but his phone was flashing with an incoming call.

Being CEO of one of the most progressive tech companies on the East Coast had its pitfalls, like being on call twenty-four hours a day.

Lincoln remained standing. "Not too far away. Don't move out of my eyesight."

I squeezed his hand and nodded. Normally I would have teased him about his overreaction, but when it came to our girl, I was completely on board with being good.

I led her onto the floor, happy that there were no

paps in here. It meant when Star started swaying her hips, I could move up behind her and let her grind up on me. She moved like she felt the music in her soul, and I moved with her. She was like a beautiful instrument as she threw back her head and laughed, and I desperately wanted to learn to play her. She was so free in the moment, so fucking gorgeous. The song shifted to something with a real slow beat and loads of bass. Oh, shit. It was one of my songs.

Her eyes lit up as she spun in my arms, palming the back of my neck as she undulated to the music with me.

"You have such a beautiful voice," she purred. "It makes me want to touch myself."

Shock stilled my feet, my eyebrows almost all the way up to my hairline. I leaned closed. "Is that right?"

She nodded. "I just imagine you singing all the dirty things you want to do to me."

I pulled her tight to my body. "Like how I want to run my tongue over every tempting curve of you?"

She swallowed hard. "Uh huh."

"Or how I want to eat your wet little pussy until your juices make my cheeks shine?"

"Vincent..." she whispered. Fuck. I wanted to find a dark corner and bury my cock in her wet heat right now. But I wouldn't do that here, among these people. These posers and people who were desperate to make a few bucks by selling off a grainy photo taken on a camera phone in the dark.

"Later, Star. Let's just dance for now."

Her eyes were burning hot with lust, and I felt it brand me right across my damn heart.

I hated Halloween. Vincent would say it was because I was a killjoy, but it was because everyone hid themselves on Halloween. It was hard to discern friend from foe when everyone was dressed as Disney characters.

I watched Vincent and Celeste grind on each other on the dance floor and it was making me uncomfortably hard in my tailored tux. Reese slammed his phone onto the table and sighed. "Problems?"

He shook his head, taking off his black cowboy hat. "No. I'm just tired, you know? I'm tired of being CEO, tired of the twenty-hour work days. Celeste..." his eyes drifted to the dance floor too. "She's changed things. I want to be with her all day, not in meeting after meeting, going around and around over the same thing."

I nodded. Ever since the night I'd fucked her

against the windows and bared my soul, we'd turned a corner, I guess. Also, being forced together all the time helped. Making love to her all the time helped too.

Reese downed his glass of champagne in one mouthful. "What do you want to do?"

He shrugged. "I don't know. But I want to be around when the baby is born. I want to see it take its first steps. Maybe I can hand over some of the day to day running of the company to an executive board. I've built a good team. I don't need to spearhead it all the time, do I?"

He was asking the wrong damn person. I knew the easiest things to make a shank out of, but not much about Chief Financial Officers. "Do it, man. You're richer than God. The company is doing well. One of us needs to be a good dad, and you had the best role model," I joked. Reese just got this soft look in his eye, the same one he always did when I mentioned how different our upbringings were. It's not like I was trying to make a big deal of it, it was just a joke.

I turned back to the dance floor before he wanted to have a deep and meaningful conversation right here. "They are like two layers of clothing away from having sex out there," I grumbled, and Reese laughed.

"They aren't the only ones."

His complete lack of jealousy blew my brain. I was lucky, I understood that. And honestly, the idea of Celeste making love to either Reese or Vincent didn't bother me as much as I knew it should. But when another guy, I think he was a famous DJ from memory, tried to dance up behind Celeste, every single one of my hackles raised. Fuck that.

I narrowed my eyes. "We're going home. This was stupid," I growled and Reese had the audacity to laugh. But he began gathering Vince's purple Willy Wonka jacket that he'd kept on for all of two seconds and Celeste's purse as I strode across the dancefloor to where Vincent and Celeste were dancing.

The party boy was dancing closer, his hands out like he wanted to grab her ass. Vince was too caught up in Celeste to even notice.

When I was close enough, I slapped the man's hand, and when he looked up at me outraged, I let death fill my face.

"Touch her and you'll want to hope that you don't need hands to be a pill-popping jukebox. Fuck off."

The guy snarled and I kind of hoped he'd start something. But he just muttered something under his breath and walked away, and I watched him until he left the dance floor.

"Have you come to dance, Lincoln?" Vincent yelled over the music, gripping my jacket and pulling me closer, until my body was pressed along Celeste's back. I grabbed her hips to steady her, and the little minx rubbed her ass on my crotch. In her sky-high heels, we were more similarly matched in height, and if I slid my hand up her dress, pushed her panties to the side, I could probably fuck her right here on the dancefloor. As if she knew the direction of my thoughts, she looked over her shoulder and grinned.

Temptress.

I smirked and leaned forward, scraping my teeth down the back of her neck the way she liked, and I was rewarded by her full body shudder. My semi-hard dick was well and truly on its way to being achingly hard.

"We should go," I shouted to them both, and Vincent's eyes met mine. They were filled with lust, and I knew he was probably as hard as me.

Celeste frowned. "We only just got here," she pouted, and I thrust my hard cock against her ass. She grinned again and this time it was all heat. "Oh, I see. Just because you can't control your dick, we have to go home?"

"Yes," I whispered into her ear, and she trembled beneath my palms again.

"We'll make it worth it, Star," Vincent crooned, and she gave us what I liked to call her snow leopard grin. It was wide and predatory, and it made me feel like a mouse that was being played with.

"You better," she cooed back, and then stepped from between us. Vincent winked at me and then stepped back. We tried to keep our relationship on the downlow in public. Vincent loved his music, but as it was, his sexuality was the only topic he was ever asked about in interviews. But if he got caught making out with me in public? His music would come second to his sex life in most people's minds.

I wondered what the press would say if they knew we were basically polyamorous now?

Reese was standing on the edge of the dancefloor, Vincent's purple velvet jacket over his arm. He just looked so fucking wholesome, like the kinda guy you could trust with your drink, your wallet, and your girl.

Celeste bounded up to him and kissed him, uncaring about the fact that we'd been all but mauling her on the dancefloor. I was kind of glad that it was so packed out there otherwise we were definitely going to be front page news tomorrow.

Who fucking cared?

Not Reese, given the way he wrapped her in his arms and kissed her deeply. "Have I told you how beautiful you look tonight?" he asked her, and she flushed so red that I could see it even in the darkness. She wasn't great with compliments, and I could understand it. When you grew up being told how shit you were, it seemed unreasonable when people complimented you as an adult.

But Reese wasn't wrong. She was so fucking beautiful.

We were almost at the coat check when Vincent's manager finally caught up with him.

"Vinnie! I've been looking for you all night," he

panted; he always looked like he was one line of coke away from a coronary. His eyes slid over me like I was part of the furniture, but he nodded respectfully at Reese. "Good to see you, kid."

Reese gave him a tight smile because it wasn't in his nature to cause conflict. But Celeste had noticed his dismissal of me and I could almost feel her vibrating with anger beneath my hand. Vincent gave us an assessing look and threw Celeste one of his charming winks. "How about I meet you guys in the car? This won't take but a minute."

I ushered Celeste away before she turned into the hulk, or Vince's manager asked too many questions. She managed to stomp even in her heels.

"He just ignored you like you don't exist!" she raged, and I shrugged.

"Vincent's manager is one of the few people who know Vincent and I are a couple, and he likes to pretend I don't exist or I'm just security. Doesn't matter to me, angel."

Still, she looked absolutely pissed. Hormones? The line to the coat check was long, and Celeste kept throwing dirty looks back over her shoulder at Vincent's manager. Reese gave her Vince's purple Willy Wonka jacket, and smiled. "How about you guys go wait for the car and I'll get your coat and wait for Vince?"

She nodded, but still looked a little peeved. I

guided her through the side entrance, away from the paparazzi. This was the side that the non-A list guests would arrive and depart from, and it was bustling.

I quickly sent a text to the driver, and he replied that he was seven minutes out. I helped Celeste into the purple velvet jacket, and it hung down to her knees, and I couldn't help my smile. She looked like a tiny pimp from the seventies. She wrapped her arms around my waist, still grumbling against my chest about social injustice and I laughed.

"It's the way it is. Vince and Reese? They are a big deal. I am just the muscle."

She stepped back and punched me in the shoulder. "Don't talk bullshit, Lincoln. You are just as important as Reese and Vince."

I pulled her back into my arms. "To you? I can only try to be. But to the rest of the world? I mean next to nothing. Replaceable security. Just another gorilla in a suit."

"I like gorillas," she muttered and I grinned. I leaned down and kissed her softly, with more tenderness than I thought I possessed.

I saw the limo coming up behind a town car, and I walked further down the carpet, past the clusters of people already swaying on their feet. It was barely even ten yet, and these people were completely high.

The town car shuddered to a stop and two clowns climbed out.

I narrowed my eyes. They looked wrong.

It was my final thought as one lifted a gun and the sound of the gunshot echoed off the surrounding warehouses. The slug to my chest pulled me from Celeste's arms and my world went silent.

Shock blanked my vision, and when it came back online, the second clown appeared, dragging Celeste from my arms as I sunk to my knees. She kicked and screamed, but it meant nothing as they stuffed her into the car, a gun to her head.

My body stopped working and my legs gave out completely. I sunk to my knees, my hand desperately trying to find my gun beneath my jacket, but instead came away stained red with blood.

The town car peeled away from the curb as security surged from the building, and I slipped to the side.

I'd failed again. She was gone and so was I.

18

CELESTE

I watched Lincoln fall to his knees, a flower of blood spreading across his white shirt. "Lincoln!" I screamed, but a second hunter appeared from nowhere and dragged me toward the town car. I struggled but my eyes remained locked on Lincoln. I was screaming, but no one stepped forward to help. Not me. Not Lincoln, who was fishing under his jacket with useless hands, looking for his gun.

"Help him!" I screamed at the useless, gawking crowd. They all stood as still as statues; statues dressed in stupid Halloween costumes. I should never have convinced Vincent to take me to this party. I should have known better.

I swung around, kicking and hitting at the man dragging me. He grunted as my elbow connected with something soft, but he didn't loosen his grip. Should I shift here, save myself? Would the Shifter Council come for me, because I knew while most of the paparazzi were around front, at least one person would have the camera out filming this rather than helping me.

I procrastinated too long because I was being stuffed into the back of the town car. It happened in seconds. From happiness to tragedy in the blink of an eye.

The hunter holding me slammed the door shut. "Fucking drive," he growled and the driver floored the car into the darkness. I caught the shocked face of Reese running from the doors as we drove away. Thank god. He'd help Lincoln.

My brain refused to acknowledge that he'd been shot in the chest. Often fatal. But Reese would not let him die. I knew this deep down in my soul. Reese would make sure he lived, even if he had to reanimate his corpse, like Frankenstein.

I snarled as my snow leopard took over, shifting. She knew we were better protected in our shifted form, even if she was mournfully crying over the loss of Lincoln too. We had to protect our cub.

"She's fucking shifting. Give her the sedative before we're shredded," the kidnapper behind me screeched, but too late. My fingers were claws, and I was shredding at the hunter in front of me. He stabbed me with a needle before I was fully shifted and my change slowed. By the time I was fully snow leopard, my reactions were sluggish.

The man with the needle swore. "She goddamn shifted before I could inject her."

"You double-dosed her? You fucking idiot," the driver yelled. He looked over his shoulder at me with cold eyes. "You've poisoned her. The witch who gave us that shit said we had to be careful." He slammed his hand against the steering wheel. "Dammit!"

He pulled off the main road and onto the back streets. "We're going to have to wait till the baby is born and then sell it instead. She's useless now." He swore again and my brain was screaming. Lincoln. The baby. Lincoln. The baby. Eventually, darkness took me.

I woke up on a thin blanket in the darkness. I struggled to my feet, but my legs were wobbly and I sank back to my belly almost straight away. I yowled in frustration, struggling to my four feet again.

"I wouldn't bother. The drugs are too strong and there's nowhere for you to go anyway," a voice said from the darkness. I tilted my head in the direction of his voice. He was right. I was in a cage, thick bars between me and freedom. "I was hoping the drugs would wear off a little more but no such luck. There's too much and eventually your organs will shut down. But we've got awhile, long enough that the cub will survive if we cut it out of you." He seemed annoyed, and I wished I was briefly in my human form so I could tell him to go and fuck himself.

I got a good look at him as he stepped forward from the shadows of the room. "It's a pity. We would have gotten a good price with you as a with-child shifter. Infants sell okay, but it's the long game and you have to care for them." He sighed like it was really an arduous task to kill me and steal my child. I snarled in his direction but he wasn't even looking at me. He was pretty, in a dead kind of way. Close cropped blonde hair, strong jawline despite the scars on his cheeks. Brilliant blue eyes, slightly more blue than mine but not by much. Cruel and mean, there was nothing human about him except his bi-pedal nature and an opposable thumb. In his eyes, there was nothing but death.

I turned my head away, though I kept watch on him from the corner of my eye. Never turn your back on a predator, and there was no doubt in my mind that this guy was a monster. He banged on the bars and made me flinch, but then he turned back toward the doorway. "I'll get them to bring you down food. Try to eat it. You are no good to me now, but your stay here can be pleasant or very, very unpleasant."

My skin rippled with fear at his words. When the door shut, I let myself collapse back to my belly. I curled around the swollen stomach, nudging it with my nose.

It'll be okay, Little One. Daddy will save us.

I just hoped I wasn't telling my child its very first lie.

True to his word, someone arrived with food. It was the guy who overdosed me with whatever the hell they jabbed me with. He slid me a sandwich and a small carton of milk through the bars of my cage. The milk reminded me of Lincoln, and then I wanted to cry. The guy didn't say anything, but he looked... almost apologetic. Like he was sorry for sentencing me to a slow and apparently painful death. I wanted to claw his face into ribbons.

I snarled uselessly from behind the bars.

The guy didn't say anything more, he just left. I transformed back, wrapping the thin blanket that I was sitting on around me toga style. I lurched toward the cage doors, rattling them uselessly. Whatever they were, I wasn't big enough or strong enough to do any damage to them.

Fuck, fuck, fuck, fuck.

My knees gave out and I slurped down the milk and ate the sandwich. I was getting out of here. I needed my strength and so did the baby. I would not die here, and neither would he.

As soon as I finished, I shifted back to my snow leopard form. I curled up and let the lethargy of the drugs pull me back under. Whatever they'd given me was killing me slowly. I could feel it already.

Madness.

The worst ten seconds of my life were pure madness. I'd heard the screams, burst through the door too late. Too late to get to Celeste. Too late to get to Lincoln. Too late.

I ran, faster than I've ever ran, but it was still too slow. I caught the number plate as it sped away, but that was it. This wasn't Hollywood. There was no convenient car to hijack while screaming "Follow that car!"

All I had was my brain and my brothers to get her back. And I would get her back. I refused to let myself even contemplate any other scenario. I turned and ran back to where Lincoln was bleeding out on the red carpet.

Vincent was beside him, and security was on the

phone to 911. A man from the crowd had Lincoln's shirt pulled open, hands over the wound in his chest. Not a man, a damn kid. He looked pale. "It went through. Fuck, those guys just came out of nowhere." His arm shook with the force he was using to apply pressure. "I'm only in my third year at med school, but we studied gunshot wounds." I tried to ignore the way his hands shook. "I need tape and a piece of plastic."

A cameraman burst forward, his camera undoubtedly still rolling as he rested his equipment bag on the ground. He pulled out duct tape and a small plastic baggie that contained some cords. He handed both to the med student.

Vincent had Lincoln's jacket jammed against an exit wound in his back, his body half under Lincoln holding him up. "Hold on, Linc. Helps coming," he crooned even as his voice caught in his throat. "We've got you."

"Celeste," Lincoln wheezed, forcing blood to bubble up through the gunshot wound in his chest.

"Shh, don't worry. It's going to be okay. Star is fine," Vincent lied, tears gathering in the corners of his eyes. Lincoln was gasping for breath, and the med student created some kind of temporary valve over his chest wound by taping three sides of the plastic baggie down with tape. The gunshot had gone in just below his right nipple and I was acutely aware that if it had been a few inches to the left, my best friend would be dead. As it was, he was as grey as a corpse.

The impromptu valve seemed to ease some of the gasping, but Lincoln still couldn't breathe. I almost cried when the ear piercing scream of sirens and lights lit up the night.

Paramedics were soon there, working with calm efficiency, asking questions of the med student as they worked. One pulled out a huge needle, piercing it into his chest and Lincoln sucked in a gasp. The other paramedic put an oxygen mask over his face, talking to him quietly. Everything was a blur, a whir of sound that made no sense, like I was hearing it under water. They were loading him onto a stretcher and wheeling him toward the ambulance.

Vincent clung to his hand. "I'm coming with you. I'm his boyfriend."

The medics didn't fight him on it, loading them both into the back of the ambulance. I stood there, useless, everyone I care about gone in an instant. The med student began to shake beside me, and I turned to him.

"You did good," I said, but my voice sounded flat. I was in shock.

The kid looked at me. "You're in shock," he said, echoing my thoughts.

"I think we both are." The cops arrived, rushing in

with their hands on their guns, but the offenders were gone. They took my girlfriend. My child.

I fell to my knees, uncaring that I was kneeling in the lifeblood of my best friend. A cop was talking to me, and although I could hear his words, I couldn't understand them.

A cop was kneeling in front of me then. "Sir? Can you tell me what happened?"

He had big brown eyes that turned down at the corners, and a small frown line between his brows.

I shook my head. "They took her. They shot Linc and they took her."

"Who, Sir? Who was taken?"

"My girlfriend, Celeste. She's having my baby."

"She's pregnant?" I nodded and he said something over his shoulder. "Do you know who might have taken her?"

I shook my head, because I didn't know. I had no fucking idea who they were, or how I'd get her back. "I don't know. I don't know."

SOMEONE DROVE me to the hospital hours later, and we were outside the doors before I realized it was the med student who was in the driver's seat. When I looked at him surprised, he shrugged. "I just need to know..."

He needed to know if Lincoln lived or died. I needed to know too. We strode through the emergency room until we reached the desk. The nurse behind the counter seemed calmly concerned. I didn't think that was possible, but she embodied it perfectly. I realized both me and the med kid were covered in blood.

"I'm the brother of Lincoln Prescott. I need to know about his condition." I implored her with my eyes and she typed away on the computer. "Mr Prescott has gone up to surgery. I'll show you to the family waiting room. Do you need help?" she asked softly, and I nodded. I did need help. I needed help to ensure my best friend didn't die. I needed help to ensure that I got Celeste back. But there was nothing this nurse could do for me.

"I'm fine," I said, despite my nod.

She led me to a waiting room, and I saw Vincent pacing inside. I was across the room and holding Vince in my arms in a moment. "He's in surgery." He whispered into my shoulder. "They took her, Reese. She's gone."

I squeezed him tight and let him go. "I know. We're going to get her back. It's going to be okay."

I stepped away and looked over to the med kid. I should ask him his name. "What's your name?"

"Bryant Cole."

"I owe you so much." I pulled out my card. "In a week, call this number. Tell them who you are. They'll have orders to pay for your college tuition."

Bryant didn't have time to respond because a

doctor was walking into the waiting room. Both Vincent and I pounced on him.

"Are you the family of Lincoln Prescott?"

I nodded, and he gave a short nod. "The surgery went well. The bullet went through, and we managed to repair the damage to his lung. I don't have to tell you that he is very, very lucky. A little bit further either way and we'd be having a far different conversation right now. The field valve gave him precious moments." I wanted to cry, but instead, I wrapped an arm around Vincent's shoulders. I shot Bryant Cole another thankful look. "He's in post-op, but you can see him. He'll be sore and sorry for a couple of weeks, but he should make a full recovery."

I reached out and shook the doctor's hand, as Vincent's body trembled beneath my arm. When I looked at him, his face was perfectly blank.

"We'll come through and see him. Thank you so much, Doctor."

The surgeon gave me a tight smile and directed me toward post-op, and a kind-faced nurse walked us to a curtained-off room.

Lincoln was asleep, attached to machines to help him breathe and monitor his vital signs. He looked grey, but not the near-death look of before. He was shirtless, bandages over his chest wound yellow and slightly bloody. He was alive, and the steady beep of the heart rate monitor eased the tightness in my chest.

Vincent walked over and rested his forehead against Lincoln's. I went to the other side of the bed and held his hand. It felt warm and dry, and I held it tightly in mine. I needed to be out there looking for Celeste, but what could I do? I'd called the police, told them everything I know. What was my next step?

I squeezed Lincoln's hand and then stood. "I have to find her, Vince."

Vincent nodded, but he looked torn. I knew he wanted to find her too, but he'd almost lost his lover. He was shaken, and a shaken Vincent was a reckless Vincent.

I walked to his side and rested my hand on his shoulder. "Stay. Someone should be with him when he wakes up, otherwise, he's likely to freak the fuck out and storm out of here like the Terminator." I gave him a weak grin, but Vincent still looked torn. "I'll keep you updated every step of the way. They both need us right now. You do your part here, and I'll do mine."

Vincent let out a long sigh. "Okay. But let me know if there's any news. Anything at all. Promise me, Reese."

I swore it all over again and dragged myself out of the room.

MY HOME WAS LITTERED with reminders of Celeste. Every box filled with baby stuff, the fluffy rug she liked to lay on in the sun, her discarded tshirt still strewn over the bed, it was a tsunami of reminders that she was out there, scared and worried. Maybe she was suffering.

My anxiety ratcheted up to twelve. I sprinted to my bedroom, grabbing my laptop out of my desk. I opened up my secure browser, mashing keys to make it hurry.

The police couldn't help us, not really. Celeste wasn't an ordinary missing person. They weren't ordinary kidnappers.

I needed help.

I opened up the secure chat to Talbaloo.

Buttercup: Celeste has been taken. They stole her straight off the street in front of dozens of humans. I need help. Please!

The next line remained painfully blank, but I would wait. While I waited, I scoured the dark web for any hints of auctions, black market deals for cubs and shifters, and what I found made me sick. They were selling tiny kids. Women, teenagers. Rage mixed with my fear, but I wrote down times and dates. I would buy her back if I had to, as much as it killed something inside me to put money in the pockets of these monsters.

My computer dinged, and I clicked into the chat.

Talbaloo: Shit! When?

Buttercup: Tonight. Shot my best friend in the process.

Talbaloo: Tell me everything. Don't leave out a single detail. Descriptions, number plates, how many. I need to know everything

I let out a shuddering breath. I don't know how my internet pen friend could fucking help me in a time like this, but I had no other options. Maybe he knew someone. So I told him everything. I pulled the police reports, because hacking into their database was child's play. I grabbed CCTV footage from the back dock of the warehouse across the alley. Watching the footage of Lincoln getting shot and Celeste being dragged into the car made me want to put my fist through the wall.

I'd give myself over to the rage later.

Buttercup: Can you help?

Talbaloo: I've got you, Man. Your girl and your cub will be back in your arms before you know it.

Talbaloo has left the chat

I stared at the computer screen, my heart thundering in my chest. He was my only hope, because, without him, I had nothing.

I'd woken up in my fair share of hospital beds. I'd been stabbed and stomped but I have to say, none of that hurt like being shot.

Shot.

Celeste.

I rocketed up in bed, pulling at the cords and tubes attached to my body, especially the one down my throat.

Fuck, I can't breathe. I can't breathe.

Vincent was suddenly all I could see, his hand on my shoulders, steadying me. "Hey, Linc, it's okay. It's okay. You're okay. Just wait up and I'll get someone. Nurse!"

An older lady with a tight face but kind eyes came in. "Hi Lincoln. It's good to see you awake."

She looked at the monitors behind my head. "Your

oxygen levels look really good, so I might extubate you now if it's causing you discomfort. You're a very lucky guy. But right now, I just need you to try taking some deep breaths while I get everything set up."

She bustled around the room and my eyes went back to Vincent. I begged him for what I needed to know with my eyes. Was she safe? Did they get her back?

But he was ignoring the questions, and that in itself was an answer. The pain in my chest was unbearable, and it had nothing to do with the bullet wound in my chest. She was gone and they hadn't gotten her back.

I laid still as the nurse went through the process of removing the tube from my throat that I assumed was helping me breathe. I wanted to be tube free so I could get out there and look for her myself.

Vincent's eyes never left mine, and soon enough the nurse was gone and I just had nasal oxygen. I wanted to tear it off too, but first I needed Vincent. I lifted my chin and he was across the room and had his face pressed to mine.

"Fuck. Fuck! I thought you were going to die, Linc. I thought you were going to die and leave me here by myself and I couldn't take that. I love you. I love you so fucking much. You aren't allowed to get shot again."

"Love... you. Too," I gasped out because it hurt to speak, my throat a little damaged from whatever else they'd jammed down there during surgery. "Celeste?"

I needed to hear him say it. Needed to know everything.

Vincent straightened, and the sadness in his eyes made me want to drag him into the bed with me and curl myself around him until we were both okay.

"She's gone. Cops have nothing. Reese is out there, doing whatever the fuck Reese does. He'll find her, Linc. He loves the hell out of her. I love her. We will find her, I swear it."

He was trying to appease me, probably to keep me in this bed, but he was honestly fighting a losing battle. As soon as I could stand, I'd be out of here and on the streets looking for her. I'd lost her on my watch. I wouldn't rest until she was back in my arms.

But not while I was this weak. I tried to fight the closing of my eyes, but I couldn't. My body overruled my mind and I slipped back to sleep.

WHEN I WOKE AGAIN, I was in an ordinary hospital room. Well, not an average one. A private room. Vincent was asleep in a chair, his head resting on the edge of my bed. I ran my fingers through his blond hair. Fuck, he was beautiful when he slept, despite the fact that his face was scruffy and he had black smudges under his eyes from exhaustion. Had he even left?

Even as I thought it, I knew he hadn't. He was still in his Willy Wonka outfit.

I stroked his face gently until he blinked awake.

"Hey."

He sat up and rubbed his face against his arm. "You're awake? How do you feel?"

How did I feel? Like I'd been shot. It hurt to breathe, my chest felt like it had been torn apart and reassembled wrong. "I feel good," I lied.

Vince raised an eyebrow. Yeah, he didn't believe me either. "I need to get out of here, Vince. What is Reese up to?"

Vincent leaned closer. "Well, he hacked the police departments files for one."

Shock made my eyes go wide. Reese? Honest, law abiding Reese, hacking police files? Fuck, shit was really getting wild. "The cops have nothing. Lost the car in the side streets out in the suburbs and didn't pick it up again." His face crumpled into a mask of tortured guilt. "This whole thing is my fault. We should have been at home where we could keep her safe. We knew! We knew the threat was real. Fuck, we should have packed up her and Reese and moved as far away as possible. Across the country. Hell, maybe to a different country. Somewhere where she would be safe and I wouldn't have to worry about you jumping in front of bullets and shattering my fucking heart in the process."

I couldn't tell if he was angry or sad or just some unholy combination of the two. I grabbed him and pulled him onto my chest, wrapping my arms around his shoulders and holding him tight. I didn't care about the wound in my chest, only about the wound in his. "I'm okay. I'm harder to kill than this." I kissed the top of his head. "In my defense, they just straight out shot me. Didn't jump in front of any bullets."

Vince scoffed against my chest. "Like you wouldn't if given the chance."

Well, I couldn't argue with that.

I held him for a little longer, and when a nurse peeked through the doorway, I shook my head. She could come back in a little bit. I needed Vincent and he needed me. She gave me a disapproving look, but her eyes were soft. When I realized his breathing became gentle snores, I nudged him awake.

He stood up, blinking wearily. "You need to go home. Have a shower. Change out of that god awful outfit," I said gruffly, because this was too much emotion for one day. Too much chaos. Too much of everything. "Get a cab. Have some sleep. I promise I won't do anything stupid while you're not watching."

"Like getting shot."

I smiled sadly. "Like that." He kissed me goodbye, gathered up his stuff and left. He must have been exhausted, because he didn't even protest. Not really. He just did what he was told, and that was so unlike Vincent I would worry he'd been body snatched if it wasn't for this situation.

I waited until he was gone for fifteen minutes before I pressed the buzzer to call the nurse. She walked in smiling, but the expression on my face must have been fierce, because I could see the joyfulness just die.

"I'd like to leave."

She tensed her jaw. "Lincoln, you had major surgery less than two days ago."

"Will I die?"

"Probably."

I gave her my most charming grin. "That wasn't a yes. Now get this shit off of of me, I have to go."

"No." She crossed her arms over her chest and gave me the dead eye. I was pretty sure that expression could have quelled the fiercest of people, but I had a really good reason to leave.

"Look," I read her name badge, and softened my voice. "Look, Daphne. I'm leaving, so either you take these things off properly, or I tear them off with about as much finesse as a wrecking ball. Either way, I'm out of here."

She huffed angrily and stormed out of the room. I gave her a couple of minutes, but she didn't return. Okay, so the hard way it is.

I was about to yank out my cannula when she bustled back in, muttering about pigheaded stubborn stupid men. All under her breath though, probably so I didn't take her to the review board for slander or something. Not that I would. It isn't slander if she was 100% correct. I was being stupid and stubborn. But there was someone bigger than myself out there, someone or should I say someones, who meant more than me lying around in a hospital bed trying to recover.

She removed the cannula from my arm, still gently even though she looked at me like she wanted to beat me over the head. When I was free and clear, she stood back and let me stand. She watched me as I stood on wobbly legs, looking a bit like a baby giraffe, but she didn't move to steady me. She just crossed her arms and looked a little furious. My ass flapped in the breeze as she thrust a bunch of forms at me.

"You need to sign these to say you are releasing yourself against medical orders and that the hospital holds no responsibility if you get onto the street and die of a pulmonary embolism." With that, she turned and left the room.

Someone, probably Reese, had dropped me in a t-shirt and sweats, for when I was back in the land of the living, and I was eternally grateful. I slipped them on, leaning almost completely on the bed for support, and when I was done, I was gasping for breath. Still, when Nurse Daphne walked back in, I tried to regulate my breathing like I wasn't struggling. Given the look on her face, she wasn't fooled.

She pointed to the wheelchair. "Get in. One of us

has to wheel your ass to the curb, and I drew the short straw."

Daphne the nurse was growing on me. Her tight grey hair and her no-nonsense face made her look like someone's stern great aunt. She looked like she would whoop my ass and then give me ice cream. So I didn't argue. I sat my ass in that chair like a good boy and let the tiny five foot nothing nurse wheel me out of the hospital, bumping my toes into shit on purpose as if to make a point.

"Glad it wasn't my leg that got banged up," I teased, and she huffed.

She purposefully let me roll into the door of the elevator. "You aren't 'banged up' Mr. Prescott. You were shot. You had major, near fatal surgery. What you have is an incurable case of the stupids."

She walked me through the sliding front doors of the hospital and right to the curb. "Is someone picking you up?" Her tone says she knows I was waiting for Vincent to leave to check myself out. "Let me hail you a cab."

She whistles and a cab pulls in from a rank just up the road. Daphne relents and opens up the door for me. Finally, I can see the concern win out against her frustration. "Please, try to rest, Mr. Prescott."

I gave her my most charming grin, somewhere between Vincent's smirk and Reese's disarmingly wholesome smile. "I promise."

She just shook her head and slammed the door shut. "Where too?" the cabbie says gruffly. I gave him the address of a place I swore I'd never return to. A place where weakness was an easy way to end up in the gutter.

But I'd climb into the gutter for Celeste, and wallow around in the filth until I got her back.

21

CELESTE

Four days. I'd been here four days and I could barely lift my head. I was going to die down here, and I knew it. Die in a cage, and if life was fair, maybe my cub would die with me. Even thinking that made me snarl, but what was the other option? Dead, I couldn't protect him. If I was dead, he'd be cut from my womb and sold to the highest bidder, if he survived at all.

A tear leaked down my cheek but it was the only one I'd shed. I was going to be strong, and if that meant dragging myself to the food plate they thrust into my cell once a day, that's what I'd do. I'd continue to fight until I couldn't any longer.

I switched back to eat the bread, because even half starved, my snow leopard turned up her nose at anything that wasn't meat. My baby moved happily in my stomach, oblivious to my outer turmoil. If I was this weak after four days, would I even be strong enough to deliver? I knew the answer to the question.

I waited for my captors to return, because seeing them was better than this nothingness. At least I could gather clues to where I was, what the hell was wrong with me, if I could talk to them. I could make them slip up, though to what avail was beyond me right now. But knowledge was power, and it was a power I would need while my body was failing me.

The bounty hunter crew was a three man job. There was the leader. He was the first guy who stood outside my door, taunting me when they'd first captured me. The second guy would just come and pace in front of my cell, leering at me like he was waiting to catch me as a human again and do something horrific. The third guy was younger than the other two, but not by much. He was the one who brought me food. Who'd accidentally overdosed me on whatever the hell they'd given me. He looked at me with something like guilt. Like he felt bad for giving me a death sentence. Why would that make him feel guilty, but selling me off to the skin trade didn't? The morals of humans in pursuit of cold hard cash knew no ethics, I guess.

But he fed me regularly, and for that I was grateful. I snorted and threw my bread across the cage. Grateful to my captor.

I was fucking going crazy already. I needed Reese to work his magic, or the cops, or something. Maybe Eden would find me. I clung to all these ideas, even though logic would tell me that it was an impossibility. I had no clan, no support network in the supernatural world. My mother had made sure of that as a kid, and I'd never met another snow leopard shifter. I'd met a couple of wolves and some other big cats, but we were generally solitary by nature. No one would know how to find the bounty hunters in time. Reese would figure it out, sure. He was super damn smart and I think he loved me. He would tear the world apart to find me. I knew it deep down. Because he was my mate.

My snow leopard purred at the thought. That was why I'd gone home with him that first night. That was why I'd gone back to him when I'd gotten pregnant. That was why I'd been trying to keep him at a distance this whole time. Because I knew that if I let the thought creep in, no matter how impossible it seemed, that there would be no going back. I couldn't leave both my mate and my cub. I wasn't that strong.

It didn't matter now. I could think about it as much as I wanted because they'd found me anyway. Reese was my mate. He was adopted, so I guess there was a chance he was some kind of shifter. Didn't matter if he wasn't a snow leopard, or couldn't shift. Blood spoke to blood. Soul spoke to soul.

Heart spoke to heart. He was my mate. We'd made

a baby because we were meant to be together. And I was never going to see him again.

I curled into a ball on the blanket in the corner. I was so fucking cold. I was going to have to shift back to my snow leopard soon just to be warm.

There was an odd popping noise outside the door of my room. Fireworks? Gunshots? Just three single pop, pop, pops.

I screwed up my nose as the smell of gunsmoke hinted at the edges of my senses. Target practice? There was no yelling, no screaming.

I settled back down, but when the door slammed open and the hugest man I've ever seen walked in, I screamed.

I shifted back to snow leopard before he'd made it to the door of my cage, baring my teeth. The huge guy grabbed hold of the bars of my cell and wrenched it right off.

Fuck. This was it. This is where I died.

He strode into the cell, and I tried to dart around his legs. I was a big cat, but compared to this guy? I may as well be an alley tabby. He was quick too, obviously a shifter. He grabbed me with gentle hands.

"Woah there, little mama. My name is Talbot. Someone called Buttercup sent me to bring you home."

Reese. Reese had found me. In my shocked relief, I shifted back to human and fell to my knees. I sobbed as Talbot whipped off his shirt and dropped it over my head. I just cried and cried tears of happiness. I couldn't have stood, even if I'd tried.

Two more huge guys walked into the room, and the biggest one was an Alpha. I could feel it in my bones. I tilted my head to the side. "Clear," he said and lifted his ski mask. He grinned at me, and he was the perfect all-american guy. That was, if you couldn't feel the waves of power he shed like a fur coat. Tall, blonde, with a white smile that was almost blinding, he was beautiful. But he wasn't mine. My snow leopard whined for her mates.

Fuck. I shut the thought down. Not mates. Lovers, yes. But they were humans and that meant heartbreak.

A little part of me thought perhaps it meant happiness too.

"Well aren't you just the tiniest little thing," the Alpha cooed happily. "I'm Vance, Alpha Bear of the Cold River Sleuth. You have a worried mate at home, so how about we blow this popsicle stand." He leaned down and scooped me up into his arms, holding me like I was a doll. He inhaled deeply and frowned. "Search the place. They've given her something and I don't like the smell of it."

Talbot took off, giving me another reassuring smile. The last guy stepped forward, peeling back his ski mask too. I realized he was Talbot's twin. "Ma'am, I'm

Franklin. Rescuer of beautiful damsels, destroyer of bounty hunter pieces of fuc-"

Vance slapped him on the back of the head. "Go help Talbot. I'm pretty sure we'd all like to burn this place to the ground, and my zippo finger is feeling itchy."

He carried me out of the room, through the maze-like corridors of what I assumed was some kind of warehouse. I could smell the reek of fear, the old stench of other shifters in mortal terror.

We ran back into Talbot and Franklin in the outer hallway, and Talbot's face was solemn. He held up a vial to Vance, and his deep, rumbling growl had me tensing in his arms.

He shot me a quick smile that didn't reach his eyes, and squeezed me tight. "Sorry, Sweetheart. Bear problems. We are grumbly."

Franklin held out his arms and made a gimme gimme action with his hands. "I'm nicer than you are."

Vance didn't protest, just eased me gently into Franklin's waiting arms. Franklin squeezed me tight, a rumbling vibration in his chest soothing me. It was a bit like a purr, and it calmed me down. But he did hug me tighter. Maybe that was a bear problem too. But it was a problem that I was more than okay with.

Vance pocketed the vial and nodded toward the door. "Lets burn this bastard down."

Ten minutes later, I was ensconced in the back seat

of a white SUV, watching a warehouse downtown go up like it was bonfire night.

The bears climbed in, squishing me in the back between the twins which, let's face it, was probably every girl with a preference for dick's dream, but all I wanted to do was be at home with my guys. I wanted to hold Lincoln in my arms, and make sure he was okay.

Because if he wasn't, if he was...

I'm not sure I'd ever recover.

I shook my head as I found a pale, gasping Lincoln sitting on a stoop in his old neighborhood. It was a shithole of a place, one where I would never have left my car unattended. It was inner city, and hadn't been gentrified yet. There were streetwalkers, boarded up windows and the word fuck was liberally tagged on every available blank wall.

It was hard to imagine Lincoln had come from these streets now, but then, this place had molded him into the man I loved. So I guess I could only be thankful for the piss-covered sidewalks.

I double-parked and walked over to him. "You checked yourself out of the hospital," I chastised a little redundantly. "A nurse named Daphne looked like she wanted to wear your balls as earrings as she told me that."

Lincoln gave a pained laugh, and attempted to stand. He weaved badly, and I lurched toward him. I got my shoulder under his arm and led him toward my car. He huffed as he got into the passenger seat and I leaned across him to belt him in. Yeah, that wouldn't sit well with the control freak, but fuck him. He should still be in the hospital and I was holding back the urge to yell at him as it was.

He must have sensed my frustrated anger, because he didn't protest despite all the huffing. And I was doing it in his old neighborhood. How you were perceived was everything here. Lincoln no longer belonged here, but it was hard to change the mindset. You could take the guy out of the hood, but it had done some damage first.

I slid into the driver's seat and roared out of this shithole. I waited until we were back on the expressway in traffic before I spoke. "What the fuck were you doing there, Linc? I get you hated the hospital, but the old neighborhood wasn't exactly a tourist stop on the way home." I patted myself on the back for how calm I sounded.

"Had to see a guy." That was it. That was all he was giving me. I was tempted to throw him out of the car and onto his dumb ass head in the middle of the freeway. "How'd you know where I was?"

I was tempted to make a smartass joke, but for once, I wasn't feeling like a joker. Nearly losing him.

Actually losing Celeste. I was dying on the inside and I had nothing left to save myself.

I shrugged. "Reese."

I didn't elaborate. Let him think that Reese had inserted a tracking chip beneath his skin, and not that he'd bugged his phone.

We sat in silence for a while longer, but it was Lincoln who eventually broke. "I was tracking down my brother."

I nearly slammed on the brakes in rush hour traffic. "What the fuck, Lincoln? Why would you do that?"

He didn't turn to look at me, just shrugged. "I heard he started dealing in shit on the black market. Thought he'd be able to get us an invite. We could buy Celeste back."

I shook my head. Both he and Reese had the same idea. Buying women made me want to vomit, like they were a commodity or something. But we were playing in a different world and if I had to give up my entire fortune to get her back, I would.

The idea shocked me. Celeste had gotten well and truly under my skin, and now I couldn't imagine a world without her.

"I don't think it will be that easy."

My phone rang, and Reese's name ran across the stereo screen. I tapped the answer button, not taking my eyes off the traffic. "Hey. I found him. He looks half dead but I'm bringing him home."

I heard Reese's relieved sigh. "They found her."

This time I did slam on the brakes, and the horn of the guy who nearly rear-ended me drowned out the rest of what Reese was saying.

"What?" Lincoln yelled. "What did you say?"

"They found her. They're bringing her back here now."

My heart stuttered in my chest. "Is she okay?"

"I don't know, Vince. She's alive, and that's all I know. Just get back here."

I COULDN'T STOP Lincoln sprinting to the elevator from the underground parking garage. I swiped my key and the elevator hurtled to the top floor. It seemed like it went on for ages, and I bounced on the balls of my feet. Lincoln was gasping for air and looking so pale I was worried he might pass out, but I didn't tell him to slow down. He needed this as much as I did. Maybe more.

The doors slid open, and three huge guys stood in the foyer. Lincoln's hand went for a gun that wasn't there, and the biggest one, fuck he must have been 6'7, gave us both an appraising look. Finally, he grinned, and fuck me he was hot as hell. The other two massive guys turned and I realized they were twins. Normally, I would be all over that idea, but my heart was in this room somewhere and I was desperate to hold her in my arms.

They all parted and I saw Reese on the couch, his arms curled around a heartbreakingly familiar body.

"Celeste," Lincoln whispered, and she turned, looking over her shoulder. She gave a weak smile, and blood rushed in my ears. Something was wrong. She had huge, dark circles under her eyes. She looked like she was fading away right in front of me.

The big guy, and he had some serious skull crushing energy, gave us both a soft smile. "You're going to have to go to her. She's weak."

Celeste snarled, and the guy laughed. "In body, Little One. Not in spirit."

Lincoln's knees started to shake, and I could tell he was close to collapsing himself. I sent an imploring look to Reese. He stood with Celeste still in his arms. He looked at the big guys. "Make yourselves at home. There's beer and food in the fridge. I'll be back in a second," he said, even though he hadn't really moved his face from Celeste's neck the whole time we'd been here. It was like he was trying to breathe her into his lungs.

I nudged Lincoln gently. I wanted to reach out and help him to the bedroom, but he'd hate being seen as weak in front of strangers, especially these guys.

He straightened his shoulders and walked to the bedroom on shaky legs. The big guy, who was definitely their leader, nodded to him on the way past.

"Alpha," he murmured, though there was a small, indulgent smile on his face.

Fuck. These guys were shifters. I knew it deep in my soul, right down there with the part that warned you to run the hell away when you got too close to a predator. "Elephants?"

One of the twins threw back his head and laughed. "Only from the waist down," he said and winked.

"Bears," the Alpha one replied, and I nodded like that wasn't the most fucking far out thing I'd ever heard.

Lincoln turned even paler, if that was possible, and I hurried him down the hallway into my bed. Reese laid Star down on the pillows and Lincoln climbed in beside her. He dragged her into his arms, and his eyes were huge and shiny.

"I thought I'd lost you."

She nuzzled against his throat, dropping tiny kisses. "Same."

They twined themselves around each other, and I walked over, resting my forehead against her cheek. "Thank god you're back. Someone needs to talk some sense into this lunatic," I joked, even though something eased in me at the scent of her skin.

She turned her head and caught my lips. "Love you, Vincent."

I kissed her back softly. "Love you too, Star. If you think you are ever leaving again..." I let the threat trail off, mostly because both she and Lincoln had passed out from exhaustion.

Reese and I stood there for a little longer, watching these two opposing forces become one. I looked up at him on the other side of the bed. "Where did they find her?"

"Warehouse. They said it smelled like fear and death, but they didn't find any other shifters there. They have removed the hunters who caught her as a threat and burned the place to the ground."

The Bears had killed them. I should feel worse at the idea of murder, but all I felt was a grim satisfaction. "Lincoln was downtown, looking for his brother. Had the same idea as you. Finding the underground auction and buying her back."

Reese's face folded into a frown. Lincoln's brother wasn't a good person. In fact, he was the worst kind of person. A bully, a manipulator, and a criminal. He would drag Lincoln back into the world, and he would have done it too, for Celeste.

"Did he find him?"

I shrugged. We hadn't gotten that far before Reese had called. But I hoped not. I hoped we could leave that nightmare in the past where it belonged.

We left Lincoln and Celeste asleep and crept back out into the living room. Vincent came up beside me and whispered in my ear, "They're bears."

I stopped in front of the biggest one. The twins were sitting on the couch, and one was wiggling around, trying to get comfortable. "Honestly? I've sat on rocks more comfortable than this," he growled and Vincent laughed.

I held my hand out for the big one to shake. He was easily half a foot taller than me, and built like a linebacker but somehow more athletic in appearance. "Reese Townsend. Thank you. I owe you a massive debt that I can never repay."

The guy didn't hesitate to grab my hand, and I swear to god he held it like I was made of china.

"Vance, Alpha of the Cold River Sleuth." He pointed to the twins on the couch. "These are my Betas, Franklin and Talbot."

Bears. Talbot. "Baloo? Like the bear from the Jungle Book?" I asked the one named Talbot. "Talbaloo. Makes sense." I couldn't help my smile.

"Reese, like the peanut butter cups," he said with an answering grin.

The other twin, Franklin, took a deep gulp of beer. "Nerd humor. They are a match made in heaven."

I grinned at him too. "Thank you as well. I appreciate the risks you took."

Franklin snorted and shook his head. "No risk at all. It was almost pathetically easy." His face transformed into a scary mask that had more than a little teeth. "Bounty hunters are the worst kind of scum. A couple less in the world will make hundreds of women and children safer. Consider it a national service."

Vance grunted in agreement. "We should go soon, it's a long trip back to Black Mountain. But first, we need to talk about your mate." He pulled a vial out of his pocket, and handed it to me. I didn't recognize the brand, but I wasn't a pharmacist.

"This is a tranquilizing agent for shifters. In small doses, it makes us docile. It isn't like your human drugs. It's a cocktail of silver and magic, with a good dose of horse tranqs."

I tipped it toward the light, and it moved in a gelatinous roll, almost like mercury. It shimmered under the downlight, looking beautiful but deadly.

I looked back at Vance. "I think they overdosed her with the tranq. It would explain why she's so weak." His jaw tensed, and that should have been a sign that the next thing he said was going to be devastating. "Her body can't process that much tranquilizer, and given her pregnancy, her body will be working twice as hard to protect the cub. If I'm correct, without intervention, she will die. Just fade away before your eyes. Maybe the cub too," he said gently.

I felt like he'd just punched me in the face. I reeled backwards, squeezing the vial in my hand until Vance reached over and plucked it from my fingers.

"How do I fix this? There has to be a way. An antidote or something?"

Vance looked pained. "There's no antidote, as such. You're going to need a witch."

"A witch?" I repeated back dumbly.

Vance nodded. "A witch."

I slumped down onto the couch. Why wouldn't there be witches? My brain kept short-circuiting. Apparently, I'd hit the line. Skipped right across a bridge too far.

I whipped my head around to look at Vincent, who looked comically shocked. I had no doubt my face looked like that too.

"Do you, uh, know a witch?"

Vance smiled and clapped me on the shoulder. "No, thank fuck. But I know who would."

THIRTY MINUTES later I was sitting across from Vance at a booth in a cafe down the street from my apartment. Vance was so huge that he took up one side of the booth, and when he'd ordered half the menu, I thought the waitress was going to smash him over his head with the coffee pot. Then he'd smiled and her face had done a rapid montage of anger, surprise, then lust. It was fascinating to watch.

She sauntered off without even getting my order, but I didn't blame her. There was something supremely charismatic about the Bear Alpha. "Who are we meeting?" I asked, glad that the waitress had topped off my coffee before she'd been blinded by Vance.

"Has your girl ever talked about Eden? It's a group that operates out of the city. Anyway, they are kind of like a halfway house for supernaturals. Well, preternaturals."

"What's the difference?"

"They help humans with extraordinary abilities, not just different races like shifters and witches."

"So, are they shifters too?"

Someone laughed from beside me, and I looked up, up, up into the face of someone who just seemed golden. I couldn't even explain why, but I knew in my bones he wasn't human. Even less human than Vance or Celeste. Maybe he was a witch?

He smiled down at me. "Unlikely. The back hair must be insane."

Vance grinned and stood, slapping the man on the back heartily. It would have sent an average man into the wall, but the big, golden guy hardly moved. "Locke! It's good to see you."

Every woman in the room was staring now. Like a fork halfway to their mouth staring. It was enough to make a guy feel inadequate, if I didn't completely adore the woman at home in my bed. I didn't need anyone else's adoration.

I stood and held out my hand. "Hi, I'm Reese. Thanks for meeting with us."

Locke gripped my hand and shook hard. "It's nice to meet you too. I know who you are of course. My organization uses some of your tech." He grabbed a chair from an empty table and pulled it across. Thank god. I didn't think he'd fit in the booth with me.

I sat down too, and the waitress bustled over, her arms filled with food. She stared down with starry eyes at Locke too. "Oh, can I get you something too? Pancakes? Breakfast?" She didn't exactly offer herself, but it was subliminally there.

Locke gave her a megawatt smile. "No, thank you.

I've just eaten." Somehow he made it sound pornographic and the waitress's face went bright pink.

The bell from the kitchen rang, and she raced back behind the counter. I cleared my throat and they both looked at me. The weight of their presence was like a lodestone on my chest. How anyone thought they were human was beyond me.

But less than six months ago, I would have written them off as charismatic. The human mind can only accept so much.

"Thank you for coming," I said again.

Locke shrugged. "I owe Vance one, so this was an easy way to use up a debt. How can I help you?"

I lowered my voice and told him a story. From the very beginning, every sordid, exceptional, terrifying moment that led me to this point. Should I have worried about telling this to a complete stranger? Maybe. But I trusted my gut. My gut said these guys were good people.

Locke, for his part, didn't interrupt, but his face grew stormy when he heard about the bounty hunters, sad when I told him Celeste planned to give up the baby to go on the run, and then downright fucking scary when I got to the part where she was abducted and injected with whatever the fuck she was dosed with.

He breathed deeply through his nose, and his body relaxed. "I'm saddened she didn't come to us. Don't get me wrong, I'm glad she came to you, but we could have helped her. Could have helped them both. We are trying to set up a refuge for young preternaturals. Somewhere they can run and be safe and cared for. My partners are up negotiating a location, but eventually, we'd like to make it a school. A place where they can explore their abilities in a protected environment so they don't end up trapped in a life on the run like your Celeste." His eyes were bright with passion.

I thought of fourteen year old Celeste, on the streets, alone. If these people, this Eden, could save even one girl in Celeste's position, it was a worthy cause.

"What's stopping you?"

Locke shrugged. "The things that stop organizations like ours all the time, human or supernatural. Not enough funds to feed everyone, let alone buy up a large portion of the wilderness. Not enough safe locations. We can't advertise so we rely on word of mouth, and not enough people know about us. We do what we can, but that's only so much."

I cocked my head and grinned. "I can help with one of those problems. On one proviso."

Locke waved a hand. "I'll help you find a witch to save your mate and child. I am not leveraging you for that." He seemed a little miffed, even though I hadn't even suggested such a thing.

"Thank you, but that wasn't going to be the proviso." I leaned forward. "Locke. I have money. More money than I will ever spend. If I can use it to go to a good cause, I will do it in a heartbeat." Locke narrows his eyes at me. "What I don't have is a safe place to raise my child. A place where Celeste can finally relax and be free. I'll buy the land, build your school, whatever else you need, it's yours. But I want to have a home on the grounds, within the protection of Eden, for my child and my family."

"Your pack," Vance added helpfully through a mouth full of fries.

I chewed on my lip, turning the word over in my head. "Yes. My pack."

Locke stroked his chin, his eyes boring into mine like he could see my soul or something. Finally, he nodded. "Okay. I have to pass it by the others, but we aren't exactly rolling in billionaire philanthropists, so we should be good. How do you feel about Canada?"

I raised both eyebrows. "I really like maple syrup and poutine?"

Vance snorted, and Locke laughed. "Great."

24

She seemed insubstantial in my arms. She'd only been gone for four days, but in that time she'd turned into a ghost. I pulled her sleeping form closer to my body, wrapping my whole body over hers. I couldn't have her close enough. I would protect her with my life.

While she seemed like she was fading away right before my eyes, the baby kicked happily against my palm, blissfully safe from the trauma of the last week, protected by Celeste to the very end.

I could hear the faint sound of the television playing in the living room, and I knew two of the bear shifters were still out there, drinking beer and laughing to each other. They seemed like good natured guys, but still, like their animal counterparts, they had an underlying menace that was belied by their congenial exteriors. I could vaguely hear Vincent out there, making conversation, and I wanted to call him in here. To be pressed between them both, just for a little while.

I kissed Celeste's nape, inhaling her scent into my lungs. She wiggled back against me, and I groaned even as I smiled.

"Lincoln?" her voice was the faint whisper of someone who was still mostly asleep.

I kissed her again, nuzzling my face into her hair. "I'm here."

She let out a soft sigh and relaxed back against me. "Can you bite me?"

I pulled away. "Excuse me?"

She didn't roll to face me, but she caught my hand and pulled it up so it rested on her chest over her heart. "Bite me. My leopard is restless. We both almost lost you."

I was trying to connect the dots, but it didn't really matter. I would do whatever she needed right now. If it was in my power to give it to her, I'd hand her my heart carved straight from my chest.

I twined my fingers in hers, so both of our palms were resting over her heart. "Is this a shifter thing? Does it mean something?"

She nodded. "If you were a shifter, your bite would link us together forever. We would be mates." She turned over so I could see her beautiful blue-grey eyes.

They were sunken in her head, but they still shone brightly.

"Is that what you want? To be stuck with me forever?" I asked quietly, unsure which answer I am more nervous for, yes or no.

"Yes." There was no hesitation in her voice, only complete conviction. "Yes, Lincoln, I want to be stuck with you, and Reese and Vincent, if they'll have me."

"What happened to running?"

She leaned forward and kissed me softly. It was hard to imagine a more pure kiss, and I sat still, savoring the warmth of her lips against mine. "I don't want to run. I don't want to be sad. I want to grab hold of the love that's offered to me with both hands, because someone could steal it from me in a moment."

I held her closer, kissing her back. "No one is stealing you from me again. Ever. I swear it, Celeste."

She closed her eyes and gave a shuddering sigh. "I believe you. Bite me, Lincoln. Make me yours."

I was helpless to resist. We were both weak and broken, but not beaten. I kissed my way down her jaw and ran my hand over her body. Reese had removed the oversized t-shirt she was wearing when she was rescued and put her in one of his own. I couldn't blame him, we all wanted to have her branded as ours, wrapped in our scent. Maybe we weren't as far from our primal urges as we'd like to think.

I pulled her leg over my hip, continuing to kiss her throat, pushing Reese's tee up so I could pull it over her head. When she was pressed into my body, chest to chest, skin to skin, I shuddered. So perfect. I ground my cock against the apex of her thighs and she gasped a little.

I took her nipple in my mouth, sucking it and humming happily. She gripped my hair and curled into my body. I release her nipple with a pop. "Easy, baby. We are taking this real easy."

As much as I wanted to ravish her, neither of us was up to the feat. My mind was willing, god knows my dick was harder than a rock, but the rest of me was still fucked up. My hand dipped between our bodies and I rubbed her clit in lazy circles, watching her face as she closed her eyes to the sensation. Her free hand grabbed my shoulder and her nails dug into my flesh, anchoring herself to me. I loved it. Loved the pain, loved the pleasure.

"Lincoln, please," she whispered, and I didn't know what she was asking for at that moment but I was happy to give her everything I had left.

"Roll over," I whispered, and she turned so her sexy ass was pressed against my cock.

I shoved down my boxers, freeing my cock, and my dick knew its job because it honed in on the wet heat of her pussy immediately. I pulled her leg up over my hips so I was notched against her entrance, and I moved my lips to the meaty curve of her shoulder, pressing a light kiss there.

She rocked her hips against me, and panted a little. "Do it, Lincoln. Make me yours."

I was helpless to resist her siren's call. I slid my cock into her warm heat, huffing out a sharp breath as her body gripped mine. I thrust shallowly, and she mewled in my arms. This was home.

I pressed teeth into the flesh of her shoulder, and she purred. Actually purred. "Harder. Please," she whimpered as I hit that magic spot over and over.

"You're mine, Celeste. I love you," I whispered against her skin, and then bit hard, the slight pressure of breaking the skin horrifying me but that deep down part of me, that primal animal, howled in satisfaction. She moaned and curved back against me, and I thrust into her harder and faster. The metallic taste of her blood on my tongue was sending me wild. I reached around, pressing on her clit, and she came all over my cock, her body milking mine. I released her shoulder, licking it clean even though I didn't know why. It just seemed so natural. I gritted my teeth as her body fluttered around mine. But I wasn't ready to fill her yet. I needed something else too.

"I want you to bite me too," I growled and she stiffened, but the slight rumble in her chest increased.

I pulled out of her body, even though it was basically torture, and she rolled to face me. "Are you sure?"

I understood her hesitation, really. I was a fucking dick. Was it because I was fighting this feeling? I don't know but I didn't want to fight it anymore. I didn't want to fight her. I tried to show her that with my eyes, because I was shit with words.

"I've never been more sure of anything. When I thought I'd lost you..." I couldn't even finish the thought.

Celeste gave me the sweetest kiss that made my heart pound in my chest, and then she climbed delicately onto my body. I lifted her hips so I could line my cock up with her entrance, her body weight scarily insubstantial, but her eyes were alight with desire.

I slid her down my cock. She leaned forward, but her stomach stopped her from getting to my lips. I pushed up on my elbows, ignoring the pulling of my stitches, the pain in my pecs. I needed this more. This would heal me, I knew it in my soul. She kissed me and then dropped her mouth to my pec, and bit hard. I roared as my cock twitched in her body, and I gripped her hips, pounding into her. I forgot the weakness of my body and hers. Forgot everything but the feel of her around my cock and her teeth in my flesh. She came again, her teeth still embedded in my flesh, and this time I came with her. I filled her, marked her as mine and it was beautiful and primal and perfect.

She collapsed against my chest, and I rolled her to the side, pulling out. I struggled to my feet, my legs weak and my chest was on fire. But I grabbed a towel from the back of Vincent's door and brought it over, carefully cleaning her up as she panted.

She looked at me with those big, luminous eyes and I was weak for an entirely different reason. "I love you, you know? I don't know how it happened, because I hated your guts for weeks. I don't even know when that changed to something else. But when you were shot..." she let out a shuddering breath. "I thought I was going to die too."

I smiled, because how could I not? "I know the feeling." I climbed back in beside her, pulling her back into my arms. She'd put Reese's shirt back on, and I didn't protest because there were still two strange shifters in the apartment. One day soon, I was going to strip her naked and make love to her for an entire week.

I kissed the back of her head and smiled. "Love you too, Celeste. You wormed your way under my skin and into my heart. Maybe you're a heartworm shifter."

She groaned. "This is why Vincent is the funny one and Reese is the romantic one. That was terrible," she chuckled, but her voice was slurred by the edge of sleep. I tightened my arms and we both went back to sleep.

25

CELESTE

The bears had left two days after my rescue. They'd looked at me with such softness in their expression, I'd wondered if they were considering abducting me themselves and taking me back to their den. Vance all but insinuated that he would have taken us all in, if the guys had been shifters and not humans. But there were still shifters in his sleuth who remembered the persecution by humans, and that made them afraid.

A true alpha did what was best for their pack, no matter how hard. Even I knew that. I was glad he hadn't mentioned it to the guys though, because I didn't doubt that they would ship me off in a heartbeat. They would do anything for me, as long as I was safe.

It was a weird sensation, being loved like this. I

don't think anyone had loved me the way these three guys did.

Reese fussed, making sure I had every comfort I needed. It was Reese who carried me to the couch every day, or to my fluffy rug near the window to get some sunshine. Vincent hovered. Either he was hovering beside me, or beside Lincoln, like he was worried that we'd disappear if he wasn't watching us.

Even now, I was spread across his lap as he stroked his fingers through my hair. Lincoln was lying on the chaise lounge, and Vincent had one hand out, entwining his fingers with my mate.

A small smile curled my lips. We hadn't mentioned what had gone down in the bedroom to the other guys. I didn't want to rush them, but almost losing Lincoln had created an almost insane need to have his mark on me.

I knew it would happen with Vincent and Reese. My snow leopard already decided that Reese was our mate when we'd first met him. She just wasn't being a pushy bitch about it like she was with Lincoln.

Reese walked into the room, his eyes coming straight to mine like they were magnetized. I tried to hide how weak I really was from the guys, but I doubted it was working much anymore. With every beat of my heart, I was one second closer to death. The poison working its way through my body was sapping me.

He came over and kissed me gently. "How are you feeling?"

Kissing Reese was a silver lining to being abducted. I decided I didn't need to keep myself distant from him anymore. I wasn't going to run, because no one was safe while the hunters were still out there. Not me. Not my baby. Not even Reese was safe really after harboring us for so long .

I gave him a tight smile that probably didn't reach my eyes. "I feel better today."

Vincent snorted. "Liar."

I jabbed him in the ribs and he chuckled down at me, his face shining with so much love I thought my chest would explode. Reese squatted down beside the couch so we were face to face. His eyes saw too much, looked too deeply.

"I got a call from the secretary to the Witch Member of the Convocation," Reese said, and I screwed my nose up. Supernatural politics was not something I wanted to wade into. Hell, just Shifter Politics was a nightmare. But Vance, and by extension this guy from Eden, said this was the only way I could get better. I needed a witch, the more powerful the better.

If that meant playing politics for a little while, so be it.

"What did they say?"

"They are sending a witch out in the next couple of days. Apparently, the member of the Convocation-"

"Wilde," I corrected

"Uh, yeah. Wilde. Apparently, he's too busy to come himself, despite the favor he owed Locke."

I smiled and reached out, pulling his face down for another kiss. "That's good."

I was a little worried two days would be too long, but there was nothing we could do about it. Maybe they'd have time to save my baby, and Reese would care for him. Or her. I had a feeling it was a him though. He was tough in there, kicking me in the ribs like a karate champion.

Vincent was tense underneath me, like he could sense my defeat. I swallowed hard and smiled again. I didn't want to die, lord fucking knows I didn't, I didn't spend this long running from certain death to just give up now. But suddenly being strong seemed to take too much energy.

Vincent ran his fingers through my hair once more. "It'll be okay, Star."

I nodded, and then turned my eyes back to the television so they didn't see the shine of my tears.

Reese swore, dragging me off Vincent's lap. He lifted me into his arms easily. "Fuck this shit. Fuck their secretary and a couple of days. I'm getting you the help you need now, because I can't live without you, Celeste, and I'll be damned if I will let you suffer for the next two days because you are inconvenient to some glorified bureaucrat."

"Reese, what the hell are you doing?"

I wrapped my arms and legs around him as he strode toward the door. "If it's inconvenient for this Wilde guy to come to you before you *die,* then I'll take you to him. Pompous asshole." He grabbed his keys and phone and swiped his card on the reader beside the elevator doors.

However, when they opened, a beautiful red headed woman stood there, her face twisted in a barely contained smile.

"I'll tell Wilde that you have such a glowing opinion of him," the woman crooned, the smile she'd been trying to contain finally curling her lips. "Hello. My name is Miranda. I hear you have a problem."

I looked at her with wide eyes. Her power felt like it was too much. It tingled across my skin, but her face was soft. I wiggled, and Reese let me down onto shaky legs. I locked my knees, wanting to stand on my own two feet against what could be a threat. Miranda had obviously spent some time around shifters, because she held my gaze for a moment, showing me that she was just as tough as I was, and then looked away. My Snow Leopard huffed but we recognized her for what she was. Our savior.

Reese wrapped an arm around me, a silent show of support. And possibly to keep me on my feet. "Thank you for coming so quickly. Your, uh, office said you would be a few days."

Miranda shrugged, walking further into the foyer.

She took in Vincent and Lincoln who were now sitting on the edge of the couch. "I was in the office, and heard about your situation. No offense, but you do not have a few more days." Her voice was gentle but firm.

Was she chastising me?

"Can you fix me?" I asked softly, and she reached out, gripping my hand.

Immediately, a warm reassurance flowed through me. "Darling, you will live a long, happy life with your cubs and your mates," she said. "This is not how you die, I promise you that."

I took a few more steps before my knees gave out and I snarled under my breath. I hated being this weak. Reese cursed and picked me up, striding to the couch and placing me down between Vincent and Lincoln. He introduced us all, and the Witch Miranda nodded politely.

Lincoln eyed the beautiful woman, but not with lust. With suspicion. I didn't know if I found that amusing or reassuring. He gripped my thigh, giving it a squeeze. Reese, ever the gentleman, offered Miranda a glass of water, and I got the distinct impression that she was bemused by us.

"Thank you, Mr. Townsend, but I think it would be

best for us all if we could get this done. With every breath, Celeste gets a little closer to death, and while I know I can heal her, the recovery time grows longer with each second."

Vincent climbed to his feet. "What do you need? I can get you anything?" He seemed about three seconds from offering her eye of newt and tongue of toad. She waved him away, and pulled a pouch out of her pocket. She wasn't dressed in typical witch fashion. She was in a blue tea dress that fell just below her knees, and had little lightning bolts printed across it. But it did have pockets, and that was pretty damn magical in my opinion.

"Unnecessary, I have everything I need. But thank you." Her eyes fell on Lincoln. "You're injured too? Do you wish to be healed? It's a little different to performing it on a shifter, but honestly, I could probably do it in my sleep."

Lincoln's body went stiff. "I'm healing fine." He cleared his throat. "Thank you."

Miranda rolled her eyes and mouthed, "Men," at me, and I smiled. She wasn't what I was expecting. Actually, I wasn't sure what I was expecting; some mix of old crone and Sabrina the Teenage Witch, maybe?

My heart thudded sluggishly and her brows drew together. She pulled out a small bowl from her pocket as well. Were her pockets bottomless? If they were, how did I get a dress with bottomless pockets?

I must have been starting to hallucinate a little, because when she laughed, I realized I'd said that out loud.

"Unfortunately, Child, you do not possess the magic necessary, but I'll leave you the card of my dress-maker. Every woman needs a dress with pockets. Please, lie down?" I did as she asked, Vincent shifting from the couch to stand beside Reese, but Lincoln didn't move as he watched her like she was about to pull out a gun and shoot me. .

I noticed Miranda's eyes dropping to the edges of my bite on Lincoln's neck, and a low rumble began in my chest. My mate.

She chuckled softly. "You chose well. Protective mates will be a boon for you in the future. Though I have to say, an all human harem seems like an odd choice."

I shrugged, watching her hands as she mixed powders in the bowl. "Making the logical choice isn't really in my repertoire," I muttered back and she huffed a laugh.

"Girl, I hear you." She added another vial of liquid to the bowl and pulled out a knife.

Lincoln reached out and grabbed her wrist with almost inhuman speed. I didn't even realize I'd gasped until the sound echoed around the room.

The temperature dropped, and Miranda's eyes cooled with it. "I promise you, Lincoln Prescott, that I intend your mate no harm. But if you do not let go of my wrist in the next four seconds, I will burn your hand off from your arm."

I swallowed hard. "Linc. Stop," I whispered, and he looked at me agonizingly. But he dropped his hand, not taking his eyes off that knife.

Miranda mumbled under her breath, but I don't think it was a spell, unless they'd swapped out latin for insults about the male gender. Finally, she dipped her finger in the bowl goo, writing a rune on my forehead, one over my heart and one on the soles of my feet.

Then she picked up the knife again, giving Lincoln the stink eye, before gripping my hand.

"Are you ready? I should warn you that it will be uncomfortable, but when I'm done, your body can finally start to heal."

"Will it hurt the baby?"

She shook her head. "No, your magic is already keeping the chemical from your womb. There is no magic there to burn away." She stroked my cheek. "I'm sorry."

She lifted her knife and then there was nothing but the whiteness of pain.

Star's scream of pain had me lurching toward her, only Reese's hand gripping my bicep stopped me. She was bowed on the couch, and the Witch stared at her in consternation.

"I am glad I made the decision to come here today. Your girl was lying to you. She wouldn't have lasted another two days. She wouldn't have lasted another ten hours." She shook her head. "So strong."

I wanted to see a healing glow or some other kind of mystical shit, but all I saw was the love of my misbegotten life, writhing in pain. Miranda was mouthing something, her eyes closed in concentration, her tongue poking out between her teeth in a completely bizarre expression on someone who was meant to be so powerful.

Finally she raised her hand up, and with the ceremonial dagger still clenched in the other, she sliced through the air like she was severing an invisible string. Celeste's body slumped back down, but she was no longer conscious. I was glad of it.

She wiped some of the paste from the magical bowl that was somehow in her pocket, onto Star's lips.

The woman's eyes met mine. "You may want to grab a bucket. This bit tends to be messy."

Not questioning her words, I grabbed a big mixing bowl from the kitchen cabinets, and sprinted back to the couch just in time for Star to roll onto her side and vomit. But it wasn't normal vomit, because trust me, I'd laid in pools of my own before. No, Star's vomit shone silver in the downlights and moved with an odd viscous intent that made me want to throw up right along with her.

Miranda patted Celeste's back, making soft, soothing noises like a mother might do to a sick child. I looked up at the woman, who looked about twenty-five in body, but one peek at her eyes let you know that she was far, far older than that. She had the kind of depth to her eyes that you rarely saw outside of veterans and hundred year old ladies. They'd seen things. Done things.

I had no doubt that I would never, ever want to delve into the depths of this woman's mind.

Star continued to vomit, and I sat up beside her, dragging her into my lap so I could comfort her with my body even as she was miserably expelling every-thing she'd eaten since she was five. Well, at least it seemed that way. Her body was rocked with wave after wave of shudders, and she whimpered quietly.

"Shh, I got you baby. Get all that badness out," I whispered in her ear as I held her long hair back.

Miranda stood and walked over to where Reese stood, watching us all with worried eyes. "She'll be okay now. The magic has been severed and she'll expel the toxins for a few more hours but then her body will be ready to heal." She shook her head. "I must tell you, Mr. Townsend, but I don't believe this apartment is safe for you anymore. It was disturbingly easy for me to get to your floor, and with two of your number down, you are nothing more than prey. Celeste will be incapacitated for a few more weeks as her body tries to heal the internal damage caused by the magic imbued silver. I suggest you get out of the city. Even out of the country if you can. Find somewhere safe until she has the cub."

Reese raked his fingers through his hair. The blond curls were already haphazard from the amount of times he'd done it today alone. "I don't know where that is. I know where would be safe for a human, but supernatural bounty hunters? Politics for species I have no idea about? I'm so far out of my depth that I'm drowning," he whispered, even though Star could obviously hear with her head hung over the bowl.

Miranda just quirked an eyebrow at Reese. "Didn't you just come to some kind of an agreement with Eden? To bankroll an academy in Canada?"

Reese reared back in surprise. "How do you know that?"

Miranda just smiled enigmatically. "I happen to know a place you can stay nearby. A pack that owes me a favor, and there's another snow leopard there. Their Alpha is a good man, you'll be safe."

We all looked at Celeste. Reese didn't even try to drag his eyes away as he said, "We'd appreciate that. Thank you."

It took three days to wrap up our lives, and Celeste threw up for two of them. But by the third, she looked a little better. Weak, but with a light flush to her cheeks that loosened something in my chest. I finally believed the Witch Miranda. My Star would be okay.

It took three days for Reese to appoint a management team that could operate without him at the helm. It took three days for Lincoln to see the best surgeons that money could buy, who all looked at him like he was stupid for being out of hospital already, but gave him as much follow up information as they could.

I sat in the Label's office, the exec looking at me like I was scum. Fuck him though. I wasn't his bitch, or his fucking lapdog. If I said I wanted a break, I was having a damn break. If I wanted to quit, I could do it without a damn care in the world. And he hated me because he knew it. I didn't need to be a famous singer. I didn't need to bring them millions of dollars in record sales every year. I did this job because I loved it, and as much as they hated it, they needed me.

"I need you to stay for three months, cut another record and we'll look at postponing the tour until the end of the year."

I rolled my eyes so hard that I saw my synapses rolling their eyes. "You aren't listening to me. At least twelve months off, or I walk."

The Exec snorted. I didn't even remember his name, he was the fifth one the label had had since I was signed. They tended to get caught up in parties, filled with meaningless sex and way too much cocaine.

God knows, I had. But not anymore. Not really since I'd started hooking up with Lincoln. I hadn't been to a single party since Star had landed in our life like a H-Bomb.

"Listen, you take twelve months off? Then another three months to cut a half decent record. Another six months to organize a tour and you won't be back in people's face's for 2 years at a minimum. In 2 years, you're obsolete Brazz. Nothing but a hit of yesteryear. And I'm not going to lift a finger to help you resurrect yourself from the depth of nothingness."

I stood. I was done with this dick measuring bullshit. "So be it. But I'll ask your successor if he feels the same way."

The exec stood, and I yawned. "Is that a threat?"

I couldn't help but roll my eyes once more. "Just history repeating itself."

I stuffed my hands into my too tight jeans and strolled out of the office like I owned it. Which, I possibly could if I wanted it. I was rich enough to buy the label if I wanted it. But I didn't. I wanted to sing. I wanted to make love to Star and Lincoln. I wanted to help her raise the baby.

If Rolling Stone could see me now, their Playboy Prince, they would laugh hysterically.

Nah, fuck that. I was proud. I had a purpose now. I wasn't just fucking my way through the world, high enough to dull the loneliness. I walked past the receptionist and winked. Once upon a time, her heated look would have had me tempting her into the bathrooms on this floor and fucking her against the door before promptly forgetting her.

But not anymore. There was only one woman I wanted to stick my cock in, and I'd do it with so much passion that it could only be love.

I stepped into the elevator, ignoring the fresh faced musicians who were staring at me with wide eyes. Maybe Star had made me a better person, because instead of staring at my phone and pretending to be immersed in whatever the fuck people got so caught up in their phones about these days, I gave them a warm smile.

"Don't let him fuck you, or you'll spend your career on your knees sucking his cock. Confidence is key. You want them to believe that there is no label without you. You're artists. Control your music and your fans will be for life, not just for the summer."

With that, I strode from the elevator like I was fucking Mother Theresa. I met the town car at the curb and I headed home. Well, home for now. Who was I kidding? Not to be gross, but wherever they were, that was home. If it was in the middle of fucking nowhere Canada where she was safe to be her snow leopard, then I would be there with her.

27

LINCOLN

I looked around the apartment. It wasn't packed up by any means. The cleaner would still come once a week, the place would still be ours, but the little signs of life were all stuffed in boxes and suitcases. Vincent's guitars lined the wall of the entry foyer. All the baby stuff was now packed in the SUV downstairs or in a shipping container ready to be hauled to Calgary, to a storage place there. We'd collect everything a little bit at a time. No need to make our trail too easy to follow.

Celeste was gritting her teeth as she shuffled to the kitchen, and when I stood, her glare told me to not even think about offering to help. To say she was not a good patient would be a gross understatement. She hated being so weak; it chafed against her very nature.

I raised my hands in surrender, but I still watched her like a hawk, waiting for her to stumble.

The elevator doors slid open, and Vincent walked in, a happy smirk on his face. He walked over to Celeste and wrapped her in his arms, nuzzling her neck as he spun her around. I didn't miss the fact that he spun her almost all the way to the kitchen though.

Damn. I loved that guy.

Celeste was murmuring something at him as she laughed and pushed at his shoulders. Reese was drawn from his office by the sound. Her laughter was electric. It warmed the coldest tundra of your heart.

Whatever Vince was saying to her was making her flush the prettiest pink, and Reese groaned beside me. I got it, I did. She was like sex personified, and I wasn't sure she even realized it.

Reese cleared his throat to hide the noise. "How'd it go, Vince?"

He pulled his face away from blowing raspberries on Celeste's neck for long enough to make a rude noise. "He tried to strong arm me to make another record first. I told him to fuck off."

Celeste frowned, and Vince kissed the expression away. "Don't look like that, Star. I was beginning to hate the thing I'd always loved. That would be fucking devastating. Like losing a limb. Like losing you."

Romantic bastard.

The elevator door dinged, and I turned toward it.

Everyone with a pass was in this room.

I pulled my gun, ignoring the tug on my stitches once again. When the doors slid open, there were machine guns pointed at us on the other side.

A man who was all too familiar stepped out. His smile was wide, and his eyes were dead. "Hello brother. I heard you were looking for me?"

My heart stuttered to a stop in my chest. I stood in front of the man who haunted my childhood. Who abandoned me to my mother and her crack addicted boyfriend. Somehow, I was more angry at him than either of them combined. More angry at him than my father, who ran out as soon as my mother got an addiction.

Because he was my big brother and I'd idolized him. And he destroyed that. He did worse than destroy the pedestal I'd put him on. He'd thrown me beneath its rubble and then built his career as a criminal on top of it.

In those tense seconds, I was a nine year old watching him stuff bags of coke in his pockets and punching me in the face when I asked what they were. Then I barely saw him. Unless it was late at night, or with The Dealer. I refused to say his name. To even think it. Names had power, and as far as I was concerned, the best thing that piece of shit ever created died by the poison he pumped into my mother's veins.

"No emotional hello, Little Brother? It's been what... fifteen years?"

I'd been robbed of speech. It was pure muscle memory that my gun stayed raised. My finger itched to pull the trigger in the same way I wanted to sink to my knees like a scared child again.

"What are you doing here, Logan?" I said, but the words came out rough.

Logan seemed to take that as an invitation to wander into the apartment. The goons stepped in just in front of him, and he looked at them, clicking his tongue against his teeth. Like well trained dogs, they lowered their guns. "This is a friendly visit, Lincoln. After all, it was you who came looking for me. Word is that you turned up on my streets looking half dead. I guess I wanted to see if that was true or not."

His eyes travelled over Reese and Vincent, but they settled on Celeste. The bigger guy on his left, a dark eyed monster the size of a truck, leaned forward and whispered something in his ear. Logan's eyebrows raised high, and his eyes took her in, a predatory interest lighting them.

Celeste bared her teeth at him in an action that wasn't entirely human, and Logan laughed. "Did it have anything to do with this gorgeous creature?"

Reese pushed Celeste behind him, and Logan cast him a bemused expression and I firmed my jaw. I lowered my gun, but only slightly. "You need to leave.

You aren't welcome here. I don't need your help anymore."

I might have imagined the flash of regret in his eyes, just the wish of the kid I once was. "That might be, but I'm here now, and I think we'll catch up. We can catch up at gunpoint, or we can be civil. The choice is yours."

I clenched my jaw so tightly it was a wonder I didn't shatter my back teeth. I looked at Reese and Vincent, and Reese inclined his head slightly. I dropped my gun to my side and tilted my head to the side. "Fine. Have a seat."

The smaller of his enforcers stayed by the elevator, and the other one travelled with his boss to the couch. "Thanks for the hospitality, little bro." He looked over at Reese. "You might be surprised, but I've been keeping track of you. I was very surprised when you hitched yourself to a billionaire and a rocker. But Mom was like that too. Seemed to be able to find the most influential people in the room and con them into believing she was worthy."

I growled low in my throat. "She was a victim."

Logan snorted. "She was a manipulator. You don't remember. You were too young." He shook his head. "No good comes from bringing this shit up. Do you have anything to drink?"

We all stood like statues around the room, until Vincent swaggered over to the wet bar like he didn't give a shit about dying. Up until a few months ago, he really hadn't. He poured a couple of fingers into a glass, and then looked at the big guy who was reclining on the couch like he hadn't a care in the world. He wasn't even holding his gun anymore.

"Do your *friends* want a drink?" Vincent asked, and Logan waved a hand. "Brut doesn't drink. And Reggie is a raging alcoholic with bad enough aim sober. He's fine."

Brut chuckled, but he was eyeing Celeste.

Vincent shrugged and handed Logan his drink. "So, let's get business out of the way. Why did you come to see me this week, Lincoln? I'm going to assume by my not-so-warm welcome, it wasn't just to shoot the shit and catch up."

I kept my mouth firmly closed, staring him down. Logan looked a little like me, we had the same eyes and the same strong nose. But Logan's face was a little rounder, his eyes hooded like a sleepy lion that could turn in a moment and eat you.

He shook his head. "No? Let me take some guesses, hmm? You needed my connections for something, because there is no way you would sully your fucking honor seeking me out for anything less than an illegal activity. You don't look like you need guns or coke, so I'm going to guess it has something to do with the fact that your girl over there is some kind of shifter." He looked at the man beside him. "Snow leopard?"

I stared, my mouth falling open. Celeste sucked in a breath, her legs falling from underneath her, but luckily Reese had fast hands.

I was on my feet and my gun was back in my hand in a second. "I won't let you fucking have her. Brother or not, I will put a bullet through your brain."

Logan rolled his eyes like I was a fucking child again. "Calm down, Lincoln. If I wanted her, I would have shot you all before I'd sat down on this truly painful fucking couch and saved my ass the misery. Honestly?"

I didn't lower my gun, and to Logan's credit, he didn't ask me to. "This is going to surprise you, brother, but I've been looking out for you a lot longer than you'd ever believe."

I snorted. He was right. I wouldn't fucking believe him. I'd been shot, stabbed, gone to juvenile detention. I'd been on the street and in foster homes. If he was looking out for me, he did a fucking shit job of it.

He must have seen the look on my face, because he sighed. "Yeah. Whatever. That ancient history isn't why I'm here. Just know that I mean you no harm, or the shifter."

Another growl. "My name is Celeste."

Logan raised both eyebrows at her. "I don't give a fuck?"

Brut chuckled, and that seemed to make Celeste relax a little, but for the life of me I had no idea why.

He didn't get less imposing or deadly. I looked over at Celeste and raised an eyebrow. She shrugged. "He's a supe too. Don't know what variety, but not a shifter," she said in a low voice.

That didn't make me feel better at all. Not even a little bit. What if he was something with superspeed, or like, I don't know, fucking tentacles?

Brut stood and I raised my gun. He put his own gun on the entry hall table. "Really?" Logan drawled. Brut shrugged. "It's the best outcome."

Brut stepped toward Celeste and I was across the room with my gun pressed against his back in a second. "Not another step," I growled. I looked over my shoulder at Logan. "Call him off."

Logan snorted again. "I don't control Brut. He's his own man."

"He'll be a fucking splatter painting if he doesn't stop."

Brut continued to chuckle. "I believe you. I'm an oracle."

A burst of laughter escaped Celeste's lips, and she slapped a hand over it. "I'm sorry. But I thought they were wispy women, all cloistered and delicate. And rich as hell."

Brut waggled a finger at her. "That is a common misconception. But I can read your future as quickly as I can end it." He cracked his knuckles and I slid the safety off my gun. "Makes for a more satisfying business practice."

"I'd watch your next words, because you are the only person with an uncertain future in this room right now."

Brut just chuckled. "Can we just skip this part and move on to the bit where your girl is laughing at my jokes and you and your brother settle your differences already?" He looked back at Celeste. "Worst part of being an oracle. The present is always so fucking tedious."

Celeste chewed on her bottom lip. Then she nodded. "Fuck it. I'm tired. Let's sit down, get this over with, so we can leave already. Or are you going to stop us leaving?" I didn't know if she was talking to Brut or Logan, but the effect was the same.

Brut shook his head. "Your future shows you on your way to Canada by nightfall. But only if you follow the right stars."

Well, there was no way he could know that we were going to Canada unless he was a fucking psychic, because we'd told no one but Miranda, and somehow I didn't think she was likely to blab to a gangster.

"See all that in your crystal ball?" Vincent quipped, but his eyes watched the man closely.

Brut grinned, all shiny white teeth and crinkled laugh lines. "Yeah I did. I'd show you, but I left it at home. I can show you the ones in my pants instead if you want?"

Celeste laughed, slapping her hand over her mouth again, and Brut gave me an 'I told you so' look.

I lowered my gun and put the safety back on. "Fine. Let's get this over with."

Logan gestured to Reese and I. "Please. Come and sit."

I edged around Reese's stiff back and past Brut. He was aptly named. He was huge, with nearly ageless brown skin, except the crinkles around his eyes from smiling. If it wasn't for those laugh lines, I'd put his age anywhere between twenty-five and fifty. The only real tell were the scars. He had scars across his face, his hands, his neck. He looked like he'd been in a fight with a tiger, and only one of them came out alive. If that wasn't the case, then he'd been around for a lot longer than he looked.

His arms bulged, his chest bulged. Hell, everything about him bulged. He looked like he could snap me in half and then use my corpse as a travel pillow.

Completely terrifying, until he smiled. It morphed

his face from the stuff of nightmares to something altogether warmer. It was a smile that would lure you into
a trap before you realized you were there, so I edged
around him a little more. He looked down at the bulge
of my stomach, and that smile reared its head.

"Ah. Congratulations." He looked between me and
Reese. "Do you want to know if it's a boy or a girl?"

I shook my head, even though relief washed
through me. I didn't need to know the gender of my
baby. It was enough to know that Brut had seen it, and
it had been okay enough to be dressed in blue or pink.

Logan looked between me and Lincoln. "Not
yours?"

"It's mine," Lincoln growled, and a smile curved my
lips. God, I loved him. If it had just been us, I would
have made love with him right now just to show him.
Unfortunately, this room was crowded with strangers.

Brut gave me another conspiratorial look, but
didn't correct Lincoln.

I wanted to sit on Lincoln's lap, let him hold me so I
could in turn soothe him, but he'd hate me being so
close to his brother, so instead I sat in the armchair on
the other side of the room. Vincent sat beside me and
Reese sat closer to Lincoln, offering support. Brut
sauntered over with an ease that shouldn't be possible,
and sat beside Logan.

We all sat there in awkward silence, until Vincent

couldn't take it anymore. "So, are you two a couple?" he asked, and I whipped my head toward him.

Jesus fucking christ. Had he never watched a movie in his life? You don't ask the gangsters with guns if they were gay. Pretty sure that's a major plot point in every single Hollywood blockbuster ever. I watched them for any sign of aggression, but Logan just threw back his head and laughed.

"I'm strictly pussy, but even if I wasn't, have you seen the size of this motherfucker? If everything is in proportion, he'd paralyze a man for life. No thank you. No offense, Brut."

The man in question just shook his head. "None taken."

I let out the breath that I was holding. Maybe they didn't mean to torture us with kindness and then kill us at the end.

Unless Vincent opened his mouth again. When he went to say something else, I squeezed his thigh and talked over the top of him.

"I assume there's a reason for you being here, aside from Lincoln being on your turf a few days ago. A man like you doesn't make the trip just to say hi."

"What do you know about the kind of man I am?" he asked, narrowing his eyes, and I curled my lip and showed him my useless human teeth.

Brut just continued to laugh like this was the most

hilarious conversation ever. Logan gave him an annoyed look.

He stood and paced around the room, and I watched him with predator eyes. "I trust Brut in all things. He told me that if I didn't come here, clear things up with Lincoln, that I would choose the wrong path and I would die. Needless to say, I'm not ready to be fucking compost anytime soon."

Lincoln sucked in a sharp breath, and it whistled loudly between his teeth. For a moment, he looked panicked, but he shut it down quickly. If you didn't know him well, you would miss it. Unfortunately, everyone in this room was either psychic or knew his tells. "Well, you've come now. You can leave and hope-fully the stars will save your ass."

Logan looked hopefully at Brut, but he shook his head, suddenly looking so solemn that it was like Logan was already dead. They seemed to be actual friends. Close.

He huffed and sat back down on the couch. "Lincoln, I'm sorry."

We all stared at Lincoln's brother, the gang leader, drug dealer, all around bad man, as he apologized. And he sounded like he meant it, even if his face was twisted like it physically pained him to say the words. That was the freakiest part. Linc was holding himself so tightly, it was a wonder he didn't snap.

"Okay. You can go now."

Logan reached out and I growled, the sound pure snow leopard. No one touched my mate unless he wanted it. Logan quirked an eyebrow and dismissed me. Apparently, that arrogance was a Prescott Family trait.

Lincoln shot me a reassuring look but still, I wanted to tear off his brother's arm and beat him with it.

Brut snorted. "I'd resist that urge. It does not have a good outcome in the stars."

I narrowed my eyes. "Has anyone ever told you that you sound like a bad horoscope?"

He laughed. "No. But you will many more times in your life, if we all choose correctly."

Logan wisely dropped his hand. "I know what happened when we were kids fucked you up. It fucked me up too. You know what I wanted to be when I was ten? A cop." He huffed out a laugh. "Didn't work out that way, obviously."

Lincoln rolled his eyes. "Obviously."

I tried to judge the man in front of me now that my heart wasn't trying to beat out of my chest. He held his body with barely restrained violence, tense and ready to fight at any given second, even in this room where no one but Lincoln was really a threat.

That irked to even think.

I am a threat. Normally. When I wasn't this weak little fawn with wobbly knees. I huffed and Vincent pulled me closer. Lincoln and Logan were locked in some kind of silent battle, and the hard lines around Logan's eyes softened a little. "I hated leaving you. I hated that you had to stay there with her. And when the baby was born..." He visibly shuddered, and I could hear the hard pound of his heart. Lincoln's jaw just tensed, but he didn't acknowledge anything that Logan had said. "I have so many regrets. I should have told someone that she was neglecting you guys so bad. But I worried they'd take you away from me. So fucking selfish of me. Look how it ended."

I remembered Lincoln's story, told to me in the quiet safety of the darkness. About his mother freaking out, the accident that ended his sister's life. His mother attacked him until he stabbed her in self defense. It was horrific and tragic.

Something broke inside of Lincoln. "You should have fucking been there, not out selling drugs for that fucking scumbag. For this fucking gang," he spat out, indicating Reggie and Brut.

Logan looked tired in that moment. Completely bone tired.

"You don't understand."

Lincoln was on his feet now. "Get the fuck out of my house."

Logan just shook his head. "Not until you forgive me."

"Never. You chose them over your own flesh and blood, you chose-"

"Mom was going to sell you."

I gasped, and the weight of the silence in the room was deafening. Lincoln slumped back onto the couch like he'd physically been hit.

"What?"

"Gary said that he wasn't feeding her drugs and supporting her brats for nothing. Her body wasn't fucking enough, apparently. Neither was her soul. He knew a guy who liked little boys, and they were going to send you on 'play dates' over there in exchange for money."

Lincoln was shaking his head and I was going to throw up. "She wouldn't have..."

Logan snarled. "She was a fucking addict, Lincoln. She would have sold us all in a heartbeat for her next fix by the end. We were an inconvenience." He took a shuddering breath and I watched him compose himself. "I offered to sell for him instead. I didn't keep any of the cut, the whole lot went to him. Lower reward but less risk as well. I pledged into the gang, and lived hand to mouth while I rose through the ranks. By the time you ended up in juvie, I had enough sway to get you watched inside."

This was crazy. Just plain insanity.

"I was shanked inside!"

Logan nodded, but there was a bit of death in his

eyes now. "And the guy who shanked you ended up dead."

Vincent hissed. "Fuck me. This is like watching Wimbledon but they're throwing knives instead of hitting balls."

Lincoln was shaking his head like the truth wasn't computing in his brain. "It doesn't matter now. I don't want or need your help anymore. I'll give you your forgiveness or absolution or whatever the fuck it is you came here for. But I don't need you anymore."

Logan smiled, and I wondered if he wasn't part-shark shifter. "That's where you're wrong, Little Brother. Because without me? You end up dead and your girl ends up recaptured before the week is out."

Well. He really should have led with that.

In the end, what Logan was offering us was simple. He was offering us a roadmap to the future, and as long as we didn't deviate from the map, we all lived happily ever after, or so Brut said. He was vague with anything outside of this week, but I got that too. He said there were a hundred different futures, depending on what you chose to do in the present. One change, and your whole future would be different.

We had to cross the border to Canada in one particular place. Nowhere else. We had to travel through the night until we hit some little backwater town in the middle of nowhere, and we had to stop at a cupcake store.

That was it. Then we would be home free. Sounded fucking insane to me, but who was I to argue? It was close enough to our original plan already, but a lot more specific. I liked specifics so it should be fine.

The other thing they did for us, and this is what freaked me out the most, was provide us with a full set of fake identification. They'd known, before they'd even rolled into our apartment, everything about us. Ages, heights, birthdays. Everything. They either had a very good hacker, or the detail in Brut's visions was scarily accurate.

When Logan and Brut had laid out their plan, they'd left without a fuss, like they'd come over for a drink and not to hold us all temporarily hostage. The air between the two brothers was loaded with so much tension that it would have killed a canary, but you couldn't expect a decade and a half of issues to disappear with one apology. People didn't work like that, especially when the scars ran that deep.

Brut had waved at us, giving Celeste a grin. "See you all soon."

I still wasn't sure if that was a promise or a threat. The guy didn't give me a bad feeling, but the fact he knew the shit he did gave me the creeps.

When they left, Lincoln collapsed onto a chair like all the air had been sucked out of him. His face was ghostly, and I got him a shot of whiskey.

Celeste sat in his lap and wrapped her body around his, like she was trying to consume him into her body so she could keep him safe. Vince sat down beside him, close but not smothering him.

"Are you okay?" he asked quietly. It was a simple question, one I knew Lincoln would just grunt out a 'fine' in answer to, but there was so much more to it. Lincoln had built his life around hating his brother.

As much as I wanted to know what he was feeling, I knew he needed time to process, so I didn't pry. I looked down at the piece of paper in my hand. It told us that we had to leave at exactly 4:03.

It didn't matter how we got to Montana, but once we were there, we had to cross the border at exactly 1:55 in the afternoon. Then it was just through the wilds of Alberta until we reached this town. I looked at the piece of paper. Dark River. I tried to google it on the map, but it didn't even have a street view. I'd had to google the actual coordinates to even get it to come up on the map. But if we were going to take this leap and trust Logan and Brut, then I'd have to trust them with this too.

"Are we sure they aren't just fucking with us?" Vincent asked, and I didn't know what the hell to tell him. Maybe they were? Maybe they were walking us right into a trap. I looked between Celeste and Lincoln.

Lincoln's opinion was probably biased, but Celeste just shrugged. "My snow leopard seemed okay with them, and I trust her instincts. I say we follow the plan but be wary. I don't trust anyone completely. Except you guys."

I tried not to glow at the compliment. Until a few weeks ago, she didn't trust even us. But we were a family now; I could feel it in my bones, and it made me happier than I ever thought possible. The cars were all loaded, and I walked around the apartment a couple more times to make sure everything was right. The cleaners would be paid by automatic transfer. Everything was set to run without me for at least twelve months. My lawyer had authority to take care of my affairs, and when I'd seen him on the weekend after hours to update my will, he'd looked at me like I was insane.

If I learned anything, it was that I wanted everyone to be okay if anything happened to me. I know Vincent and Lincoln felt the same.

"We should go." My watch said it was 3:55. Brut was extremely specific, but at the same time vague. Did we have to close the door to this apartment at 4:03? Did we have to be in the car and on the road at 4:03? Would a couple of minutes either side make a life or death difference?

I was hoping it was the former, because otherwise we'd have to sprint to the car to make it.

Celeste stood, swaying lightly on her feet. I longed for the day she was strong again. She picked up her tote bag, until Lincoln stood and took it off her, swinging it over his arm. Vincent had both of his guitars in his hands, and Lincoln had a single backpack that I knew was packed full of guns. I grabbed my own backpack and briefcase, filled with tech. Apparently, we all had our own crutches.

I called the elevator and at exactly 4:03, I pressed the button for the basement parking lot. The silver doors slid closed on my past. I wrapped an arm around Celeste's shoulders, and she looked up at me sadly.

"I'm sorry."

I kissed her temple and held her tight. "For what?"

She waved a hand at the doors. "For destroying your lives. For uprooting you guys from everything you worked so hard for. I'm just... sorry."

I gripped her chin and turned her to face me. I took a quick, sipping kiss of her lips. "I've never been more scared or happy in my entire life. I wouldn't change a moment of this. Not yelling to save you at the alley, not the baby, though I could have skipped the whole abduction thing. Let's not do that again, okay?"

She chuckled but it sounded strangled. I dipped my head down and realized she was crying. I pulled her into my chest. "I love you Celeste. Please don't cry."

She slapped my chest. "Well stop being so damn sweet then."

We decided to only take one car, none of us wanting to be separated. Vincent climbed into the back with Celeste, and the cargo area was so filled I couldn't see out the back windows. Lincoln sat in the front, and he leaned the seat back a bit so not to put strain on his stitches. They looked raw and oozy, and I was a little worried they were getting infected. We'd have to find a doctor straight away, and I silently thanked Logan for the fake Canadian identities.

I slid into the driver's seat, and looked in the rearview mirror. "Ready?"

Vincent kissed Celeste. "Sure am. Brut said that I had to give Star at least seven orgasms before we hit the Montana border, and I am eager to get started. Can't doom us early."

Celeste laughed. "He did not."

He laughed. "You never know. Let's get started."

I shook my head as I drove away from the city and toward our future.

Montana all looked the same. Mountains and cows. Cows and mountains. A horse. Another ten horses. Damn I was bored.

Everyone else was asleep and it was my turn to drive. Reese was beside me in the passenger seat, and Celeste was curled around Lincoln in the backseat. She'd lost her seatbelt and was just lying between his thighs, her head on his chest as he spread across the seat. I wish I was a painter rather than a musician at that moment, because I wanted to be able to paint them like that. So innocent and carefree.

It was almost time to cross the border into Canada, and we were running on time. So far, the whole trip had been completely uneventful. I wasn't sure if it was because Brut's predictions were correct, or because we never would have run into trouble anyway as the Bears had destroyed the bounty hunters. We might never know, but so far so good. I knocked my knuckles on my head so I didn't jinx us all.

"What are you doing?" Reese asked sleepily.

"Knocking on wood."

Reese looked at me like I'd lost it, and maybe I had. We'd been driving on and off for an entire day, not stopping for anything but bathroom breaks. I needed to be out of this car before I went insane. Once we were over the border, we could stop for a night somewhere, sleep in an actual bed, make love to Star in an actual bed.

Reese and Linc still hadn't forgiven me for making good on my promise to give her seven orgasms before we got to Montana. Hell, we were at seven before we even got halfway through Wisconsin.

It really broke up the drive though.

Reese checked his watch and then Brut's instructions. It was starting to get crumbled from Reese constantly opening and reading it. "It's almost time. He said if we were early we had to pull into a copse of trees just up here."

I nodded. We'd been driving down a gravel road for awhile now, and I hadn't seen a single other car. I was pretty sure it was because there wasn't another freaking person in this wilderness. We could probably park right here, in the middle of the road, and it would be enough. But Brut hadn't led us astray yet, so I continued to drive until I found the big stand of trees that Brut must have been referring to in his note, reversing right in and shutting off the car. We'd be hidden here in this odd, dense section of woods, at least for a little while.

The sound of the car turning off, or maybe it was the lack of noise woke Lincoln, and as he shifted awake, so did Celeste.

Lincoln was quickly alert, taking in the surrounding woods. "Where are we?"

Reese gave them both a reassuring smile. "On the border. We're a little early, so we are hiding out like Brut said."

Lincoln snorted but didn't protest. I'm not sure he believed the whole thing either. "How long do we have?"

"About ten minutes."

Celeste sighed and rubbed her belly. "Should have stopped to get something to eat. I'm so freaking starving I could eat an entire mountain goat."

I laughed, but Lincoln reached into his bag, sifting through the weapons and ammo, and finally pulling out a bag of jerky.

"If that is mountain goat jerky, I'm getting the hell out of this car right now and giving up," I quipped, and Lincoln shot me his first real smile all trip. "Just normal beef jerky." He turned to Celeste, kissing her softly then handing over his bounty like a freaking caveman. Like he'd hunted the cow, then dried it into jerky himself.

She accepted the food with more gratitude than jerky really warranted, leaning forward to stroke her cheek over his. I narrowed my eyes at them. Something hinky was going on between those two. They'd been extra touchy for the last couple of days. I'd lived with Lincoln for years; the man wasn't a huge proponent of PDA's.

"What's going on with you two?" If I had any doubt before, the quick look that passed between them would have erased all doubt. They were definitely up to something, and I tried to squash down the little part of me that was hurt to be excluded. It was probably some PTSD side effect of my childhood. But Celeste's face softened, and she climbed her cute pregnant butt between the seats, with a lot of cursing and some gentle maneuvering from Lincoln until she could plonk down on Reese's lap.

"We weren't keeping it a secret, I just didn't want to pressure you guys or make you feel rushed." She started, her fingers stroking down my cheeks as she caught me with her eyes and refused to let me go. "A couple of days ago, I mated Lincoln. It was something my leopard pushed for. Something I couldn't ignore."

She what? Somehow, I didn't think she meant making the beast with two backs. Apparently, Reese didn't either. He frowned, but dragged Celeste a little closer. "What does that mean?"

She chewed her bottom lip, and I reached out to tug the tender skin from between her teeth. I stroked my thumb over it and she gave me a crooked smile. "It means, I guess in human terms, that my snow leopard married him?"

I dropped my hand in shock, my eyes flicking back from between Lincoln's guarded face to Celeste's worried one. "You got shifter married and hid it from us? Were you even going to tell us? Tell me?"

This hurt. It wasn't Freudian at all. It wasn't a remnant of my childhood. It was very real, very now kinda pain. The two people I loved more than anyone else in the world got married and didn't even tell me. Didn't include me.

Didn't love me.

Okay, maybe that one screamed mommy-issues just a little. I opened the driver's door and got out. I needed space.

"Vincent..." Star started, but I shook my head, walking toward the back of the car. I heard Lincoln's door open and closed, and when his warm hand landed on my shoulder, I shrugged it off. "This changes nothing between you and me, Vince. You know that. You know I love you. Celeste loves you. Fuck, Reese loves you, and if he liked dick, pretty sure he would have become your housewife years ago."

My lips twitched, but I didn't turn around. "It changes everything."

He grabbed my shoulder and spun me, gripping my face and slamming his lips into mine. He pressed me against the back of the car and I realized I'd missed this. Missed him. He kissed me like he was trying to brand me, and I kissed him back, gripping his hips close to me.

When we were panting and half-wild with lust, he pulled away. "She will make you hers as well. She didn't want you to feel pressured, but when she looks at you there's a longing in her eyes. Just wait. If I could have waited, I probably would have. Not that I regret it, but I'd want her to choose me because the moment was perfect and she was happy. Not because we were both half dead and she was scared of losing me. You're mine, Vince. Forever. You were mine first and you'll be mine until we are both buried six feet down." He roughly gripped my chin. "Do you understand me?"

I took a deep breath in, inhaling the comforting scent of Lincoln, even if he did smell a little like corn chips after sitting in a car for nearly sixteen hours, and nodded. "Okay. Though, when you say it like that, it sounds a little serial killerish."

He laughed and bit my lip, and I chuckled. But when I stopped, the rumble still went on. Cars. Lincoln looked up, searching for the road between the trees. "Get back in the car, Vince." We scrambled back into the car, me climbing in the back with Celeste, who wrapped her body around me in her favorite position that I liked to call baby koala.

"I'm sorry. As soon as this is over, and you're ready, I'd love to take that step with you too. When you're ready. No pressure. If you don't that doesn't change my feelings for you at all. I don't want to rush-"

I kissed her, stilling the spew of words. "I'd love to be your shifter husband."

A relieved giggle passed her lips and she nuzzled my neck. "Thank god."

The sound of vehicles got louder and louder until a black SUV sped past, followed closely by Border cops. They were flying along the straight gravel road in the direction we just came.

"What are the chances they were bounty hunters?" Reese asked no one in particular.

I wanted to say it was unlikely. How could they possibly have known we'd come this way, cross at this crossing? No, it was likely they were just trying to jump the border like we were. It was fine.

No one said anything as we waited until we no longer heard the wail of sirens and the heavy rumble of cars. Reese looked at his watch.. "It's time. We should move."

He didn't make eye contact with Star, and I had a feeling he was hurting. I mean, I was, and I was a whole lot less sensitive than Reese.

We slowly pulled out of the weird copse of trees and drove dangerously fast down the aptly named 'Border Road' until we came to a T intersection. Turning into Canada, I held Star close and breathed a sigh of relief. Thank fuck. We made it.

31

LINCOLN

"Welcome to Dark River. Population... does that say 0?"

I looked toward the sign Vince was pointing to, and it did look like whatever the first number was had fallen off. Hell, maybe it wasn't a typo. Who would live out here, so far from civilization, on the way to literally nowhere.

The sun was just beginning to set when we rolled into the town Brut told us to head to, and considering he hadn't been wrong yet, I couldn't think of any reason to stop following his directions. If this was an elaborate plan to capture us, well, there were fucking easier ways.

Honestly, this place kind of gave me the creeps. It was almost empty, and there wasn't a car in sight. Maybe they were a group of traditionalists or something, like the amish? But that didn't explain why the place was practically deserted. Maybe the sign wasn't wrong after all.

I followed Brut's instructions, driving slowly around a center town square that was hung with fairy lights, and past the police station.

A man in a Sheriff's uniform stepped out onto the front lawn and looked at our car, and it sent goose-bumps skidding down my spine. The fuck was up with this place? I looked at Celeste in the rearview mirror, and her whole body was strung tight.

"Babe? What's wrong?"

She shook her head, but I could see her shifter was close to the surface. You know what, screw Brut and his cryptic instructions. "You say turn this car around, and we are out of here. Just say the word."

Her focus was still on the Sheriff, but when she looked back at me, her eyes were that of the snow leopard. She shook her head. "Stick to the plan. It hasn't led us wrong yet."

We rolled past a diner, and my stomach rumbled.

"I think this is it," Reese said, pointing to a well lit building in front of us, the light colorful through stained glass windows. We pulled up in front of 'The Immortal Cupcake', at least we knew we had the right place; it smelled amazing.

I looked around, assessing for threats, and a part of me wanted to pull my gun. Something in my hindbrain was yelling to stuff my mate back in the car and run away, but I resisted. I was going to have faith that my brother wasn't just sending me to my death, that he was actually sorry for the past. Maybe that made me naive or just plain fucking stupid. Only time will tell. Celeste shuffled out of the car, her body taut. If she'd been in her snow leopard form, she'd have been perfectly still, looking for predators.

Vincent, the beautiful, self-destructive disaster seemed completely unaware. He stepped up to the door of the cake shop, peering through the windows. "It's still open," he called back, and Celeste forcibly relaxed her shoulders. Reese wrapped his arm around her, and she snuggled against his chest, but it was an unconscious act. She was seeking comfort from her mate. I'd been googling the habits of big cats. I knew that there was a huge difference between shifters and actual animals, but obviously some of the more animalistic traits carried through to the shifters. Like mates. And biting.

A shiver of pleasure ran over my skin at the memory of her blunt teeth piercing my skin. I don't know what it said about me that even the memory of that bite made me uncomfortably hard, but I was desperate to let her do it over and over again. Soon she'd be strong enough. Soon we'd both be invincible.

Vincent pulled the door open, and a jingling bell announced our arrival. I stepped in first, and the amount of people in a cupcake shop at 7 p.m. astounded me. What was even more confronting was that every person in the room stopped and turned all at once. It was fucking creepy.

There was a girl at the counter with the name Everly stitched into her apron, and she was the last one to turn. When she took us all in, her nose twitched and her eyes narrowed on Celeste.

"Brody!" she yelled, as Reese and Vincent came up behind me. The group of us stood awkwardly just inside the door, and I was tempted to grab up Celeste and leave. There was something so, so wrong about this place.

"They're dead," Celeste whispered, as a smiling indigenous Canadian man came out of the kitchen, followed closely by a woman with fire engine red hair.

"Well, not quite dead," a voice said from behind me, and I spun on my heel to see the Sheriff from across the town square now standing right behind us. He was either an Olympic sprinter or...

"They're vampires," Celeste whispered.

I pulled my gun before I thought through the consequence of the action. Would a gun even work on these guys?

The Sheriff raised his lip, showing pointed teeth. Sharp fucking fangs.

"Holy shit, the fucking guy has fangs!" Vincent whispered loudly.

The Sheriff didn't take his eyes off me though, and my gaze ping ponged around the room, trying to work out where the greatest threat lay. That was a stupid idea. We were in a room of vampires. The threat was literally everywhere.

The Sheriff gave me what I assume was meant to be a reassuring look. "You can put that away. I'm not a threat. I'm here for your safety and to make sure everyone keeps their head." He looked past me at the inhabitants of the room. "We've been practicing for this, isn't that right?"

Reese's eyes were way too big in his head, and his face had turned pale. Deathly pale. Probably not a very apt description in a town filled with dead people.

The girl with the red hair stepped forward. "They've got this, it's fine, Walker." She gave the crowd the stink eye, like they better be fine or someone was going to get their ass kicked. Then she turned back to us. "Hi, I'm Raine. Owner of The Immortal Cupcake. This is my consort, Walker," she indicated the Sheriff behind me. "And this is my Mate, Brody, Alpha of Nîso Pack and the greater NorthWest Shapeshifters. We don't get many, uh, humans through here, but I promise that you're safe. In this building, at least."

Brody met Celeste's eyes, and she dropped her face immediately. When he looked at me, I clenched my teeth, holding his gaze until my eyes slid away, almost like my body had betrayed me.

"I'm guessing by the pregnant shifter, that you're probably here for me?" Brody asked, like he hadn't just bent me to his will with his Alpha mojo or whatever the fuck it was. "Come on upstairs. Everly?"

The girl behind the counter threw him a key she fished out of the front pocket of her apron, and Brody caught it without even looking. "Come on up. It's safer for humans in the upstairs apartment than down here among the death dealers."

Raine nudged him in the ribs with her elbow. He bent over and kissed the top of her head. "You know I mean that in the most affectionate way possible, Red. Besides, most of them are eyeing our guests like they are a turducken."

The woman screwed up her nose. "A what?"

"A turkey, stuffed with a duck, stuffed with... You know what, never mind. I'll explain later. Come on up. Everly, come and stay at the house tonight. Our guests will probably need the wards for the night."

The girl huffed, and I realized she was still quite young. "You just want me to babysit so you guys can run off to the woods and have an orgy or something."

The door opened again, and another vampire stepped in. This one had me raising my gun and pulling Celeste behind me. If the Sheriff gave me the creeps, this guy made me want to piss myself.

"Did someone say orgy?" he said happily, before his eyes landed on us. "Are we starting with drinks first?"

I pointed my gun at his face, and he smirked at me. Literally laughed in my face. "Unless you want me to take that gun from you and stick it-"

"X!" the redhead, Raine, shouted, and the guy shot her a loving look. "You're lucky I've ascribed to the whole Kumbaya bullshit of this town, otherwise you would have been a juice pouch in a second, human."

The Sheriff was shaking his head, and Brody the Alpha smiled. "Impeccable timing, X. Just taking our guests upstairs. You should probably see Tex and the Pups home though?"

The man looked around, and finding whoever his charges were, started striding across the room. Even the other vampires kind of shrank from him. Brody cleared his throat. "Follow me."

I had no other option, though following a stranger to a secondary location went against everything I'd ever learned, but I had no other options.

"Is everyone here vampires? Other than you, of course," Celeste asked, frowning. "And the girl behind the counter."

"My niece, Everly." He looked over his shoulder and smiled softly at her. "Mostly vampires. There are a few more shifters downstairs that you missed, but Dark River is 99% undead."

My heart thudded against my ribs. I'd driven us into a trap. I couldn't fight my way out of this. Brody must have sensed my panic, because he stopped and clapped a hand against my bicep. "Don't stress your-self. They have very strict laws. They can't feed from humans, turn humans, kill humans... you get the drift. The penalty is death. Permanent, irrevocable death."

He opened the door to an apartment, and indicated we should enter. I hesitated, unsure whether to step in first, or guard our backs.

Vincent took the decision from me, wandering through the doorway, his eyes taking everything in. He looked at the back of the door. "Is that blood?"

We all filed in after him, and Brody shut it tight. "Yep. We had a witch create a ward to keep out vampires."

I frowned. "Why, if all the vampires in the town are what, dieting?"

Brody waved a hand. "It's a long and complicated story. Just trust me when I say there are very few vampires in this town that can cross those wards. The ones that can, I trust with my life."

"But can I trust them with ours?" Celeste growled out.

Brody went to answer, but Reese interrupted. He was still staring at the bloody handprints on the back of the door. "The witch that did this ward, her name wouldn't happen to be Miranda, would it?"

What the hell had Brut got us into? The room smelled a little like residual blood, but mostly like the shifter girl downstairs. The apartment looked lived in, like really lived in. Everly wasn't a neat freak, that was for sure. There were dishes in the sink, and a bra strewn over the back of the couch which everyone pointedly ignored.

Brody gave me a reassuring smile. "You've met Miranda then?"

I'd made them let me walk up the stairs by myself, but I was paying for it now as my thighs felt like they'd give out. But I refused to appear weak in front of that many predators. Tame or not, weakness wasn't viewed well in the natural or supernatural worlds. It made you prey.

I sank down on the couch, hopefully not looking as relieved as I felt. I looked up into the Alpha's face quickly, and noticed him watching me with a soft look on his face. I couldn't hide my weakness from him, but my snow leopard liked him. She wanted to bare her belly to him, but not in fear. In respect.

Reese sat beside me, threading his fingers through mine. "We met briefly. We owe her a lot."

Brody raised his brows. "I wouldn't go saying that out loud in the supernatural world, friend. Miranda is inherently good, even though she wouldn't agree, but there are many other types of supernaturals that can bind you to that gratitude."

Reese frowned, but Brody moved on. "Was it Miranda that sent you here, to Dark River?"

Vincent wandered around the room like he was in a museum exhibit, until Lincoln grunted something at him. He sat down beside me and hooked an arm around my shoulders. Brody raised an eyebrow, but didn't comment.

I shrugged. "Kind of. Miranda suggested we head to your pack, because you have a member that might be able to help me. Another snow leopard shifter."

"Ghost?" Brody said, this time surprise making his jaw drop slightly. "Are you kin?"

I shook my head. "I have no idea. I've never, er, had a pack."

Brody's surprise slowly morphed to a frown. "I think you better start at the beginning."

So I did. From the very beginning, the whole, ugly truth of it all. About my mother throwing me out, which made both Brody and Lincoln growl, to growing up on the streets and running from bounty hunters. The fateful meeting with Reese, when he saved me. The awful plan that came afterwards, about leaving my baby with them and running.

Around that point Brody started to pace, his energy getting real big until I let out a tiny whine. He stilled his feet immediately, and gave me a gentle look. "I'm not mad at you, Celeste. I'm mad that you had no pack to help you. That there's still shifters out there who make progeny and abandon them to their fates. I'm sorry I interrupted. Please, continue."

I got to the hard parts. Lincoln being shot, being kidnapped by the hunters and getting overdosed.

Brody's growls started back up and Vincent pulled me closer to his body. When I got to the part about being rescued by the bears, Brody suddenly smiled.

"Ah, Vance. I know of him and his Sleuth." He looked at Reese. "You got very lucky. The ancestors were smiling down on you to gift you with one of the shifter world's most elite mercenary teams as penpals."

This time, it was my jaw that went slack. "Excuse me?" I mean, logically I'd already known that. The way they operated when they rescued me, the way they were dressed, held themselves, burned down the evidence all screamed spec-ops. But I thought they must have been mainstreaming in the human army. Not some kind of supernatural black-ops.

Brody just winked and motioned for me to continue. I mentioned how they'd hooked me up with Eden, who in turn had hooked me up with Wilde and Miranda. When I got to the last part, I was purposefully vague about Logan and Brut. I just mentioned that he was an oracle who gave me specific directions, directions that ended up with me here.

By the time I was finished, it was dark and I was starving. "Celeste, that is quite a tale. The fates really wanted you to be here, didn't they?"

I cocked my head to the side. Did they? Had my whole, tortured existence been the not so gentle prodding of destiny?

"You're welcome in my Pack, Celeste, as are your mates. We don't have many humans, and it's a bit unusual to have three human mates, but well, after the Alpha Mate turned out to be a vampire? A couple of humans seems almost vanilla in comparison," he laughed, and I relaxed. "Ghost would be glad to meet you. His history with his clan is... rocky. So he is in much the same situation as you. A two-natured shifter abandoned by his own kind. There aren't many snow leopards left. But he is my brother. I love him as if we were littermates, he is my Pack." I didn't need to be supernatural to see how much he loved this other Snow Leopard shifter. A male. For some reason I thought the snow leopard shifter Miranda was pointing me to would have been another female, and I frowned as I looked at the Alpha of the Nîso Pack.

"I'm not looking for another, you know, mate." I wasn't starting an endangered shifter breeding program. Or participating in it either, for that matter.

Brody snorted. "Uh, no. Ghost has found his mate, or at least he would have if he pulled his head out of his ass. If they both would. And no offense, Annie would eat you alive. She's all soft and gentle unless you take something that she considers hers. I still have the scars from trying to use her blocks as a pup."

I heaved a sigh of relief. "Good. I have enough on my plate with these three."

"Hey!" Vincent protested, and I leaned over to kiss his cheek. He gave me a mock stern look but his eyes were laughing.

There was a knock at the door, and Lincoln tensed. It opened and Raine stuck her head around the door-jamb. "I just brought up some food. I thought you guys might be hungry and I wouldn't suggest heading over to the diner. Or leaving the apartment for anything really."

She flushed a little, and it made her go from pretty to a little enchanting. She was softness personified, she had a gentle face, and a softly rounded body. But her eyes held some serious wickedness that led me to believe she probably kept all the mates I'd met on their toes.

Brody wandered over like he couldn't help himself, wrapping his body around hers. "Probably best. I'll take them back to Nîso tomorrow so they'll be safer."

Raine nodded, planting a soft kiss on his lips. "I better get back downstairs before someone tells the Town Council there's humans about and I have to run interference." She looked back at our group. "It was nice to meet you all. I'm sure I'll see you again soon."

If I hadn't been a shifter, I would have missed Brody's words when he leaned into Raine's ear. As it was, I heard them as clearly as if he'd been whispering them into my ear as well. "Eden approached them to fund the academy. Apparently they've offered safe haven in exchange for the money necessary to complete the build."

"Humans?"

"With a shifter child on the way. Apparently, they are collectively richer than a small country."

I grinned. "Only like, Monaco or somewhere like that," I said conspiratorially, and Raine laughed.

"Looks like we are about to become neighbors," Raine said with a smile, then small lines marred her forehead. "You don't feel, coerced or anything like that right? Like you need to pay to be safe? Because I'm

Alphamate and if you guys want to stay in Nîso forever, we'll welcome you with open arms, won't we Alpha?"

Brody looked at her with absolute adoration, and more than a little amusement. "If you say so, Red." He looked at us. "She is absolutely right. You don't need to buy your protection anymore."

Reese shook his head. "Thank you, but Locke was very... persuasive. I believe in what they are trying to create."

Raine huffed, but she was still smiling. "Yeah, so do we. We've already agreed to let them set up on land between here and Nîso." She stepped up to the door. "We'll have to have a barbecue when I'm up at Nîso. You can meet my pups."

Her pups? She was dead, and from what I can remember about biology, dead things can't procreate. I didn't say any of that though. I was a shifter with three human mates and an accidental baby. I was hardly one to point out the improbability of things. "I'd like that."

With that, Raine left quicker than my eyes could follow. She was there then gone. "Holy shit, it was like she teleported," Reese whispered and I laughed.

Dark River had been full of surprises.

W e followed the winding road toward Nîso behind Brody's Camaro. I wasn't a car guy, but Lincoln had nearly had an orgasm when he'd seen it. It was a couple of hours drive between the two towns, but it was large stretches of wilderness. It was beautiful in a way that I couldn't begin to truly comprehend. Wild and silent, we seemed to be intruding on the natural order. It sung to me in a way that was almost primal.

Celeste stared silently outside the window as well, seemingly relaxed for the first time since I met her. Was it the presence of the Alpha, or being out of the city that calmed her? She just seemed happier out here, stronger even.

We pulled onto a dirt road, over a small rise that dipped down into an impressive size town, just sitting out here in the middle of nowhere. If Brody was to be believed, a town filled with shapeshifters. It made a good counterpart to the town of vampires we just left. What the hell had happened to my reality, that I could think about vampires and shapeshifters in the same sentence with such ease. She must have felt me watching her, because she turned and caught me in those bright eyes. Celeste had happened, and I couldn't be happier.

Nîso was a weird town, like it had been built around the forest to cause the least amount of damage. So roads wound around ancient trees, some as round as cars. Houses were set in between trees like they were neighbors.

Vincent pulled Celeste onto his lap. "It's beautiful, Star. Don't you think it's beautiful?" He sounded as awed as I did. We drove up a slight incline to a big log cabin with a wrap around porch. Brody turned into the driveway, and I parked alongside.

Two people stepped out of the house, a short, curvy woman with a big smile, and a tall pale man who seemed to hover just in the shadows.

"Ah shit," Celeste muttered, and then she was out of the car, her body shifting even as the gravel crunched under her feet. I raced out of the car after her, and Lincoln looked harried. Brody gave him a tight smile. "I'm going to have to ask you not to draw your weapon in Nîso. We can be easily killed, unlike the vamps. Drawing a gun here will be seen as a sign of aggression and will not be tolerated. I can assure you though, your mate is fine. She just sensed another of her own kind, and overruled Celeste. It happens sometimes when our other halves have strong emotions."

Lincoln dropped his hands to his sides, thrusting them in his pocket, but the way the man watched him for any sign of aggression, ready to pounce, set my teeth on edge. I visibly relaxed my body.

Celeste's snow leopard edged up toward the man, and the woman cooed. "Casper, look at her. Oh my god, she's so beautiful. She makes your snow leopard look like a brute."

The guy, I assumed he must be the infamous Ghost, shot her a frown but said nothing. He shifted, and his snow leopard was far bigger than hers and at least twice the size of a wild snow leopard. He was scarred, long stripes across his fur where claws had ripped at his skin. He made Celeste's snow leopard look almost dainty in comparison.

He leaned forward and sniffed her, a chuffing noise coming from his throat that had her down on her belly, submissive. It was weird to see my fierce Celeste cowering before anyone, and I felt Vincent vibrating beside me, like he wanted to drag her away. I shot a quick look at Linc, who seemed to be handling this better than I thought. It might help that Brody was standing beside him companionably, though I had no doubt that if Linc did something stupid, he'd quickly put him down.

The big snow leopard of Ghost chuffed again, and Celestes floofy tail flicked back and forth. Then she rolled onto her back, her belly slightly bulging, and reached out her paws in his direction.

I swear the snow leopard grinned, as he batted back at her paws.

"Well, that's cute as fuck. I kind of want to shift to a snow leopard and play too," the woman sighed, and Ghost butted his head against her hip, the invitation not needing words. She reached down and scratched his ears. "I'm Annie, by the way, seeing how my cousin has forgotten his manners. It's nice to meet you."

Celeste's ears flicked, and she backed away from Annie. The woman looked horrified that she'd scared Celeste, and Brody laughed.

"My bad, Annie. I told Celeste that you'd kick her ass if she went after Ghost."

Annie's cheeks flushed. "Why would you say that? Ghost isn't my mate, he's free to pursue whoever he damn well likes."

Ghost the snow leopard yowled, and Lincoln growled, and Brody laughed some more. "Don't worry guys, our new friends are all one tight knit unit. They aren't looking to add anymore, I believe?" he asked me, and I just blinked at him.

Celeste gave an annoyed chuff, and I laughed. "I think that's a no."

Annie had her hands on her hips. "For the love of the Ancestors, Brody, you make my life difficult." She looked at Celeste. "Sorry about him. I promise, the only ass I'm going to kick is my dickish cousin's. Us girls have to stick together."

She put out a hand, and Celeste wandered forward, sniffing at her hand. I wonder if she could scent deceit or ill-will or whatever. Finally, Celeste stroked her cheek over Annie's outstretched hand.

Brody shook his head. "Let's go inside and get you settled. You hanging around, Ghost, or you going to shift back at your place?"

The snow leopard tilted his head toward the street, and Brody nodded like he'd spoken. Hell, maybe he had. What did I know about shape shifters. Celeste walked down the steps, scooping up her discarded clothes in her mouth. She was swaying gently on her feet, so I knew the shift had taken something out of her. Lincoln reached down and scooped her into his arms, her snow leopard rubbing her cheek all over his face.

By the time I looked up, Ghost had lived up to his name and disappeared. Annie fussed around, straightening and dusting things as Brody gave us the grand tour. "There's only three bedrooms, but the couch pulls out if you need it. Annie stocked the fridge, but you're free to wander around Nîso. We have a small grocery store, but also some great cafes. There's a group mess hall where we all eat dinner together on Sundays in a big cookout. Raine tries to come up for those with the pups and Tex, her other shifter mate."

He pinned Lincoln with a look. "Like I said, you're free to roam. But this isn't the human world. You're just as likely to walk past a tiger as you are a human. I'd appreciate it if you left your weapons at home, so I don't have to execute you because you were too trigger happy."

He must have read the shock on my face. "This is the supernatural world. We live by a different set of rules and moral code. We take care of each other, and sometimes that's in a more animalistic way than human society."

Lincoln nodded, and I made a mental note to check him for weapons whenever we left the house. "No one here will be a threat to my mate? To my family?"

Brody tilted his head. "This is a community, like any other. There are bad elements, but they are a hidden minority. I can assure you of your safety, but I can't one hundred percent guarantee it. But I'll leave you Ghost as a guide, and we can take down two rabbits with one arrow. He can explain to Celeste all the intricacies of being a snow leopard that she seems to have missed, and he can make sure that you are safe and protected at all times. Don't let his diminutive snow leopard form fool you. Ghost is a predator through and through."

Vincent choked on his tongue. "Diminutive? Did we all see the same big cat?"

Annie chuckled. "He's practically petite. I wouldn't say that to his face though."

She rinsed a rag under the tap and wrung it dry, apparently happy with the cleanliness of the kitchen. "I'll probably be around to help translate for Ghost as well."

"He doesn't speak English?" I asked.

Brody shook his head. "He's mute."

"Physically unable or by choice?"

Annie gave me a weird look. "Physically. It causes him a lot of pain. But that's not really our story to tell."

I frowned but nodded. I wonder if that extended to his snow leopard form. I wondered if I could create a program that would read his brain waves and help him communicate without the need for a translator. I wondered if that was something he was even interested in. I wondered...

I realized Vincent was chuckling softly and everyone was looking at me. "That's the face he makes when he's trying to solve a problem. It usually results in some insane tech that the government snaps up."

Both Brody and Annie looked at me with shrewd eyes. "We'll leave you guys to get settled in. You're welcome here as long as you need. Maybe in a few days, we'll discuss Eden and their academy?"

I nodded and they left with a wave.

I looked around the homely log cabin. Celeste shifted in Lincoln's arms, and he had to juggle to hold a woman where there was once a big cat.

"I'm exhausted. Let's go to bed," she whispered, and it didn't matter who she was talking to, we all wanted a moment to lay with her. To touch her skin and know that she was there. That she was okay.

"Vince, help me get the bed from another room? We'll push them together. I don't think any of us want to be apart from Celeste tonight."

I meant me. Lincoln, Vincent and Celeste had become an easy ménage, and I was worried I was going to get left behind, especially now that she'd mated Lincoln first. Something in my gut burned, maybe jealousy, maybe fear.

I always thought she'd be mine first. Did she not want me the way I craved her?

As if she sensed my doubts, she wiggled from Lincoln's arm and sashayed naked toward me. I could have been seconds from death, and my dick would still get hard at the sight of her. She stepped easily into my arms and wrapped her own around my waist. "Are you okay? You've been quiet. Like really quiet."

I squeezed her tightly. "It's been a pretty unbelievable few weeks. But I'm fine."

"Fine enough to take me to bed?" she murmured and I swallowed hard, leaning down to capture her lips. I kissed them with more tenderness than I wanted at that moment. I wanted to devour her, to mark her as mine the way Lincoln had. Instead, I cherished her lips with soft, sipping kisses.

"Always."

Despite what she'd said to Reese, and that hot as hell kiss, as soon as she'd climbed onto the cloud-like bed in the main bedroom, Star had fallen asleep. We'd let her rest, heading back out to the living room to unload the car and make some sandwiches that we stacked in the fridge. When she still hadn't woken, and the sun had started to dip in the sky, we all climbed in next to her.

The beds pushed together in the room meant that you had to climb on and off the bed, but there was plenty of room for us all. Reese slept on the other side of Star, and Lincoln was wrapped around my back. It was kind of perfect, though it had to be freaking out Reese a little. This whole sharing thing would be odd to him, where it came completely naturally to me and Linc. Like Star was just an extension of our love. A natural progression. A missing piece of the jagged, broken puzzle we'd been.

He hadn't said anything about the fact that Star and Lincoln were now mates, though I'd seen the brief flash of hurt on his face. He was more likely to internalize his feelings than make them feel bad for doing something that had come so naturally. He was a good man like that. Me, not so much.

"What are you frowning about?" Star whispered, and I opened my eyes to see her staring at my face.

"How do you know I wasn't sleeping?"

She leaned forward and kissed me like she couldn't help herself, and I loved it. "Your face is very animated, even with your eyes closed," she teased, the laughter in her voice warming my soul. "What were you thinking about?"

"You're mating with Lincoln."

She bit her lip. "Are you still mad?"

I shook my head, not sure how to describe my feelings. "I was never mad, Star. I could never be mad about something that made you both so happy," I whispered back. "I was scared that there would be no place for me with you."

If I had any lingering doubts, her look of absolute horror, followed by an intensity that made my chest ache, chased them away. "No, Vince. No. You are so important to me. I love you."

I couldn't help it, I gripped her hips and pulled her

closer to me. She was so soft, even with the hard globe of her pregnant stomach, that hit my abs like a gutter stopper.

She huffed. "Sorry, I feel like a beached whale right now. Not very sexy, right?"

"Star, you are the most beautiful creature I've ever seen in my life. You're like the fucking madonna and you make me want to write terrible love ballads." It was all true. Pregnant women mightn't have been my kink, but Star was. Star was my every desire wrapped into one tight little package. I'd take her in whatever shape she came in. From pregnant to old age, where she had saggy tits and smile lines.

I'd love her however I could get her. When she slapped my arm, I realized I'd said that last part out loud.

"Shh, Lincoln is a light sleeper. Wouldn't want to wake him. Needs his rest." I said, waggling my eyebrows, as I slid my hand down her side and beneath the oversized shirt. One of Lincoln's faves.

I slipped my hand between her thighs, and found her wet for me. I growled low in my throat as I stroked my fingers along her center, my fingers finding her clit just so I could feel her buck against me.

When she moaned, I hushed her again. "Don't wake them. They need their beauty sleep," I teased as I slid my finger inside her. Jesus, my dick was hard as a rock. I needed to be inside her so fucking bad, but first she needed to come on my hand. I pushed another finger inside her, feeling her clench against my fingers, my thumb rolled against her clit, and I thanked god I decided to be a guitarist. Yay for finger dexterity.

I curled my fingers, and by the way she was writhing around in strained silence, I was hitting her g-spot. She reached out and gripped my hair, and I groaned as she tugged at it. To reward her, I fluttered my fingers inside her, rapidly tapping that happy spot even as I stroked her clit.

She hissed a noise that sounded a lot like fuck, then she closed her eyes, letting out a heaving breath as she clenched hard around my fingers like a Chinese finger trap.

Damn that was hot as hell. But not as hot as this next part. She curled back toward me and kissed me hard. She backed up all the declarations she'd just made with that kiss. Her tongue thrust against mine, and we warred, devoured like we were starving.

"Vincent," she breathed at me, begging so prettily. I was helpless to deny her anything really. I grabbed her thigh, pulling it over my hip as I lined my steel hard cock with her entrance. I wanted to feel her around me, her wet pussy milking me until I marked her as mine.

I slid into her in one hard thrust and she bit down on her knuckles to keep from making a noise. I grinned wickedly, and pulled back, slamming into her again, and a muffled scream escaped her lips. Yeah, maybe I wanted her to wake the whole world with the beautiful sounds she made.

I set a rhythm, deep and hard, and she rolled her hips with me, until I was the one swearing under my breath. She strained forward and I curled my body over hers, reaching her lips and drinking her down in a kiss so intense, it made my eyes crossed.

"Bite me, Star. Make me yours," I purred. She momentarily stopped the rhythm of her body. "Are you sure? I don't want to rush you."

I could understand her hesitation. I was a playboy. I fucked and forgot. But there was no way in this life or the next, that I could ever forget Star. "I've never been more sure of anything in my entire life."

She curled forward sinuously, the action more feline than human, and pressed a kiss to my chest. "You're mine. Forever," she whispered. I looked down at her, her eyes almost luminous in the darkness as she bit down, the sting of her teeth piercing my flesh making my balls pull up tight and my hips slam into her more violently.

I felt another set of lips against my shoulder. A hand stroked down my spine, and I felt Lincoln's lips near my ear. "You're ours."

His lips moved back toward my shoulder and I felt his teeth bite down hard. He didn't break the skin in the way Celeste had, but the act was still pure possession. His hand slipped between us and I felt his hand grab Celeste's hip, his thumb finding her clit as he held her still and I slammed myself between them.

Soon she was clenching her teeth on my flesh and her pussy around my cock. I was consumed by her. Consumed by them both.

I came with a roar, and Star tore her mouth from my skin to capture my lips with her own bloodied ones. I tasted myself on her lips and it was the most primal, erotic thing I'd ever done.

"I love you forever, Star."

There was movement from the other side of the bed, and Reese rolled from the blankets, not saying anything as he walked out the door, closing it softly behind him.

Star whimpered softly, rolling away as if to chase him. Lincoln put a hand on her arm. "Stay. I'll go."

He kissed my head, and slipped from the bed, pulling on his sweatpants. Star's eyes looked too bright, and I kissed each of her cheekbones.

"It'll be okay, Star. He'll figure out we all have a place in your heart sooner or later, and he'll be ours forever as well."

The baby kicked against my abs, as if he was agreeing. Not going to lie, it was pretty fucking weird. But despite Reese and the fact his baby wanted to kick my ass even in the womb, this moment was completely perfect.

I found Reese sitting out on the steps of the back porch, staring at the stars. The moon was bright tonight, giving me a good view of his tousled blonde hair and bare shoulders. I sat down beside him, wishing I had a beer or something to give to him. I needed something to do with my hands.

"You okay?" I felt like that had been our mantra over these last few months. We hadn't been okay. Hell, we hadn't been okay in years, it just took Celeste arriving to point out the gaping holes in our lives.

Reese sighed, and I could see the torment in his eyes. The guilt. Fucking Reese, he was too good. There was nothing wrong with that. There seemed to be a consensus in society that you had to be cutthroat, to look after yourself because no one would do it for you. That you had to take those gentle, giving parts of yourself and kill them yourself before someone did it for you. Especially if you were a guy.

But not Reese. He was a gentle soul but he was still strong. It was because he was so strong that he could take the burdens of others so easily, without turning into a bitter, cynical asshole.

He shrugged. "I am. I'm fine. It's just…"

"You're worried that you have no place?" I could read my friend like a book. He had no poker face. "It's always been me and Vincent. Now it's me, Vincent and Celeste, and you feel like you're on the outside."

He huffed out a laugh. "I hate it when you do that, you know? Read me like I'm a fucking psychology text-book." He curled his fingers into his sweats. "We haven't reconnected the way you guys have connected. I worry that she doesn't want me in the way I want her. We've fooled around, but she's kept me at arms length. Then she was kidnapped and she's been so ill and…"

"You're worried she keeps you around because you're the baby's father and our best friend. Because we're so loyal to you. Not because she actually wants you." He gave a tight nod, and I shoulder bumped him. "Do you want my opinion?"

"Sure."

"She kept you at arms length because she feels the most connection with you. With Vince and I, it started out as hate fucking. We would be easy to leave; though I really hope that that's not still the case. But with you?

You just have to watch the way she watches you. Her eyes are always so hungry, so fucking yearning when she looks at you. You have always had the ability to make her more vulnerable than Vince and I combined. It scares her, and for someone that was used to running, that usually means fleeing as fast as her fluffy butt can move."

He wasn't looking at me, but his jaw was working as he listened to my words. I wasn't lying; something about Celeste's feelings for Reese were bigger. Not more important than her feelings for us, I was secure in her love for me. I knew it, felt it, with every word and touch. But there was something almost otherworldly about their connection. Karmic maybe.

His shoulders sagged. "You think so?" I nodded. "I can wait. I can wait for it to be perfect. Wait until she has no doubts that I want to cherish her for the rest of my life."

He reached into his pocket and pulled out a ring. The diamond was so big, it glinted in the moonlight. I looked behind his back, in his pocket.

"What are you looking for?"

I grinned. "The bionic arm she's going to need to hold up that boulder on her hand. Holy shit, dude. How long have you had that for?"

"Two months. I was going to convince her before she had the baby that she needed to stay with me. With us. Then the whole thing happened," he nodded at my chest and the bullet wound that still ached there. "And the timing seemed wrong."

I grinned, because I couldn't help myself. This was perfect. "The time has never been better, Brother. Do it. Show her you love her forever."

He stood, a determined set to his chin and I grabbed his arm. "Maybe not right now though. In the middle of the night in bed with us all."

He gave an embarrassed laugh and sat back down. "Yeah, that might not be the most romantic gesture." The soft smile was back on his face and something loosened in my chest. I didn't want to have to choose between Reese and Celeste. Reese had saved me and I owed him everything. But Celeste? She was my everything. I couldn't have given her up if I tried now, not for Reese and maybe not even for Vincent. That made me feel disloyal as fuck to the man who I had shared my body with for years. I prayed to a god I didn't believe in that it would never come to that. That we would always be together, even if it wasn't always smooth sailing. Because a life without either of them caused an ache in my chest at just the thought.

We sat in silence for a little longer, and he stuffed the ring back into his pocket. I shuddered to think how much that rock was worth. "Do you think the big guy, Ghost, is related to her?"

I shrugged. Was there a way to tell? A shifter DNA test of some kind? Did it even really matter? "There can't be that many snow leopard shifters in North America, so maybe?"

As if we summoned him with our conversation, the huge snow leopard stepped from the darkness like his name. Invisible until he wanted to be seen. A ghost. He stopped beside something that looked a little like a post box, but when he shifted and reached inside, I realized it was like a clothing drop box. That made sense in a town of people who lost their clothes frequently, though he didn't seem overly perturbed about his nudity.

I noticed that the huge scars that had been on his shifted form were also on big, raised stripes along his back in human form too. There seemed to be a lot of others too, from round puckered scars to even, controlled slices. I'd spend enough time on the streets to know what that meant. He'd been tortured.

Ghost slid on the pants and wandered over to us. He didn't say anything, because he was mute obviously, and I wasn't sure how we were all meant to communicate.

"Do you know if she's your cousin or sibling or something?" I mean, if her father had been particularly careless, it was possible.

Ghost shook his head and shrugged. Okay, so it wasn't something they just knew. He frowned, a look of frustration crossing his face, until Reese grinned. "I've got an idea. Here, type what you want to say here.

Then press that little button and it'll read it out for you." Reese hesitated. "I'm not sure what Brody told you, but I'm in tech. I know there's equipment out there that can help you speak, and I could try and modify it so it can speak for you using your brainwaves. Or I can try at least. If that's something you want. Maybe you like that strong, silent thing. Lincoln certainly does," Reese teased and I snorted rudely.

Ghost stared down at him, his brows pulled together in a frown. Then he typed on Reese's phone.

"I'd like that," the robotic voice replied. Except it was a woman with a slight British accent, and that made the side of his mouth curl in a grin. It was completely ridiculous. Still, he continued to type. "I don't know if we are related, there's rituals to find out. But it doesn't matter. We are both snow leopards and that makes us kin." He looked at us both, and his face went hard. "That means if you hurt her or her cub, I will skin your flesh from your fucking bones," the robotic woman replied with her sunny inflection, and I didn't know whether to laugh or shit myself.

Reese laughed, and then slapped a hand over his mouth. "I'll fix that for the prototype, I swear." He stood up, so he was eye to eye with Ghost. "I would never hurt Celeste or our child. I'd die first. You don't ever have to worry that we will do anything but cherish them both for the rest of their days." He hesitated slightly, and then went on. "But I understand from talking to Brody, that you guys are a lot longer lived than the average human. That means we will die long before Celeste, god willing. And then I hope you remember the oath you just made, and protect them when we can't." He softened his words with a smile, but his eyes were fierce. "Excuse me, but I want to go and wrap my body around my soon-to-be mate. See you in the morning, Ghost." With that, he strolled inside, and I remember how fierce his goodness could be. Because he could kill you with kindness, and you'd go down with a smile on your face.

Over the next few days we settled into a routine. Every morning at ten, Ghost and Annie would turn up and take us out to see Nîso. I'd shift into my snow leopard form and I'd explore the wildness of the town, and honestly, it was the greatest feeling to be able to be free. No one even blinked an eye at our group as we walked by. No, that was a lie. They did stare; at the guys. Humans were far more of an anomaly in this town than another snow leopard just strolling around.

It was like an alternate universe and I never wanted to leave. Ghost wasn't a big talker, and not just for the obvious reasons. Annie would translate for him when he signed, but she did most of the talking. I totally got what the Alpha Brody was talking about now, it was so freaking obvious that they were mates. I didn't know what was holding them back, and honestly I had enough of my own relationship drama to last me a lifetime.

I looked over at Reese, who was laughing at something Vincent was saying. We hadn't spoken about the other night, or my mating with Vincent, but he didn't seem mad anymore. He still held me and kissed me; there were no repercussions. No silent treatment. None of the anger or jealousy another man might have had in that situation.

Reese wasn't another man. He was one of a kind. But still, I was a little worried that he was bottling it up inside and one day he was just going to explode. Maybe he'd be one of those people, that when he commits a mass murder, all his neighbors would say "I just can't imagine it. He was such a nice man, he always mowed his lawn on Saturdays."

He threw his head back and laughed, and I felt my own lips twitch at the sound of his happiness. Okay, maybe he wasn't that close to a mental snap. Still, I wanted to sort this stuff out with him soon.

My snow leopard huffed her agreement inside my head. She hated that we hadn't made him our mate yet. He was the first one she wanted, the reason why we couldn't stay away. He was our mate, the connection so deep that I wondered if he wasn't part shifter way back in the beginning. But he'd exhibited no other traits except knocking me up when I wasn't all the way in heat, and this pull in my chest to make him mine.

As if he felt me watching him, he looked over his shoulder at me. The love in his eyes was a punch in the chest. He drifted back to walk alongside me. "Are you feeling okay?"

He wrapped an arm around my shoulders, and I snuggled into his side. "I'm really happy here. This place..."

"It's shifter paradise. I understand."

We were walking toward the Sunday cookout that Brody had mentioned earlier in the week, where all the members of Nîso came together for a massive community barbecue for dinner with the rest of the pack. Brilliant idea, but we'd yet to be in a large mass of the town's occupants.

I was a little nervous. I could see them all gathered in a large clearing, kids running around, the steady hum of voices coloring the evening air.

I spotted Brody, his Alpha power like a beacon. He had his arm wrapped around Raine's waist, and a group of kids played close by. I spotted an all white head of an omega pup, and raised my eyebrows in surprise. Annie noticed, and she smiled fondly.

"Thats Enit. She's one of Alpha and Raine's kids. They're wolf shifters."

The shapeshifter and the vampire had wolf pup children? There was a story there for sure.

A hush went over the clearing as we stepped in, and I tried not to feel awkward. The socially awkward part of me wanted to hide, but I remembered it wasn't me that they were gawking at. It was my mates. So I stood tall, lacing my fingers with Reese, comforted by the feel of Vincent and Lincoln at my back. I didn't care how... unusual three human mates were, they were mine and I would fight for them.

A low growl rumbled in my chest, and Ghost cast me a wary look. "You think this reception is weird? You should have seen it when Brody brought home a vampire as a prospective mate," Annie whispered conspiratorially. "It did not go well."

We walked toward Brody and I dropped my eyes in deference, turning my head to the left to bare my throat. "Alpha." I looked briefly at Raine, and did the same throat baring thing, though maybe that had different connotations for vampires? Up until the other day, I'd never met a vamp, so I was going in blind. "Alphamate."

"It's good to see you and your mates again," she said, reaching out and dragging me into a hug. It felt oddly nice, even if her skin did run slightly cooler than normal. She stepped back and smiled at the guys, and I watched her for any sign she might leap on them and tear out their throats. She seemed in total control though. Her gaze drifted back to me. "Have you enjoyed Nîso? Has Ghost been a welcoming host?"

Annie snorted, and Raine smiled. Ghost gave the Alphamate the finger, and my mouth fell open. I didn't know much about Pack dynamics, but I didn't think you were meant to disrespect the Alphamate. I waited for Raine or Brody to put Ghost in his place, but they both just laughed.

"Ghost has been wonderful. It's been nice having another snow leopard around. I didn't realize how much mine wanted the company of her own kind. Annie has been a gem too. Thank you all," I said, and my eyes got big and watery. Fucking hormones.

Reese's arm went around my shoulders again, and he kissed my forehead. "Let's get you some food before you cry, Star," Vincent said from behind me. "She gets hangry. But like not angry, just sad. Sadgry?"

Raine laughed. "Oh girl, we've all been there. Go, enjoy the barbecue. No one knows how to do barbecue like a bunch of carnivorous shapeshifters."

I waved goodbye to them and wandered away. There were faint whispers on the wind as we walked past, exclamations of shock about my mates.

"So fucking disgusting. Vampires are bad enough, but humans? Muddying the gene pool until we are all bred out. That's what will happen," someone hissed, and I spun on my heel, looking for whoever had spoken. But there were just too many people.

Ghost cast his eye over the crowd too, his face a hard mask. He was scary as fuck. There, I admitted it.

But he seemed softer when he was around me, so I think he liked me.

"What's wrong?" Lincoln asked softly at my back, and I could tell by the frustration in his voice that he wished he'd brought his gun. I was more than glad that Reese had managed to convince him to leave it at home.

I spun around, grabbed his shirt and pulled him in for a kiss. I kissed him with all the passion I felt for him, every ounce of love. I was creating a spectacle, but I didn't care. When I pulled away, he blinked down at me kind of dazed. "It's nothing, Linc. Closed minded bigots come in all species apparently."

Annie reached out for a high five, and I gave her one.

The rest of the night went smoother, but I was always on the lookout for those comments. I wanted to say they were the only ones, but it would be a lie. There was a steady stream of those offhand comments through the pack, and it saddened me.

Reese was wrong. This wasn't shifter paradise, though it was pretty close. Real paradise would be where I could be with my mates without them being stared at, our actions judged. It was sad, because I liked 99% of the people I'd met here.

I generally had fun, as did Vincent, who began talking music with one of Raine's other mates. A blind snake shifter with the very rock and roll name of Tex.

He'd fanboyed a little when he realized who Vincent was, and it had Raine laugh hysterically. He was sweet, and although his eyes were unseeing, his body seemed to follow his mate around the clearing, like he was so in tune with her he knew where she was at all times. Maybe he did. I was a little sad that I would never get to experience that true, soul deep shifter mating, but not sad enough to give up the men I loved. I would give up the world for them.

My body grew more and more tired as the night wore on, until I could barely lift my arms. I didn't want to be rude or seem weak, so I kept pushing it. Stupid. Reese watched me, and when he realized I wasn't going to call it a night, he did it for me.

"It's time to go, baby," he whispered in my hair, and I sighed with relief. I didn't like the idea of hiking it all the way back to the house, but I would.

Reese noticed my wobbling legs, so he leaned down and kissed me, sliding his hands under my ass until he could lift me into his arms.

"I'll carry you home, let them think it's because I'm taking you home to ravish you," he whispered in my ear, and I fell in love with him a bit more.

I kissed him back. "I think that's exactly what you should do."

His smile lit up his face until he was so fucking beautiful, I don't know how I managed to breathe.

Annie shook her head. "Ghost will walk you

home." The big, pale shifter nodded decisively. I'd take his protection. I wrapped my legs around Reese's body and held on tight as he strode out of the clearing like I weighed nothing.

Beneath that good guy, tech nerd exterior, Reese was ripped. It kind of made my mouth water thinking about it.

Yeah, we definitely needed to make good on the ravishing. I tucked my face in his neck so he could see where he was walking. "You seemed tense most of the night. What's wrong?" he whispered as we slowly walked back up the hill to the house.

I hesitated, but I didn't want to lie to Reese. "There's a little bit of... bigotry about the fact I am mated to three humans."

I felt him jerk in surprise. "Seriously?"

I didn't answer, just nodded against his neck. We walked in silence until we got back to the house, and Reese placed me down on wobbly legs. He caught my hand before I could walk into the house. He looked over his shoulder at Lincoln, who nodded softly, and then randomly at Ghost, who lifted his chin but didn't move.

What the fuck?

Reese dropped to one knee, and my heart dropped with him. He reached into his pocket.

"I don't know if this is the right time, or if there ever would be a right time, but Celeste, I love you so much my soul both aches and sings. I love you so much that I can't imagine my life without you in it. Will you do me the honor of being my wife?"

My eyes locked onto his green ones, and I couldn't drag them away. Not to look at the other guys to judge their reactions. Not to look to see if Ghost was still here, witnessing this moment. I was caught in the moment with Reese, frozen in time.

She was silent and I felt my soul dying one second at a time. Holy shit, what if she said no? Only in the darkest of nights had I contemplated the idea that perhaps she didn't feel for me the same consuming love that I felt for her, but that couldn't be true. I know love when I see it.

She just continued to stare, and I couldn't look away. As if the moment would disappear if I broke my gaze first.

"Yes. Reese, yes. I want to be your wife, your mate, the mother of your cub. I want to be your everything," she whispered, and my heart stuttered back to life and my breath whooshed out of my burning lungs. Happiness filled all my limbs and I whooped as I got to my feet, indelicately sliding the ring on her finger with shaking hands. I whooped, twirling her around in my arms.

I looked at Vincent, who was grinning widely, and Lincoln, who was looking at our girl with so much love. I could relate to the feeling. I knew it intimately.

Placing her back on her feet, I leaned forward and kissed her. It was a kiss filled with promises of a future so perfect she couldn't help but be happy. She kissed me back with so much heat, my toes curled in my shoes. Her tongue stroked mine, and she tangled my hair in her fingers, holding my face to hers as she plundered. She didn't have to worry, I wasn't going anywhere for the rest of my life.

"I love you, Reese. Now take me to bed so I can claim you as mine forever too."

She didn't have to tell me twice. I lifted her into my arms and kicked through the front door, giving her short, sipping kisses. I kissed her possessively, marking her lips as mine. And her cheeks. And her throat.

She grabbed my hair again and pulled my face away. "Bed, Buttercup. I need you inside me now," she panted, and I groaned as I ground my dick against her once more.

I picked her up, nearly sprinting to the bedroom. I placed her gently on the bed, and started unwrapping her from her clothes as quickly as humanly possible.

When she was naked before me, her belly swollen

with my child, her eyes hooded in pleasure I'd given her, my knees nearly turned to jello.

"Fuck, Celeste, you are the greatest gift fate has ever given me," I said, falling to my knees at the edge of the bed and pulling her toward the edge so I could bury my face in her sweet pussy. I ate her like she was my last damn meal. I lapped and suckled, twisting my tongue this way and that until she was writhing against my face. Her fingers gripped the sheets, as she came on a scream, her juices soaking my cheeks.

She was panting, but her eyes were wild. She was closer to her more primal nature than normal, and I was dying to meet it with my own primal needs. I loved all of Celeste. I stripped quickly out of my clothes, and she grabbed at my arms as soon as I was in arms length. "Please, Reese," she begged, and I was completely undone. I slid between her thighs, lining myself up with her entrance and slamming myself inside her. This wasn't gentle lovemaking. This was a frenzied coupling that was more animalistic than sweet.

She gripped my shoulders and pulled me close. "Will you be my mate?"

I curled forward, kissing her with all the love in my soul. "I'm yours, heart and soul."

She kissed me back, then turned her head and bit me hard on the shoulder. Something settled inside me, some awareness that hadn't been there before.

Something that felt like Celeste. On the heels of that sensation was pleasure I hadn't ever known, all gift wrapped in pain. I gripped her thigh, spreading her wider as I thrust with a wildness I didn't know I possessed.

She moaned around her bite, her teeth still gripping my flesh, and the pain combined with pleasure was making my orgasm barrel toward me like a freight train. I reached between us clumsily, finding her clit with my thumb and pinching it lightly.

Her body convulsed and her teeth released my shoulder so she could scream her orgasm so loudly that I was pretty sure they heard it down at the barbecue. Her pussy felt like a vice around my dick and I came roaring after her.

I slid from her and collapsed at her side so I didn't hurt her. "I fucking love you so much," I whispered against her damp hair. She looked at me with hooded eyes, her mouth still a little bloody from her bite.

"You're mine forever, Buttercup. I love you too."

Exhaustion took her quickly, but that was okay. I was exactly where I wanted to be forevermore.

CELESTE WAS COMPLETELY EXHAUSTED, and I left her curled up in bed. I bounced out of the bedroom, the grin on my face so wide it was beginning to hurt my cheeks. Lincoln and Vincent were sitting on the couch, their heads together as they spoke softly, beers clenched in their hands.

When they heard me come in, Vincent was on his feet and his arms wrapped around my shoulders faster than my eyes could follow. "Congrats, man. I'm so fucking happy for you. For us all."

I hugged him back, because technically I hadn't clued him in on the plan, unless Lincoln had. But judging by his shocked excitement, I doubted it.

"You're not mad?"

Vincent reared back. "What? Fuck no. This feels so fucking right, don't you think? I mean, what do me and Lincoln know about what it takes to make a wife happy? Not a damn thing. But you are the perfect husband for her."

I stepped back so I could look at his face properly. "I might be legally her spouse, but we are all her husbands. The ring makes no difference to me. We are all in this together. Family."

Vincent smiled, his eyes a little shiny. "See? Perfect husband material. You always say the right shit."

I laughed and thumped his shoulder. "She's asleep. I'm just going down to see Brody about the academy proposed by Eden."

"I'll come with you." Lincoln stood, walking toward the door and I put a hand on his arm. "Stay. Watch our girl, I'll be back soon. Ghost is probably still hanging around."

As if I'd summoned him, which was pretty weird if I thought about it for too long, there was a knock on the door and I opened it to find Ghost.

I didn't know him well enough to tease him about it. So I gave him a big smile and waved at the guys.

I found Ghost's presence kind of soothing, which was probably the exact opposite of what I should feel. I mean, he'd never been overly aggressive, but he had a menace about him that had nothing to do with the fact he turned into a big cat. It was his eyes I think; they were completely blank, except when he looked at Annie or Brody.

We walked in silence, and I appreciated the moment. It was dark now, and the stars up here... they were something else. I could stop and stare at them for hours like a college kid on their first high. But I dragged my eyes away as we got closer to a well lit house. When I noticed Brody's car out the front, I realized it was the Alpha's residence. It was weird to think of people in concepts of alphas and omegas.

I got to the door, and Ghost stopped. "You're not coming in?"

Ghost screwed up his nose and shook his head. "Not a fan of talking business?"

He faked a gag and I couldn't hold in my laugh. There was laughter coming from inside, and I knocked loudly.

The door swung open before I could even pull my

fist back to knock again. Raine was there, smiling happily.

"Reese! Come in. The pups are just heading to bed, dammit." They ran around the living room in circles and I smiled at their happy squeals. Would my baby be like this? An energetic ball of chaos?

Brody smiled as I walked in, throwing me a beer that I barely caught. "Hey Reese." He looked at the pups, still tearing around. "Stop!" They all halted like they'd been caught in quicksand. "Brush your teeth then head to bed." His voice was firm, the thread of authority in it unmistakable. Almost as one, the kids huffed and he grinned at them. "Love you guys."

The little pale blond one laughed, barrelling through the room and into his arms to give him a sloppy kiss on the cheek. She wriggled back out of his arms and over to Tex. The kid looked like he was sixteen, he had a baby face for sure, but he was covered in tattoos and Raine looked at him like he was the most perfect being on earth.

Probably the same way I looked at Celeste.

The other two kids walked over for hugs goodnight from Brody, but they didn't have the infectious enthusiasm of the littlest one. Tex herded them away along with Raine, and it was just me and Brody left in the living room. I cracked my beer and raised it in a toast.

"How are you settling in?"

"Celeste has really loved it here."

"That's not really what I asked."

I hesitated, not knowing how to bring up the looks, the whispered comments about Celeste's choices in mates, the outright bigotry today at the barbecue, without sounding condemning. So I went with honesty. "I think this place is amazing, and what you've created here is something so, so special."

Brody lifted an eyebrow. "Why do I sense a butt?"

I bit my bottom lip. "There seems to be some people who are less than impressed with the fact Celeste has chosen human mates. There's been... comments. I know they upset Celeste. It doesn't faze me or the guys outside of that. Lincoln and Vincent are used to it, with Vincent being openly bisexual in the spotlight of the music industry and Lincoln? Lincoln just honestly doesn't give a fuck." I shrugged. "Other people's opinions have never bothered me, but I think that Celeste was beginning to believe this was some kind of utopia, and it just brought her back down to reality."

I braced myself for his anger, but he just shook his head sadly. "Ghost said as much, but I hoped your human senses had meant you were reasonably impervious to the peanut gallery." He took a long swig of his beer. "There are factions in my town that believe in shapeshifter purity. Ghost is used to bearing the brunt of it for most of his life, being the only two-natured in a town full of shapeshifters. Our heritage and history are quite different. But people eventually came to accept him." He looked up, and I noticed Raine was standing in the hall, leaning her shoulder on the door jamb. "When I introduced Raine as my mate, there were incidents. But I made my position as Alpha, and the position of this Pack, that I will not take that kind of secular attitude. But old attitudes are hard to beat out of people. Tex and Raine try. The pups have helped too, in their own way.

"We are a long-lived race. The old ones remember the time where we didn't mix our bloodlines with anyone other than those in Nîso and the greater North American Shapeshifter packs. To maintain racial purity. I don't hold to that bullshit. The younger generations don't have the same bigotry as the old generations, or the more radical factions." He sighed and he looked world weary. "At least I hope not. Sometimes they are easily radicalized."

I couldn't have done his job. It was bad enough running a business, but at least if I fired someone for their conduct, that was just it. But if Brody made the decision to eject someone from the pack, that person was losing their home, their family, their history. That was a big burden to carry.

"You guys might be supernatural, but you're still people at least half the time too. The beauty of humanity is that we are all individual and all have the ability to think for ourselves. Unfortunately, that means sometimes people are just too fucking stupid for life, but you have to manage the good with the bad." I gave him a reassuring smile. "You're doing a good job here, Alpha. I'm sorry it's tough, though."

Raine came over and sat beside him on the couch, and he turned his face into her neck. It was so like what Celeste did, that it made me ache for her a little. Maybe I should wrap this up already so I could go home to my fiancée.

A stupid grin crossed my face at the word. I probably looked like I had a mental break, but I didn't care.

I took a swig of my beer to get my giddy happiness back under control. "About the Academy. I thought we'd discuss some of the logistics." I hesitated. "Do you think we can trust them?" Somewhere in the last three months, my ability to see the good in everyone had taken a beating. My trust didn't come as easily as it once did.

Brody tapped the lip of his beer bottle against his bottom lip. "I think so. The members of Eden I had met seemed pretty genuine. And one of Raine's other mates has the ability to compel the truth."

I swallowed hard, because that was scary as fuck. But also, how many mates did Raine have? I didn't ask but the question must have been written on my face.

"Seven, like the dwarves or days of the week. The Deadly Sins. All the fun shit comes in sevens," she said happily. "Celeste has room for a few more if she gets sick of you guys."

I felt my face crease into a frown, and she laughed. "Don't worry, Reese. She seems pretty damn smitten with you all."

The goofy grin was back dammit. Brody saved me from answering by picking up the thread of our previous conversation. "I'm happy to lend my support. I have found them a tract of land that adjoins ours, on the Dark River side of the Packlands. They should be safe enough between us. What have they offered you for your support?"

I hesitated, but went with honesty again. "A place on the grounds where Celeste and the baby can be safe. I'll buy the land, fund the construction of the academy or refuge or whatever the hell they are making out here. The baby will go to school there, hopefully, and I can rest easy knowing that my family is safe." I paused as I thought out my next words. "They didn't seem to have a problem with us being human."

Raine shrugged. "I asked around. They seem to be an odd collection of different preternatural beings. Humans, lycanthropes, shifters. It makes sense they would welcome you. They don't have the racial purification views of some of the traditionalists in Nîso."

We spent a few hours talking about how to best create an environment that was one with the surrounding nature, while still maintaining a school feel in case any human authorities came sniffing around. I respected what they'd created here in Nîso, how the whole place seemed to work alongside the wilderness around it.

By the time I left Brody's house, the wildlife was a cacophony as I stepped out into the night. I started the short stroll back to the house we were using, but I couldn't see Ghost. It was late, maybe he'd gone home for the night.

Despite Brody's words, I wasn't worried. It was one thing to go from snide comments to violence. I stuffed my hands inside my pockets, the winter air a cold kiss along my skin. I didn't have any right to be this happy, this elated, having given up my entire life back home. I should feel guilty or something, but I felt none of that. I had a purpose, a life outside the four walls of my office.

I heard the low crunch of steps on gravel behind me and my shoulders tensed until I forced them to relax. I listened closer as the steps were timed with mine, and I resisted the urge to run. It was probably just Ghost making sure I got home. I gradually picked up my pace, and when a dark figure began to walk down the road in front of me, I tensed again. Fuck, was I being surrounded?

But I knew the swaggering gate of the shadow

coming toward me, and when I recognized Lincoln, I almost collapsed with relief.

He was lit by the low street lights, and he looked as relieved to see me as I was to see him. "I was beginning to worry."

"Just stayed late talking to the Alpha. I told him I'd call him when I got home safely," I said loudly. A blatant lie, but hopefully enough to deter whatever was stalking me out there, unless it was a real wild animal and not a disgruntled shifter.

Lincoln had known me a long time, knew my tells, and he frowned harder. "Fair enough. Let's go." But I noticed his hand creep to his hip where his gun sat. We talked softly about nothing in particular as we walked home, and when we reached the house, I took the stairs two at a time, and slammed the door closed, breathing heavily.

I loved Nîso, but we needed to get this academy underway, as soon as possible. I pulled my phone out.

When the person at the other end of the line answered, I swallowed hard. Here went nothing. "Locke? It's Reese Townsend. Let's do this."

How fast could cold hard cash push through the purchase of a chunk of forest and build a house big enough for four adults and a nursery?

The answer was 47 days and 3 hours.

I helped Celeste pack the last of her things into a suitcase, and looked around this house that had been our home for the last month and a half. We'd created some serious memories here already, but if we were going to make anymore, I wanted them to be in our own home. Reese hadn't let us out to see the house, said it was his surprise for the family, and he was so giddy with excitement, I let it go.

He'd come back spooked one night, calling up Eden then and there, and getting to work. They'd given him all the details he needed, where they wanted the land, how big it needed to be, and then they'd left the rest up to him. He'd run it through a bunch of offshore companies set up to look like logging corporations, and then through a few more shell companies, before it got to him. He was happy the ownership was all but untraceable, and the guy was super fucking smart, so I was inclined to take his word for it.

Celeste was seriously damn pregnant now, and while she felt stronger, the poison all but gone from her system, the pregnancy made her tired.

She looked like she was carrying a small football team. "Girl, you look huge today."

The look she turned on me said she was going to wear my testicles as earrings, and I laughed as I covered my balls. "It's like you want to die?" she said lightly, but I wasn't sure she was joking.

I wrapped an arm around her. "I didn't say it was a bad thing. I like 'em chunky." She growled and I back tracked hard. "I mean it, Star. You're-"

"If you're about to say blooming, stop and think if you value your balls."

"I was going to say utterly gorgeous. Every day I think there's no way you can get more beautiful to me, and every day you prove me wrong."

She relaxed into my arms and sniffed, and I felt her tears against my shoulders. That was another thing. She seemed to cry a lot now. "Good save," she muttered against my chest.

I stroked my cheek against hers in a way that I knew that both Star and her snow leopard liked, and she purred. "You know, there's time for you to bend me over that chair and fuck me before we have to go."

Yeah, the whole pregnancy thing made her horny as hell too. I liked that part much better than the tears.

As if he could hear her words, Lincoln called from the other room. "Are you guys ready?"

Star huffed, and I leaned down to press a quick kiss to her lips. "Later I'll bury my face between your thighs and make you scream my name, okay?"

She crossed her arms over her chest and pouted. I hefted her bag and walked it out to the living room, and Lincoln came over to grab the rest of Star's stuff. Reese was basically bouncing with excitement.

He grabbed her up in his arms and kissed her. "Are you excited, baby? This is it. You're going to love it."

She smiled, because who couldn't in the face of his damn joy. He hustled us out to the car, and Brody, Ghost and Annie were there to see us off. Celeste hugged them all, and Ghost looked down at her with a soft expression. They'd definitely become close, and they decided that when Miranda was down, they'd do a magic DNA test. I don't think it mattered to either of them, but they were both without biological families, so it would be nice.

Brody shook my hand. "If you guys need us, we are just on the other side of the ward. You guys have free passes, so you can crossover whenever, and it will stop most supernaturals and all Vampires that aren't preapproved. Miranda will be down at the end of the week to do the ward on the academy grounds. I think she'll bring her coven, as it's quite a big space."

Reese was nodding, shaking everyone's hands.

"You guys will have to come and see the place. You're always welcome."

Honestly though, we were moving twenty minutes away, not to a different state. But it felt big, so I got the sentiment.

Finally, we all loaded into the SUV and left Nîso for the first time in over a month. I sat with Star on my lap, and I soaked in her warmth. Soon we were out of Nîso's limits, and I snuggled into her neck. Lincoln looked over his shoulder.

"Put Celeste in her own seat, with a belt."

I sighed and strapped her in, missing her warmth already.

Celeste screamed, and I turned in time to see our car plow into a black truck that came from nowhere. I slammed forward, feeling something snap in my chest and my head hit the passenger seat in front of me as the car flipped end over end before ending up on its roof.

The last thought I had before everything went black was that maybe Linc had a touch of the oracle too.

. . .

I came around to the sound of gunshots. No. Not again. I struggled against the seatbelt. "Star!" My vision was patchy as I flailed around upside down, trying to find the buckle. "Linc!"

Reese looked over at me from the driver's seat, the puffy balloon of the airbag suffocating him. "It's okay, Vince. She's there." I looked over, and Celeste had shifted into a snow leopard on the roof of the car, having slipped the seatbelt.

I breathed a sigh of relief. "Thank fuck. Are you okay? The baby?" She purred, licking at the blood on my face. That was why my vision was fucked, there was blood pooling in my eyes. More gunshots sounded, and Lincoln swore.

Blood was pouring from his nose, and it looked broken. "They've got us pinned down," he shouted, and I covered Star with my body. "You guys have to make a run for it. I'll cover you for as long as I can."

Celeste snarled. "No way. I'm not leaving you here, Linc. Don't ask me to," I said, wanting to drag him across the seats and out the back with us.

He looked over his shoulder, firing wildly. "You have to think of the baby. Get her out of here, Vince. Protect our mate."

My heart was tearing out of my chest. I'm sure that's what this feeling was. "No..."

"Yes! Now go before I run out of ammo."

I hesitated too long, and I heard the click of Lincoln's empty clip. "Fuck, fuck go!"

He was pushing Reese between the seats, but Reese was frozen.

"Look!"

I looked around Lincoln's head, but what I saw didn't compute. My mind rebelled. A monster was in the middle of the road between the bounty hunters and the SUV. It was vaguely canine looking, but it stood on two legs, its body weirdly elongated. It looked like a horror movie werewolf.

Lincoln shook himself from his shock first. "Go!" I shifted my ass into gear, kicking open my door and dragging Star through it. Then I dragged Reese out and Linc came tumbling out last. "To the woods!" I began to sprint, Celeste's snow leopard fast despite being heavily pregnant. There were more gunshots, and I ducked low as I tore through the undergrowth, the heavy footfalls of Reese and Lincoln right behind me.

I wasn't sure how long we ran for, but eventually Celeste's legs wobbled and she went down with a pained yowl.

I fell to my knees beside her. "It's okay, baby. We're safe here," I whispered, looking over at Lincoln to make sure I wasn't lying.

"We can rest here." Reese collapsed beside us, dragging Celeste into his arms. Lincoln watched the edge of the treeline, and the gunshots turned into screams.

I stared at him with wide eyes, and he looked pale. What the fuck was going on out there?

"Reese?" A voice called. "Reese, are you out there? It's Locke!" We all hesitated. Was it really Locke? "Someone called Brut called, said we had to be out here in the middle of fucking nowhere Canada, at exactly 10:33. It was too fucking specific to pass up?"

Celeste shifted back, and let out a shuddering sigh of relief. Reese pulled off his sweater and gave it to her as we all stood and began our careful path back to the road.

Two figures stood in the middle of the road, and the monster was nowhere to be seen. We paused.

"Is that Locke?" Lincoln whispered to Reese, and he narrowed his eyes. Then his shoulders sagged.

"Yes."

We were safe. I was sending Brut a fucking bottle of whiskey and new crystal ball. We owed that big fucker our lives.

Ten minutes later, Locke had rolled our car off the road and into the trees... single handedly. Apparently the dude had some serious super strength, on top of his pretty boy looks. And boy, he really was fucking beautiful.

We all piled into their Tesla, Celeste on my lap, and drove the rest of the way to the house. Reese was on the phone to Brody and Ghost, and I could hear Brody cursing from the other side of the car. They'd send out a replacement SUV and someone to get all our shit from our now destroyed vehicle.

I knew we'd reached the right place, because there, in the middle of absolutely nowhere, was a huge fence and a set of wrought iron gates. Reese clicked a button, and the gates swung open.

The other guy, the big quiet one that I was pretty sure turned into a werewolf whose name was actually Micah, looked into the rearview vision mirror.

"Welcome home, guys. Welcome to Eden."

ABOUT THE AUTHOR

Grace McGinty is eclectic. She has worked as a choco-latier, a librarian, a forensic accountant and finally a writer. Like her professional career, the genres she writes are also eclectic. She writes romance, reverse harem romance, fantasy, contemporary young adult and new adult books.

She lives in rural Australia with her crazy family, an entire menagerie of pets, and will one day be crushed by her giant piles of books that litter every room.

Head over to www.gracemcginty.com and join my mailing list for sneak previews into what I am working on and to stay up-to-date with new releases and giveaways!

Want to know more about Eden? Learn about the members and its creation in HEART OF THE HOUNDED! Preorder it here: www.books2read.com/Heartoth

Turn the page for a sneak peek at HEART OF THE HOUNDED...

THE HEART OF THE HOUNDED

AN EDEN ACADEMY PREQUEL

CHAPTER ONE

I sighed, thinking that if I had to endure one more stare of pity than I might go fucking insane. A small, slightly hysterical voice in my head decided that it would be deliciously ironic, considering the pitying looks of my fellow townspeople were due to the death of my mother two weeks ago from a degenerative brain disease, which had gradually sent her crazy. In the end stages, she'd been barely coherent, screaming for hours in gibberish, or having moments of complete lucidity and calmly talking about conspiracy theories, my biological father, and, most painfully, about me. She would follow these episodes with weeks of not speaking at all, just sitting there mutely staring out the window of the tiny cabin we shared in the mountains of Minnesota.

The tulle of my fluro pink tutu scraped at my forearms, and it bobbed slightly as I strode down the main street, the buckles on my biker boots clinking with each step. While I got the odd side-eye, I'd desensitized this town to my 'craziness' enough that no one even commented anymore.

I never enjoyed coming into town and tried to do so as little as possible, but when I did, I liked to live up to the reputation I had fostered. They already assumed I was crazy, due to my mother's mental illness, which had to be hereditary right? Uh, no Rita, you judgemental old heffer, not necessarily.

So, at some point in my life, I realized I had two choices. One, to watch everything I said and did, so the gossips wouldn't twist every word to fit their insane narrative. Or I could embrace it completely, becoming everything they thought I'd be and more. Honestly, it was kind of freeing to live in a way where you didn't give a single fuck about what people thought of you. Want to wear a ballgown to go grocery shopping? Do it. Want to lie on the grass in the middle of town for three hours so you can appreciate the sky? Hell yeah. Want to go out on Friday night, dressed like a Joan Jett wannabe and dance by yourself in the middle of the dance floor like no one was watching? Fucking go for it.

But still, just being around these people was kind of hard work. This time I waited until I was eating canned beans for dinner before I resigned myself to a shopping trip into town.

It was worse this time, of course, because I was getting much more attention due to the fact that my mother's funeral had been the previous Friday, after which I had skipped the wake and headed straight out of town, ready to lick my wounds in private. The abandonment of proper funeral protocol had resulted in more than a few disapproving looks and clucking tongues from the older citizens of Roseau today, which was actually a refreshing break from the pity or condescending looks.

The line at the post office was way too long, and I held in a groan. Gloria was the only teller, and she had to get every person's life story for the gossip files before she could move on to the next customer.

The door behind me opened again, the cold autumn air chilling the back of my thighs. I probably should have doubled my tights.

A throat cleared, and Gregory Staynes from the bank stood behind me in the line. His eyes drifted up from where they were checking out my legs. Damn pervert. "Layla."

"Mornin' Mr. Staynes," I sing-songed in my best dazed and confused voice.

"You missed your mortgage payment. It was due

last Friday." Yeah, last Friday, the day of my mother's funeral, you piece of poo paper.

I gave him a wide-eyed look. "Did I? My house elf usually takes care to remind me of those, and she said we were paid up til next month," I exclaimed in a slightly higher pitched voice, and Shit Staynes winced a little. "I'll be right over to pay it after here, Sir. And I'll have a good hard talk with Glinda. What's the point of having a house elf if she can't keep up with the mortgage payments, am I right?"

Gregory Staynes' lip curled in something between pity and disgust, like craziness could be contagious. What a fucking imbecile. Bet if I suggested that I'd have sex with him to pay off this month's mortgage payment, he wouldn't give a shit about how crazy I was, the predatory dick cheese.

I mentally rolled my eyes and stepped up to the counter.

"Morning Layla, how are you holding up?" Gloria, was fifty-something, and she'd been the post office teller here for thirty years. She knew everything about everyone. She schooled her aging features into a mask of concern, and I gritted my teeth and answered that exact question for the thirtieth time today.

"I'm fine, Gloria. Thank you for asking."

My tone was flat even to my own ears, but who cared? I honestly couldn't understand if the towns-people really thought I would lay my wounded soul bare to any person who thought to ask, or if they were just following social norms and saying what was expected.

Gloria rifled around behind the counter, retrieving my mail, and she came up holding a stack of envelopes, which all look like late reminders for bills.

I'd been hiding from that particular problem for the past month. Tanya, my mother, hadn't left behind any savings and the medical bills alone would have crippled the average person. I schooled my face into an expression of manic happiness, with a grin that stretched my face in an almost unpleasant way, as the way-too-interested Gloria tried to read me, maybe see if I was having financial problems that she could gossip about.

I leaned in close. "I'm going to have to fire Glinda the House Elf. Do you see this shit? Good help is hard to find, even with the fairies."

I pushed away from the counter, murmuring my goodbyes. There was time to consider my financial black hole when I wasn't surrounded by nosey townies.

I headed straight for my battered SUV, sighing in relief as it came into view. It had never let me down, and was the one constant in my life these days. Striding faster towards it, I prayed that no one would stop me, but apparently, God had forsaken me today.

Police Chief Tony Hammond waved at me from down the street, his broad face turned up in a smile.

He had a round face, pink cheeks and looked like a cross between Santa and every sitcom grandpa ever, so it was almost impossible not to smile back.

My face felt weird twisting into my first real smile in... hell, I didn't even know how long.

The police chief and I had a lot of history. Most of it was good. Some of it was a little more tragic. He'd found me all those years ago after the accident. I called it an 'accident' because the word attack always made me shudder uncontrollably and hyperventilate. Basically, the dictionary definition of a panic attack, but I'd never been to see a psych about what happened that night. Or what I thought had happened. There was always something there at the edge of my consciousness, something I'd well and truly blocked out, and that drove me just as crazy. It was always on the edge of my mind, like if I had a little more sanity, I could just reach out and grab it. Instead, I had recurring nightmares that I couldn't escape, always just a little bit different so I knew it was a dream and not a memory.

I'd healed quickly after the accident, at least physically. When Tony and his wife Sue had found me, my clothes had been torn and bloody and I had eight bite marks, a broken wrist and a huge bump on my head. They'd called the hospital and the local doctor had come out to determine if it was safe to move me to the emergency room. They'd sedated me for most of the first two days, my weird ramblings and wild behavior nearly getting me thrown in a padded room, so most of my convalescence was a pleasant haze. My body healed, but the whole thing had turned me into the recluse I am today.

Then there were the rumors. They started in the hospital. I'd heard the nurses whispering as I was just coming out of my sedated slumber.

"Her neck, Tina, look at it." The voice had hissed. "She should have bled to death in minutes from those wounds, but they are already scabbed over and on their way to being scars. It's not right, not possible."

Tina, my primary nurse, had shooed the other nurse out of the room.

It ballooned from there of course, spreading like wildfire when I left the hospital. Most of the rumors were wild and unrealistic, like the one where, while bleeding to death, I had lit a fire and cauterized my own wounds with a rock from the fire. I had always laughed at that one.

Others were more malicious, the worst one was spread by the older citizens who accused my mother of child abuse. My nails dug into my palm. I always got angry thinking how much that rumor hurt her.

But teenagers? They were the worst. Teenagers could manage to be cruel just by breathing, which was quite a feat if you think about it.

The nickname 'Chew Toy' didn't take long to catch on, and it was fuelled as much by my icy demeanour as it was by the large raw bite mark on my neck. High school was half the reason I hated coming into town now, and almost the entire reason that I wrapped myself protectively in a persona of insanity.

I caught up to Chief Tony, and he wrapped me in a bear hug.

"How are you doing, Layla?" For some reason, coming from him, the question didn't irritate me like the others had, and tears actually started to well in my eyes. I blinked them back and smiled wanly at him.

"I'm okay, Tony. It's been hard, but I'm doing alright."

He smiled back. "I bet you are getting sick of being asked that question, right? Look, Sue said that if I ever saw you in town I was to invite you to dinner. Actually, she said *insist* that you come to dinner."

Tony looked sheepish, and I could almost hear Sue's commanding tone. She could be quite compelling for a plump grandmother of eight. Sue and my mother had been best friends, before my mother's mental health had turned a corner and she'd stopped coming out of the house. Even still, Sue dropped off casseroles and meals a couple of times a week, and washed the linen for me once a month.

"I wish I could but..." I couldn't think of an adequate excuse so I just shrugged. Tony, as expected, just nodded his head and smiled sympathetically.

"I should be going now. Crime stops for no man."

"Also, the diner is only running its lunch specials for another fifteen minutes."

He let out a booming laugh, and I chuckled along. Crime in Roseau was nonexistent. It was hard to be a knife wielding axe murderer in a town where your neighbors knew what time you brushed your teeth at night.

As I waggled my fingers in a goodbye wave, I headed to my SUV and took in this tiny speck on the map that I called home.

It looked average. Small town America in a nutshell.

I got to my SUV, patting the rear passenger door as if it were a faithful horse. I would probably cry when it chugged its last breath, and that day was coming soon. It squeaked where it shouldn't squeak, and chugged when it shouldn't chug. Turning the key, it roared to life, the noise in the cabin almost deafening. It probably needed a new muffler too. I didn't mind though, the rough chug stopped me from thinking the inevitable bad thoughts.

As I sped away from town, it was comforting to know that I wouldn't have to make that journey again for another month. Hopefully that was enough time for the townspeople's memories to dim and for me to decide what to do with my life. With Mom gone, there was really nothing tying me to Roseau anymore.

I navigated the straight country roads on autopilot,

my mind preoccupied with the pile of bills on the passenger seat. I knew I wanted to leave Roseau, but I couldn't. I'd planned to leave as soon as my mother died, but the time came and went and I couldn't drag myself away. It wasn't that I felt any real affection for the town of my tormented childhood. I knew I could go back to college and finish the nursing degree that I'd abandoned to care for Mom, then maybe start a nursing career at one of the major hospitals. However, the more firmly I made up my mind to go, the more I procrastinated about actually leaving.

Letting out a heavy sigh, I finally noticed the turn off to my place, the Double U Ranch. It wasn't actually a real ranch, more of a hobby farm. Its maintenance had provided an easy existence for two people, but I soon found out it was a lot of work for just one. I had a full run of chickens, two dairy cows, a horse called Monster and five acres of veggies and orchards.

I squeezed the bridge of my nose and opened the front door of the house. Fred, the Labrador, lifted his head off the rug in the living room, and gathering it was only me, promptly fell back to sleep. My cat, Pip, was more excited to see me. He was a feral kitten I'd rescued from the top of an apple tree before he was even three weeks old. That was just the kind of nature he had. Since then, he had been a mischievous little shithead who didn't take attitude from anyone, not even Monster the Horse.

After ten or so trips back and forth from the car to the house, the sun had disappeared behind the mountains and I was ready to collapse onto the couch. I had armed myself with a sandwich, a good book and the local radio station playing in the background. The snow had started up again, making the radio a little fuzzy. They were predicting a heavy snowfall, one of the first of the season, and I was glad that I hadn't procrastinated the trip to town until tomorrow.

The fire was crackling nicely, throwing off heat that was only partially blocked by Fred's position on the hearth. This was the only time of the day I ever achieved any kind of calm, where the pressures and the problems of the day disappeared with the daylight, and the dreams that interrupted my sleep were still safely tucked away.

A few hours later my legs were dead, and my eyes were beginning to droop. A scratching at the door interrupted my trek to bed, but it wasn't unusual before a snow storm. Animals knew when to seek shelter, and I had more than a few half-domesticated ones rolling around my yard. Still, I grabbed the shotgun from by the door just to be on the safe side. You never knew when you were going to get a grizzly instead of a raccoon on your front porch. Loading the shotgun, I peeked around the door, switching on the porch light to stun the animal.

At first, I didn't see anything but the inky blackness

of night that lay beyond the reach of the porch light. However, the faintest noise whipped my gaze down to the welcome mat in front of the door.

I slowly lowered my gun because there, lying face down in a pool of rapidly spreading blood, was a man. A naked man.